CHROMOSOME QUEST

DARING, DINOSAURS, AND THE CLOCKWORK APOCALYPSE

NATHAN GREGORY

NATHAN GREGORY AUTHOR DOT COM

This is a work of fiction. Names, characters, places, and incidents are either products of the author's imagination or, if real, are used entirely fictitiously. If you suspect a character is based on some real person, however loosely, you are probably mistaken.

Copyright © 2015, 2018, 2021, 2022, 2023 by Nathan Gregory

All rights reserved.

No part of this book may be reproduced or transmitted in any form or by any means, electronic or mechanical, without explicit and written permission from the author, except for the use of brief quotations in a review, as permitted by U.S. copyright law.

Publisher: Nathan Gregory,   https://www.NathanGregoryAuthor.com

Kindle ASIN: B00R8NXS56

KDP ISBN-13: 979-8378169351

Paperback Edition: Copyright © February 19, 2023

Lulu Press ISBN: 978-1-387-88103-1

Lulu Press Product ID: 1nwk27vv

CONTENTS

1. White Rabbit   1

2. Rabbit Hole   10

3. Precipice   17

4. Falling   23

5. Landing   29

6. Castle   36

7. Feast   43

8. Terror   53

9. Smiles   59

10. Training   65

11. Tranquility   76

12. Weapons   86

13. Milady   98

14. Portals   104

15. Telegraph   114

16. Commencement 125

17. New Castle 134

18. Healing 142

19. River 148

20. Dark Castle 154

21. Queen's Chambers 166

22. Muddy Water 173

23. Great Run 186

24. Battle Briefing 193

25. K-Day 207

26. Taboos 214

27. Looking Glass 223

28. Citadel 231

29. Nematode 244

30. Plaza 260

The Story Continues... 272

About the Author 274

The Writings of Nathan Gregory 278

Chapter 1

WHITE RABBIT

I suppose I could say it was all HER fault. Adam blamed Eve, after all. SHE knew that, like Adam, I, too, have a particular weakness for beautiful women. Athletic with long crimson hair, almost as if SHE had been custom-built to my innermost fantasies, even perhaps as if I had designed her myself. I was powerless the moment I laid eyes on HER.

Earlier this morning, I met with an entrepreneurial gentleman in the throes of launching a new company. Gentleman! Ha! We shouted at each other over a thumping, monotonous rap beat. The shitty music, reek of pot, the hoody, and bare feet in the office did not bode well, but it still hurt when he dismissed me as a neek! So much for the value of experience. Or even just values!

I was licking my wounds in the plaza at 17th and Market, sipping my Arabian Mocha-Java and browsing the Guardian, ostensibly searching for an opportunity. But, in truth, I was merely enjoying a bit of people-watching, languidly cycling between skimming the kitschy pages of the urban rag for ideas, scanning the crowd for interesting characters, and luxuriating in the aroma of the flavorful brew.

I was in no hurry to return to my spartan sleeping room a few blocks away. The cramped quarters, adequate for sleeping, offer little conducive to creative work. Not even a desk. Just a place to sleep between searching the classifieds for opportunities and in my current state — one of rejection, feeling down, and pitying myself following yet another failed job interview — not some place I needed to be just now.

When I wish to pursue creative work, writing, or emails, rather than trying to work while cuddling a laptop on my tiny bed, I often do so right here, relaxing at a cafe table in the plaza, people-watching, and sipping a pleasant brew.

Not today. I declared the remainder of the day to be a mental-health break, an attempt to find a more buoyant mood, a time for relaxing and restoration.

I reflected that just as my professional fortune is in a tailspin of late, my personal life is not soaring either. Not that I have problems attracting companionship, but relationships are fragile and take a degree of nurturing I have been ill-equipped to provide of late. I guess I alone sabotaged my previous relationship; between money problems and searching for work, it is hard to be a sparkling companion when feeling on the rocks.

Perhaps, I thought, I should suck it up and call one of my distaff buddies and promote a casual, no-expectations outing. Kurzweil has a book signing this afternoon. I know he is popular with several of my friends, and then afterward, perhaps we might take in a movie or even just a simple, low-budget dinner. No expectations. That's the ticket; no plans, no expectations, just a friendly face and a few smiles for the afternoon. Let her make the rules; let her call the shots this time. How hard could that be?

Before I do so, I need to screw my head on straight and perk up. My present dark mood is uncharacteristic of my ordinarily buoyant nature, and I need to stop this navel-gazing and get my head in the game.

Opportunity seldom knocks when the door is locked, and the welcome light is dark!

The morning's meeting had been the latest in a long string of frustrations and disappointments, personal and professional, and I was not in a state of mind right now to email resumes or craft cover letters. I needed an afternoon's break to regroup and rethink my plans. Despite having held fascinating jobs, started, and ran companies, and often made good money, my bank account is anemic today.

Whipsawed by the ebb and flow of the economy and the fickle nature of investors, I need a real job in my chosen field, and soon.

The morning was unusually sunny in the City by the Bay, perfect weather to bring out the colorfully disaffected the way sunshine following rain brings out the dandelions and is just as expressive. When the sun shines, diverse characters appear in all their glory. Often literally.

I had noticed a few curious characters gathering at one end of the plaza; I first paid them little attention. But soon, it became clear something was up. Several of the guys, and then I noticed a couple of gals, were shirtless. Someone had brought out the body paint and was artlessly painting on a canvas of skin: nothing imaginative, just the usual assortment of counter-cultural symbols, peace signs, and anti-capitalist slogans. I wondered what social injustice they sought to redress on this day. So far, it appeared they were protesting merely for the practice.

Nudity in protests is routine enough, though those getting their kit off are not often those one might be most eager to see unclad. I often wonder why many counter-culture types stray so far from physical ideals. Is being disaffected a cause, effect, or just an unrelated correlation of an untidy physical appearance? It seems as if there should be a Ph.D. thesis in there somewhere.

Nudity is not limited to protests. There is a vocal Urban Nudist movement in the city, although, with our ordinarily cool climate, it takes a hardy soul to lounge about in bare skin out-of-doors with abandon. But, on the other hand, warm sunny days bring out the body-freedom crowd.

Urban nudists eschew the nudity taboo and reject the traditional nudist convention of congregating with like-minded souls behind tall fences. Instead, they argue that bare skin is normal and acceptable in everyday life. Who am I to disagree? Live and let live, I say. I have no objections to skin.

A lack of protest paraphernalia hallmarks these hardy souls. No sign-waving, chanting, or body painting, not using the trappings of the First Amendment as an excuse to get naked. Instead, they go about more-or-less normal activities, reading a book, having a java, and sometimes writing or emailing on a laptop in the plaza.

I suppose perhaps they are protesting too, just somewhat less boisterously. In any case, urban nudism is a growing movement to which numerous cities increasingly turn a blind eye.

People in the city are laid back, and most citizens pay no mind, though, on occasion, the cops do show up, often when some less broad-minded tourist gets their undies in a bunch. It doesn't happen often, but it does happen.

Shifting my chair to keep the gathering activists in one corner of my eye, I savored another sip. Then, I returned to my paper, wondering if this were a day the police would choose to appear and perfunctorily enforce the ostensible nudity laws.

In the city, public nudity is an offense more-or-less akin to a parking ticket unless it takes place within a sanctioned event. Many of the city's marches, footraces, and similar spectacles have a well-accepted and popular nude contingent. Spectators can be heard cheering and shouting, "Go naked people!"

While rare, the police have sometimes ticketed unsanctioned activists. However, as a rule, they just tell everyone to put their clothes back on, and duty discharged, warning delivered, retreat to the nearest donut shop.

An advertisement caught my eye:

Are You a Boob?
This is not for you!
We badly need a man, highly intelligent, an engineer
well conversant with technology, and politically astute.
A competent man fully at home with culture and
politics as well as with engineering and mathematics.
He must be well versed in the methodology of the
sciences.
He must be tall, perfectly healthy, and physically fit,
handsome of face and figure, comfortable with his
body, fluent in English, with some grounding in the
Romance languages.
Must be willing to travel, no family or emotional ties.
Permanent employment, high pay, adventure, and
danger.
You must apply in person.

The address given was mere blocks from where I sat. I was intrigued but suspicious. It must be some con or a joke, not worth the time to investigate. I was mulling the questions in my mind when I saw . . . HER!

I almost missed her arrival. The gathering crowd of colorful characters had begun stripping. Some retained a modicum of modesty, others flamboyantly clad in bare skin and garish body paint, modesty protected by nothing more than counter-culture symbology.

Then SHE stepped from the crowd; time slowed, and the sun shone brighter — the entire plaza fell silent.

She was very tall and well-muscled, lean, taut, rather buxom, a fit, broad-shouldered, and muscular mesomorph with flaming red hair that extended to her waist, falling free and unrestrained. Although she would be the center of attention in any setting, she was well beyond merely attention-getting here in the plaza. She appeared to have stepped from a Boris Vallejo fantasy but with less clothing. She was stunning in form and figure; she was profoundly unclothed!

Skyclad!
Clothed with the sun!
Barefoot to the chin!

Unlike the rag-tag collection of characters gathering for their colorful protest, she wore no paint, displayed no slogans, and no counter-culture symbology. Nothing marred her exquisite, deep-bronzed skin, not so much as a freckle. Simply fully, totally, completely nude, she stepped from the gathering crowd, confident, poised, as though stepping from the pages of a carefully sculpted and airbrushed fantasy layout. Unlike the protesters the passersby ignored, she magnetically drew every eye in the plaza.

Unperturbed, ignoring the open-mouthed silence and staring eyes, she strolled abreast of my table, and paused a bare half-heartbeat. She looked me in the eye, her smile, an enigmatic puzzle, her eyes twinkling with mischief and delight, as though possessing a secret she dare not share. Then she joined the colorful collection of semi-undressed protesters and vanished within their ranks. I followed her with my eyes as long as possible, bewitched, drawn to her magical form.

Despite my rapt attention, she strolled into that chromatic congress and vanished. I scrambled to my feet, paper in hand, brew forgotten, and unable to track with my eyes, followed with my feet.

Futilely so, it turned out.

She should have been visible from blocks away with her height and crimson woody-woodpecker crest, not to mention that blinding expanse of sun-bronzed skin. Instead, I traveled a full half-block in the direction she had gone before I could admit she was nowhere in sight. How someone so spectacular and stunningly unclad could vanish so, defies logic.

Logic can be a feeble reed sometimes.

Recognizing my buffoonery, I slowed my pace and abandoned the quest. Aimless now, I continued to drift in the same general direction, propelled only by inertia. I glanced at the store windows, read signs and handbills, and wandered along in an introspective fog.

Then, in a plywood-covered window, I saw a familiar question. *"Are You a Boob?"* stared at me, scrawled in red. It was not a handbill, not an ad, simple graffiti. I glanced at the paper in my hand, which still lay open to the advertisement I first noticed.

I checked the address; I realized I was not looking at just graffiti; it was a makeshift sign. I stood in front of the advertised address, and applicants, or suckers, queued in line. Like Alice, I'd followed my "White Rabbit" and found myself staring at the open rabbit hole.

This Alice is not about to tumble! No red pill for this cyber nerd; I am strictly the blue-pill type!

At least I knew the answer to the question! Only a mindless boob would become so entranced as to stalk a strange woman, no matter how she dressed or didn't.

What on Earth had I been thinking? I knew the answer to that, too.

Cursing, I turned toward home. I could salvage the day if I returned to my room, curled up with the laptop, and pounded out a few job applications. Adding a dozen more to the thousands I have sent into the ether might seem pointless, but sooner or later, one must score.

Perseverance and all that!

I sauntered along, hands in pockets, drifting up the hill toward my rented berth, pondering the morning's events, wishing I stayed in the plaza and finished my Java. Why was I so drawn to a mysterious character like that? I guess I knew one answer, but the city does not lack unusual and quirky characters, including nudes. So, why had this one exerted such an influence, such an unreasoning attraction?

I wished I had carried my laptop this morning instead of leaving it locked in my bedroom. I should have stayed at my table in the plaza, working on resumes instead of chasing a mirage. I kicked myself again for such an infantile reaction to that flaming-haired woman!

It's not as if I have lacked females willing to share their charms, yet something about her presence grabbed me in a way I've never before experienced, as though we shared a strange bond of which I remained unaware. Just seeing her strolling nude through the plaza left me shaken, unnerved, and feeling almost sexually assaulted.

Who is she? She is, no doubt, a female bodybuilder. Women do not develop a physique like that without working at it. Well, neither do men. I tried it for a while; trust me, it is hard work. She didn't seem to be with the protesters. Where did she come from? How did she disappear? And most of all, why was she taking a casual nude stroll through the city? If it was to get my attention, she succeeded.

She got everyone's attention!

Please visit the Chromosome Quest Reviews Page and leave a nice review.

https://www.amazon.com/review/create-review?&asin=B00R8NXS56

If you're enjoying the story so far, why don't you help an author out by leaving a nice review on Amazon?

CHAPTER 2

RABBIT HOLE

I entered my room and extracted my laptop from its security housing, unlocking the redundant security cable. My computer is old and obsolete, not particularly valuable, but any tech has an annoying tendency to wander off in this neighborhood. Losing it would not be a total disaster, but it would be inconvenient. If I could afford to replace it, I would; I cannot afford to lose it. Hence, I take severe precautions. I opened the laptop and checked my email. The usual spam littered the inbox; ads for male enhancement and sure-fire money-making offers that had squeezed through the spam filter.

Ignoring the clickbait and timewasters, I skimmed the jobs boards checking for any new listings. Five new job possibilities were in evidence. I scanned the first three and discarded them as unsuitable without a second glance. The next one seemed interesting, so I took a moment to pull a form letter from a folder, edit the date and other minor details to match the job description, attach my resume, and hit send. One more application cast to the ether, never to return. Then I opened the last posting. *"Are You a Boob?"* stared at me from the screen — the same ad I had seen in the urban paper, now on the jobs board. A soft Anglo-Saxon monosyllable escaped my lips as I hit the delete key.

Returning to the email inbox, I checked the residual spam and started deleting it. As the spam dropped into the bit-bucket, another message popped into view. I reacted with a sharp intake of breath. *"Are You a Boob?"* stared at me. Again. Angrily, I deleted the email!

Cursing a universe that allows such cons and hucksters to prey on the vulnerable, I closed the email. Then, I headed over to my Social Media page to see what social inequity has cyberspace in a dither today. I tried to relax by paging through the usual postings of lost pets, cute kids, ribald jokes, cat videos, and religious appeals. However, I was still fuming at the persistence of that ad and, more particularly, annoyed at myself for chasing that nude woman like a sex-starved idiot. Finally, I watched a few cat videos, wishing my current situation was more conducive to owning a pet.

Cats are not, as a rule, considered the manly pet, dogs being considered more masculine by some. You know what? I don't care. I have had many dogs and almost as many cats. Both make terrific companions in different ways and for various reasons. I would have one of each if I could. But, unfortunately, right now, I can't support myself, much less a furry companion.

The comical cat left me laughing out loud as the clip ended, and I returned to the home page, still shaking silently at the animal antics. Unfortunately, a new posting had appeared while I watched the video, and once again, I saw red as the annoying *"Are You a Boob?"* glared at me from the screen.

Was the universe sending me a message? Is there some reason I keep seeing this ridiculous advertisement everywhere I turn? Am I a boob? Duh.

We've already established that!

With sudden resolve, I checked the time. Early afternoon! I still have time to get to the bottom of this and find out what sort of scam is in play. I secured the computer and charged out the door, energized by a sudden purpose.

I determined to penetrate whatever fraud they perpetrate and perhaps blow the doors off that run-down den of thieves by calling the cops and filing a complaint. I wanted to bust them and put them out of business!

I found myself out the door, down the street, striding energetically, purposefully heading back toward the derelict storefront I had paused in front of earlier.

I didn't know the mysterious red-haired woman was behind the advertisement and whatever con they were running. Pointedly, I had nothing whatever linking them. Yet, somehow, intuitively, I connected them in my mind, perhaps for no other reason than I had been reading the ad when I first saw her.

I wondered, was I searching for revenge for a supremely annoying advertisement? Or in pursuit of a job opportunity I desperately needed? Or was I hoping to encounter her there? I had no reason to think she might be present, but I couldn't shake the feeling that she was somehow connected.

After a few minutes of brisk walking, I stared anew at the dilapidated storefront with its boarded-up window. "*Are You a Boob?*" scrawled in red, staring back at me from the plywood. A line of hapless souls stood in front of the sign, queued up in front of the door. Had they, too, followed my white rabbit? Are we all just a bunch of horny losers chasing a piece of fantasy tail? Or is it just a more mundane case of job-hungry people chasing down an advertisement that promised employment at high pay? My mind insisted the latter was the case. Still, I wondered.

Men queued in front of the storefront and down the sidewalk. At least fifteen men of various descriptions waited in front of the building, and there was no way to know how many were inside. A few women stood in line too. Not that surprising, I suppose. Gender-specific employment is a minefield of social-justice legal technicalities. In our increasingly litigious society, who knows what motives a woman might have in applying for a job advertised as intended for a man. Besides, in these days of transgender acceptance, who can be confident of a stranger's sex short of a DNA test? You can't trust your eyes.

Chromosomes never lie!

A few in line did not meet the criteria listed in the ad, even ignoring gender. Someone barely over five feet tall weighing in at 300+ pounds could hardly be described as "Tall, Healthy, and Physically Fit," could they?

The line was moving slowly. It didn't seem to be advancing at all when I arrived. I took my place at the end of the line and stood placidly, awaiting my turn. Though calm on the outside, on the inside, I was seething. I was not so much angry at those running this circus side-show as at myself for allowing myself to fall sucker, falling despite my best resolve. Whatever scam was in the offing, I had pegged it as a waste of time when I first saw the ad and nothing I had yet seen suggested otherwise. But here I was, quietly standing in line, obediently queuing up for whatever sadistic game might be in the works, ready to become the butt of whatever practical joke was in play. Casually, I surveyed the scene for candid cameras.

I occupied myself studying my fellow applicants. Every few minutes, the door would open, and someone would exit. The drooping shoulders and the slow shuffle indicated rejection is in the air. The time between each exit was long enough to convince me that a significant test or evaluation was happening. Even specimens that fell far short of the announced criteria exited at the same rate as anyone else. No matter how far they diverged from the stated profile, it appears they reject no one out of hand. Whatever test they were administering appeared to be applied equally to all. The social-justice warriors would be pleased.

When I arrived, a fellow close to my height and build was at the queue head. A few minutes later, someone exited, and that fellow disappeared inside. I tried to note the other candidates as they entered to compare them to those who left. I strove to estimate how long the process might take.

An hour passed. Six candidates exited, and six new applicants entered. The pace seemed consistent at one every ten minutes, as near as I could judge.

Two hours went by. That first fellow had not reappeared. Neither had anyone who had entered behind him, but some dozen seemingly failed candidates had emerged. Twelve who queued in front had gone in, keeping the average time to process a candidate hovering around ten minutes. That did not seem very long, yet the line moved very slowly.

I surmised they were conducting the tests in parallel, every individual taking much more than ten minutes, but on average, rejecting one every ten minutes. I watched to see if any came out in a different order than when they went in, thus suggesting a parallel process wherein individual candidates could require various evaluation times. I noticed a short, chubby, balding little old guy, apparently a staff member, escorting out each departing candidate. After showing each one out, he would wave in the next hopeful.

Two of the rejects had been women. Three men and three women remained outside, ahead of me, when the guy who had been at the head of the line when I arrived emerged. I estimated I had another hour to wait. He, too, displayed the body language of rejection, yet, he had seemed much closer to the advertised criteria. Thus, I did not consider my chances exceptional. I came close to blowing it off and going home, but, having come this far and with no pressing demands, I resolved to stick it out.

Sometime later, two remained in front of me, with a much longer line behind. Then, finally, the chubby old guy appeared at the door but didn't escort anyone out nor wave anyone in. Instead, he pulled out a tiny table and chair and sat down, pulled out a stack of cards, and wrote some numbers on them as we watched. Twice he paused and counted noses, pointedly avoiding my gaze. I wondered why and whether I should feel insulted.

Clapping his hands for attention, he announced: "Everyone in line at this time is invited to return tomorrow." Groans and grumbles arose from the line. "If you'd like to take a number to retain your place, we will take your application in order, starting tomorrow morning."

A few turned and stomped off, grumbling. The rest of us queued to take a number. Chubby cut me off along with the two in front of me, saying "Not You," and pointed for us to return to our place in line. I arrived here just in time to be today's very last candidate.

While he was taking names and giving out numbers to the thirty or so candidates in line behind me, another departing candidate peeked out, glancing around as if uncertain. Without glancing up from his cards, chubby waved him on out. A few minutes later, this repeated as yet another discarded candidate appeared. Again, chubby waved him out and turned back to his cards. The two in front of me looked around as if expecting an invitation. Chubby waved a hand at them and told them to go inside and wait if they wished, he would be along shortly to get them started. They entered, leaving me standing alone at the door.

After a few moments, chubby put away his cards and pen and folded his chair and table. Then he turned to me and said, "Come on, Fitz, we may as well get you started too; we have a lot of promises to keep and miles to go before we sleep." Taken aback, I wondered how he had known my name. I hadn't so much as said hello to anyone since I arrived!

Chapter 3

PRECIPICE

We entered the dimly lit storefront. My eyes adjusted, and I decided it wasn't quite as dim as I had first thought, and it was much cleaner than I had expected from the exterior. We were in a small anteroom. The two who had been immediately in front of me were also there. One was a man, the other presented as a woman, although plain-looking, almost masculine. Our host seemed unaware that she had applied to an advertised position explicitly calling for a male.

After a few moments of fussing around with the table, chair, cards, and such, our host handed out plastic pouches. He instructed, "Remove all clothing, shoes, jewelry, piercings, and anything similar; place them along with any phones, wallet, and other items, in this bag. Please write your name on the card and put it in the bag to be visible. Your possessions will be secure and returned to you when finished. Drop the bag into that slot, and our staff will take care of it.

"Think of this as a medical examination. Don't worry; your anonymity and personal safety are guaranteed."

The woman raised her hand. Our host nodded to her. "We are expected to undress here in front of strangers?"

"Sorry." He sighed. "Normally, candidates are processed one at a time, and I have more time to explain. I apologize. It's late, and we are all a bit tired. You three kinda bunched up on me at the end of the day. I wanted to get you all processed today. Forgive my shortcuts, the impatience of a crotchety old man. Perhaps I should have told you three to come back tomorrow, but I judged we could get you in and processed today if we hustled. If you'd rather not, you may come back tomorrow and be at the head of the line."

The woman turned as if to leave. Before she could do so, he stopped her and continued. "Perhaps I should explain that self-confidence in one's skin is supremely relevant to the job. If you are selected, your post will involve continuous, total nudity, your own and that of many others in a social setting. If you join our team, you will live the next several months bereft of clothing. It is not for nothing that our advertisement stated "comfort with one's own body" as a job requirement. Conducting the test with all applicants fully nude in mixed company is part of the process, our way of weeding out those who might have a problem with the requirements.

"Demonstrating comfort with nudity from this point forward is itself a test you must pass. If you are not comfortable in a nude environment, you may as well skip on out now and save us all some trouble. This is not for you!"

The last phrase was delivered almost in a singsong as if reading the recruitment ad. I suppose he was, in a way.

He paused a moment and, seeing no further objections, continued. "Our doctor will examine you. There will be a simple blood test, a CAT scan, a brief physical fitness exam, and an intelligence test. It is of utmost importance that there be nothing on your body that is not a natural part of your flesh. Jewelry and such can cause severe problems in the scanners. There are other reasons, too, which I will not explain. At least not unless you are selected.

"Once the testing is complete, you will be given a place to rest and wait a short time while we evaluate the results. Once we complete the evaluation, we will return your possessions and escort you out.

"Unless you should be selected!

"If selected, you will go straight from this office to your formal training at another facility. Nothing you brought here today will go with you. We will provide everything you need there. You will live, train and work at multiple remote locations for several months, at the end of which you will return here, all your possessions returned. You will be well paid for your time away and handsomely rewarded if your project succeeds. If you are not prepared to abandon your life here and now, this instant, leaving behind all your possessions, this is not for you." Again, that slight singsong lilt.

With that, he turned on his heels and exited without allowing anyone the opportunity to raise further objections.

My companions and I stood open-mouthed for a moment. Then after a moment's hesitation, we all three began undressing. I discretely turned to face the wall, keeping my eyes focused elsewhere, avoiding looking at the others. I sensed the others must be doing similarly.

I have no fears or hang-ups about nudity. The Bay Area coastline is rife with nude beaches, and I have visited them all. I am comfortable in my skin and not especially shy about being 'caught' naked. Skin is skin, and we all have in essence the same amount. I have often spotted nudes in the city, the Urban Nudists, the protesters undressing openly on the street, and public events such as the Folsom Street Fair, where nudity is the least shocker.

I may have reservations about some individuals' actions, wisdom, drug use, and perhaps even their appearance, but never simple nudity.

Still, in the presence of strangers, disrobing in public can be daunting if you aren't expecting it. I wasn't.

A few moments later, bare as the day I was born with all my possessions in this tiny plastic bag, I turned to face my companions. I was only mildly surprised to note the apparent woman sported a member as masculine as my own, jarringly out of place below hormone augmented yet perfectly feminine mammaries.

As I said, chromosomes don't lie.

Not my first rodeo, nor my first transgender woman, I thought as I crossed the room and inserted my bag into the slot in the wall. My fellow adventurers followed my example and did likewise.

As we steeled ourselves for the coming examination, I pondered the other aspect of the program. What would I be leaving behind if selected and were to depart here and now, leaving all behind? Not much, I decided. A few items of spare clothing. An old and tired laptop. An unfinished novel I probably would never finish. A two-year-old Droid was in the plastic bag I had just surrendered. Would it accompany me on my hypothetical travels, I wondered?

It seemed not.

My room is paid for another month. If I don't return, I suppose my landlady will store my meager possessions for a while. After that, I don't know. Would someone call the cops and report me missing? Possible, I suppose, but I doubt it. An orphan, I have no family, few friends, few acquaintances. I will worry about that if the time comes.

We stood there, studiously ignoring each other's skin. Minutes later, after the last plastic bag hit the table behind the slot, a strange woman dressed in medical scrubs, a nurse I surmised, opened the door and called the name of one of the others. I wondered again how they knew his name. He entered, following her, and disappeared.

My companion and I passed several minutes in silence. Finally, studiously avoiding the elephant in the room, I broke the stillness by casually remarking on the singular nature of this job interview, if that's what it was.

My companion responded with a grimace. Then, the ice seemingly broken, picked up the conversational thread and ran with it. "It seemed a good opportunity to start fresh, and I need a job. Scarier in a way than I bargained for, though. I hadn't anticipated the nudity aspect, but what the heck? I'm not gonna let that be a problem. I don't hide who I am. It's never comfortable to be in a situation where you worry about the preconceptions and fears of others, but it must be faced."

I nodded and responded, "I think today, many people feel a touch of hopelessness for many reasons. Anything that promises adventure and a new life is attractive. I didn't anticipate the nudity requirement either, but it's not an obstacle. Other places may be more rigid, but people in this city do not often get exercised over skin or lifestyle."

I continued, "Most urbanites these days are too preoccupied with their troubles to spend time being upset over someone else's."

My companion nodded agreement as the door opened, and the scrubs-clad nurse again appeared and motioned to my companion. Without ceremony, I was suddenly alone. Not merely alone, but alone in unfamiliar surroundings, and utterly, completely naked, without even a toothpick. My clothes, wallet, phone, and every worldly possession disappeared, and I surrendered via that plastic bag to the slot in the wall. There was no possibility now of retreat unless I wanted to walk home naked. I suppose I could do so, but the idea wasn't attractive. So, I found myself standing alone, naked, in an empty room, feeling more than a touch vulnerable.

I had absolutely nothing whatsoever, just me, my very, very tender skin, and I.

Please visit the Chromosome Quest Reviews Page and leave a nice review.

https://www.amazon.com/review/create-review?&asin=B00R8NXS56

If you're enjoying the story so far, why don't you help an author out by leaving a nice review on Amazon?

Chapter 4

FALLING

I stood there, feeling vulnerable for many minutes. Perhaps it seemed longer than it was. Various thoughts flitted through my brain as I considered how many ways this could turn really, really dark. Am I the butt of some cosmic joke or victim of some outrageous scam? I was a fool to place myself in this position. Will the cops find my abused, naked body in some alley? Time stretched, and my imagination became frenetic. Then the door opened again.

The nurse motioned to me, and I stepped through the portal into a spartan interior room with a small desk occupied by an ordinary laptop and an elevator door opposite that. Motioning to the elevator, she indicated the obvious. I stepped inside. There was a prominent handgrip, which I instinctively grabbed. The door closed, and the elevator went up. Or was it down. Maybe both. It moved and moved; it stopped. It shook. At one point, it seemed to go sideways, then almost seemed to do a loop-the-loop. Maybe not, but still, I concluded this was one odd elevator. Perhaps it was merely a distraction intended to disorient me. If so, it worked. I was glad I had grabbed that handle.

After a ridiculous amount of time, the doors opened, and I staggered out, suppressing a twinge of motion sickness, into a vast room filled with what appeared to be high-tech medical equipment. Several other candidates were present, each accompanied by a nurse and subjected to testing at a test workstation. I was curious to note the absence of any privacy or modesty screens around the various stations.

I assumed this factor, too, must be a part of the test, judging our ability to remain self-confident in the open and vulnerable environment.

Another nurse was waiting for me; at least, I think she was a different one. I was beginning to suspect the wild elevator ride had been a simple disorientation tactic and had gone nowhere. She guided me to the first of many tests. She stood me against what appeared to be an X-Ray machine. A doctor, I supposed, cloaked and hooded behind a control panel, spoke softly, had me turning at various angles. At first, the voice was very soft, barely a whisper, and gender uncertain. Then, after a moment and a few more words that slowly became more distinct, I realized the speaker was female, her voice a rich, sensual contralto with a very slight, indeterminate accent. Most definitely female. Beneath the hood, a wisp of crimson was visible. I thought of the statuesque, well-muscled form I had followed earlier in the day. Could be, I supposed, but by no means definite.

After the 'X-Ray machine,' other tests followed in rapid succession. Some I was familiar with, some not so much. I thought I was very familiar with modern technology, including medical machines. Still, as testing progressed, I realized many of the devices I saw were incomprehensible even to my engineering mind. The few nameplates I saw on the equipment were unfamiliar. I was confused and disjointed. Nauseated by the decidedly odd elevator ride, then, without a pause, new conundrums and puzzles confounded me faster than I could absorb. Blood drawn, pulse, blood pressure, and other parameters measured, samples taken. The testing was as rapid as it was thorough.

With each battery of tests, we moved deeper into the complex. Although it defied reason, the facility seemed much larger on the inside than the outside. Much too large to have been in the dilapidated city storefront. We progressed through endless hallways, from room to room. The facility seemed entirely windowless. Were we underground? Quite possibly, I suppose.

After a time, I found myself in a small room facing a wall-mounted display. Evidently, it was a touchscreen since no mouse or keyboard was in evidence. The nurse had me stand in front of the screen, and she said, "Follow instructions on the screen. It will take just a few minutes." Hopefully, it wouldn't be too long as there was no chair, stool, or other provision for sitting or relaxing. She left, and the screen came to life a few seconds later. The instructions were simple; it seemed to be a sort of intelligence test. Questions would be displayed, and I was supposed to select the best answer. Sometimes it might look like complete nonsense, but in any case, no matter how silly, I had to choose the response that seemed most appropriate to me. If I fail to answer a question, the lack of an answer is my answer. Then, answered or not, the next question appears.

The instructions ended, and at the bottom, a button said: "Touch here to begin." I touched, and we were off to the races, an apt metaphor given the pace of the test. There were a lot of questions. I soon realized I had to respond quickly. Very quickly. Each one appeared for only a couple of seconds. I soon realized it must be watching my eye movements to determine when I had finished reading, and it then allowed less than one second to select an answer before moving on. There were a lot of questions in a very brief time.

Some questions were outright silly. "What color is the number five" (Red, I decided), some more difficult as in "Multiply 128 times 16" and some complete nonsense. After a few moments, I began to get the hang of it and adapt to the pace. As I grew more adept, it began displaying two questions, apparently unrelated, side by side, almost as if I was to select one with each hand. I started doing so, and the pace accelerated. As I mastered the two-question side-by-side format, suddenly, there were three, each one only giving me a brief moment to answer once I had read it. I experimented by intentionally ignoring one of the three and not looking at it. It stayed longer before disappearing to be replaced by another.

After a while, I began to get the hang of the three-by format. The format shifted again, and there were now four questions on the screen. The pace accelerated again. I felt as if I were picking responses wildly, at random, unable to process the data, fiercely determined to choose an answer, any answer, lest the machine decide for me. The pace accelerated again.

I had no time to keep track of the time or the number of questions, but I might guess I answered upwards of one thousand in something like fifteen minutes, an insane pace. I would not be surprised if the average were well under one second per question. I am sure I got most of them wrong, assuming there is a wrong answer. Or a correct answer. Most of the problems seemed disconnected from the possible solutions. I suspected the test was one of psychology as much as intelligence or learning. Clearly, it was testing reading and comprehension, decision-making, and more. Knowledge, not so much, as very few of the questions seemed designed to gauge the facts at one's command—the ability to assess a problem and decide on a response. Whether right or wrong is less important than making a decision; at least, that seemed to be what was at play.

After the last question, the screen displayed a series of graphics in rapid succession. The images started simple, then became more and more complicated, and came faster and faster. They were accompanied by a cacophony of sounds as if each picture carried a soundtrack. Because they came so rapidly, the soundtracks were jumbled together. Faster and faster the images flickered past, increasingly discordant the sounds, until ultimately the screen dissolved into a hypnotic Mandelbrot type of display, almost as if a screensaver had kicked in. For a moment, I thought the machine had crashed; then, I realized the pattern seemed purposeful, as though intended to elicit a specific reaction. With a start, I realized it was lulling me into a strange trance-like state. I fought back, closing my eyes, blinking, and shaking my head, intentionally turning away. After a moment, the display broke and displayed what appeared to be a numeric score: 42, it said.

Curious, I thought. What's the significance of the number? Is it a percentage? The answer to the Ultimate Question of Life, the Universe, and Everything? Is it my score on the test? Did I get a failing grade?

After a moment or two, the screen went dark, and seconds later, the door opened, and the nurse returned.

She showed me to another room. The singular fixture of the room was a low couch, covered with paper dispensed from a roll at one end, like a typical medical exam table, except lower, softer, and more comfortable. She told me to lie down, and the doctor would be with me soon.

I stretched out on the couch, paper crinkling against my skin, and waited. The room was warm, very unlike the typical medical office. My head was still reeling from the hypnotic display, and I was slightly nauseous, both from the wild elevator ride and the nauseatingly hypnotic Mandelbrot. I closed my eyes to rest them for a moment.

I realized the room had darkened, and I was in total blackness. I felt my awareness fading, almost as though drugged. I fought for consciousness but could not seem to climb over the threshold of awareness. As I struggled, the room swirled, and oblivion descended with a thud.

Chapter 5

LANDING

After a time, I became aware of bird sounds. And heat. Oppressive, humid heat, but with a gentle breeze, nothing like being in a small, closed room; I was out of doors. Not quite ready to open my eyes just yet, I lay and listened, concentrating on my senses, describing my environment in my mind. I could hear the faint rush of water in the distance. I smelled the perfume of flowers, the earthy soil, and the pungent scent of grass.

With a start, I realized I was no longer lying on the medical couch. Instead, I was lying on soft grass in an open clearing. Still naked. No matter, I had accepted the premise of perpetual nudity, and as blistering hot as it felt, clothing seemed starkly unreasonable! Every square inch of my skin became soaked with sweat as my body struggled to regulate its core temperature in the scorching heat. Like Death Valley in summer. Only hotter! I had never felt heat like this; I wondered if I could survive.

I realized I was hungry. How long had it been since I had eaten, I wondered? Will someone feed me soon?

I lay quietly, listening, sniffing the air for a few moments. Not willing to admit I was awake just yet, I wanted to determine as much as I could about my surroundings without moving. No sounds betrayed the presence of anyone else. Finally, I opened my eyes to see the sky and tropical-appearing trees. I spotted decidedly odd-looking Palm trees and a flower that seemed to be a Bird of Paradise but different.

Slowly I raised slightly and looked around. A row of exotic trees appeared to mark the edge of a forested area on one side. Fortunately, the trees blocked the broiling sun, so I lay in the shade. A good thing, I recognized, else I risked severe sunburn. That orb in the sky was brutally HOT!!

On the other side, a man sat on a rock, head down, unmoving, arms folded as if deep in thought or even asleep. He was as naked as I. As my eyes focused more clearly, I realized I knew him. He was the same chubby old guy who had set up the table in front of the storefront and handed out cards to the prospective candidates invited back tomorrow—the old guy who had unaccountably known my name.

Seeing him unclothed caused me to revise my original assessment somewhat. While compared to me, he was still slightly short and chubby; he was, I realized, astoundingly well-muscled, not unlike my white rabbit. Naked, he appeared far more fit and capable than my initial assessment. I immediately resolved not to get into any fights with him. I wondered if he had taken up bodybuilding too.

When I moved to rise, he roused and opened his eyes. "Well, well, well, the sleeper awakes. Welcome to the enchanted land of Oz, my boy. Cinch up your nut-sack, suck in your gut and get ready for the ride of your life. I am pleased to inform you that you have been chosen; you won the booby prize!"

At this, I sat up and stared at him quizzically as I fought to regain my equilibrium. I felt foggy, adrift, as if I had just awakened from a profoundly deep sleep. Then, mustering my tremendous intellectual acumen, I prepared a stream of invective designed to blister paint at 20 yards! Raging, scorching profanity welled up as I demanded to know where I was; how dare they drug me? Someone is gonna pay the piper for this, I vowed.

Then out loud, I said, "Huh?"

"Your enthusiasm overwhelms. Just wait until you comprehend the magnitude of your good fortune this day. Just wait. I'll never understand why SHE chose you, but SHE picked you out of a field of thousands. She promised you travel! Already a taste of that, I suppose, though you hardly realize it yet. Much more to come. You'll see!"

"What was that you said about Oz. The fictional Oz? Or did you stuff me on a jet, and we're in New Zealand?"

At that, he erupted in laughter, giving me a moment to shake off the lethargy of my awakening, and as a result, when he sobered, I was more engaged.

"No Jets. Not by boat or train, either. Magic. Or may as well be." His mirth subsided, and he became serious. He motioned me to join him on a rock adjacent to his and then continued in an academic tone, suddenly sounding precisely like a dour college professor lecturing to a class.

"Almost precisely 500 years before you were born, the most advanced scientist of his day, a man named Leonardo da Vinci speculated about the possibility of flying machines. He imagined helicopters and aircraft with wings. Aeronautical engineers universally agree that aircraft built to his designs could have flown if he had a proper power source and materials to create the structures he imagined. Leonardo could not even dream about the possibilities of jet engines and regular passenger flights at supersonic speeds. Yet earthly aircraft operate on the same underlying physical principles as the fantastical flying machines he described. In just half a millennium, all his wildest dreams have not only come true but have been far, far surpassed.

"Today, Earth's most advanced physicists speculate about theoretical constructs such as the Einstein-Rosen bridge. Likewise, screenwriters create elaborate imaginary worlds incorporating a colloquialization they call 'Wormholes.' Now I pose to you the question, what might become of these physicists' speculations, given another half-a-millennium or so?

"As for where we are, no, this is not Mr. Baum's mythical land, and it is not New Zealand either. So don't worry about where it is, for now. Instead, worry about preparing for what is to come."

"As for where we are, no, this is not Mr. Baum's mythical land, and it is not New Zealand either. So don't worry about where it is, for now. Instead, worry about preparing for what is to come."

"I see," I said as I absorbed his words. Then, mocking the verbal capital letters he had used, I responded, "SHE chose me and magically transported me through a wormhole to a mystical, faraway land. A land where I am to train and prepare for a grand quest, a great adventure, a Hero's Journey!"

"Hah! You got it!" he ejaculated, laughing heartily.

"So what is this mystical quest? Rescuing a Princess in Distress? Steal an Egg from the Roc's nest? Slay Talos in Cydonia? Recover the necklace Brísingamen or Odin's Draupnir? As I recall, the promise included high pay; what would be my payment? My weight in precious stones and gold? Eternal life? The pulchritudinous body of SHE who chose me?"

"All that and more, my boy, all that and more. Whatever you can imagine, all that, and more. If you survive, that is. As for her body, I can't promise you that, and you wouldn't want it anyway. In my opinion, she's rather old, you know, a bit of an old hag. SHE would kill me if I told you her right age. But, if you want a bedmate or just a quick spot of friendly exercise, let me know; I can fix you up with someone young and horny, much more fun than her wrinkled old carcass.

"But much more terrific tail awaits your pleasure right here than you can imagine! You might find yourself wanting to sleep alone to get some rest. No, my boy, you will not lack for warmth in your bed."

"So, who is this SHE that you keep talking about? She sounds like someone you're a little afraid of. You talk like she's an ogre," I asked.

"A little?" he expostulated. "Mortal terror is more like it. Trust me; you do not want to get on HER bad side. If you displease HER, she will kill you in an instant. And then, likely, I would be stuck with disposing of the body. Again!" He dropped his voice almost as if muttering to himself, "I sometimes wonder who will dispose of my corpse on the day she becomes displeased with me."

I thought he was joking, but he seemed deadly serious from all I could tell. Shifting away from the implications of that, I changed tack. "So, tell me about the mystical quest? And are we really on another planet?"

He answered in a singsong, "I don't want to spoil the surprise!" Then lowering his voice ominously, "You will find out quite soon enough."

He said, "Before we begin, let's go eat; I'm starved; haven't had a decent meal in days. It's quite a little walk to some friends' home where they will feed us. We need to get somewhere safe before night falls, too. There are seriously dangerous nocturnal predators here."

With that, he stood, and with a scant wave for me to follow, headed toward the woods, angled to the right following the tree line perhaps 150 feet or so, until we came to a broad, clear path. He turned onto the trail and entered the woods, and I followed in bewilderment. I say bewilderment because these woods were unlike anything I had ever seen. They were clean, more exquisitely groomed than any state park I had ever seen, and though we were barefoot, the trail was soft, sandy, and smooth to walk.

We hiked through these woods without shoes, clothing, or any other type of protection. Bareness had ceased to be a novelty, and given the climate, it felt pleasant to have the air caress my entire body. Still, I worried about the possibility of snakes, wild pigs, or other denizens of the woods, threats such as poison ivy, or other nasty hazards. It is not for nothing that we tend to equate nudity with vulnerability. So, I kept a sharp eye for possible dangers as I followed my companion.

I began to pay attention to the trees and plant life. They were unlike anything I had seen before. Not substantially different than any other forest, merely as if the trees were only an unfamiliar species. I noticed birds of exquisite colors and saw squirrels in the trees. Most curiously, the squirrels appeared almost ordinary except for their bright, colorful tails. I surmised that these squirrels seem to display them much as some birds display colorful plumage. Then, in the distance, I saw a peculiar, gigantic bird. For an instant, I thought I saw a pterodactyl! However, it was far away, and I decided I was mistaken, a trick of light and shadow.

My companion noticed my vigilance as he commented at one point, "Fitz, my boy, you can relax; these woods are quite safe in the daytime. But never, ever under any circumstances, let yourself get caught out here after sunset. Not even close to sunset. Always be in a secure shelter long before nightfall, as failure is certain death. There are three kinds of serious predators, all quite vicious. Fortunately, they are all nocturnal. You do not want to face them, trust me."

As we walked, I considered a million questions, not so much reluctant to ask them as struggling to decide what to ask first. Are we on another planet, as it appears? That seems evident. How did we get here? I know the answer to that one, I guess, Magic Wormholes! One man's magic is another man's engineering; supernatural is a null word. Do we get back home the same way? Do we ever get back home, period? Finally, I settled on a more mundane question to begin. "You seem to know my name, but I don't know yours."

"Call me Petch." Raising a quizzical eyebrow, I responded, "From Texas?" His turn to be quizzical. Then after a moment, realization dawned. "You mean from Nintendo. There's no one named Lonk, and I had the name long before anyone ever heard of Nintendo. It's short for Petchy, a nickname granted by a friend long ago. I haven't used my birth name in ages. I am known all over the galaxy as Petchy, or simply Petch. I am to be your guide and trainer, and perhaps in a manner of speaking, your squire. If we live that long, even the training is not without hazards." Glancing at the sky, he added, "We may not survive this day if we don't pick up the pace."

With that ominous pronouncement, he lengthened his stride, resolutely placing one foot in front of the other. I shifted gears to keep up. For an old guy, he was certainly agile; we were close to a dead run, and I was suddenly too busy breathing to ask silly questions.

Chapter 6

CASTLE

We had walked for miles when the trail opened to a large clearing. Despite Petchy's pessimism, there was still ample daylight when we arrived, although it was indeed late afternoon. In the center of the clearing was a magnificent stone edifice. A castle, lacking only a moat and drawbridge, home to many dozens, if not hundreds of residents. I was impressed by the masonry; the massive stone blocks would have taken powerful muscles, long levers, and the labors of many decades to carve and move into place. It appears to have been constructed over many decades and is centuries old. Some parts looked like they could be millennia old, as aged as the Sphinx or the Great Pyramid. Of course, I'm no expert in such things, and any opinion I might venture is mere guesswork and speculation. In any case, it was apparent we were not in California anymore.

My companion called out in a strange language, and the main door opened. As it did so, I noticed no wood was used anywhere in its construction. Instead, the door was a massive, finely balanced stone, carefully carved from a single boulder and finely polished.

A diminutive figure appeared in the doorway. For an instant, I thought it was an animal. Then I heard a high, delicate feminine voice answer in the same strange tongue, and I realized our greeter was indeed a fur-bearing mammal; she was not an animal, as I quickly saw. Instead, an entirely human, very mammalian appearing female, tiny, but no shorter than some Earth humans, lean and curvy, and as nude as we were, save she wore an elegant head-to-toe pelt of the most exquisitely sensual and luxurious gray fur. Much like a tailless cat, like a short-haired Russian Blue with which I had once shared a house.

I repressed an urge to stroke that fur, then shuddered slightly, fearing it might be bad manners to stroke a stranger as if she were a pet.

Petch held no such qualms. He went straight into her arms, giving her a big enthusiastic hug, nuzzling her cheek, and stroking her head and neck like I might have greeted my former housemate. I won't say she purred like a cat, but she did make small guttural noises in response to his caresses and tucked her head into his chest. She gyrated seductively against his body, speaking the shorthand of old friends.

He spoke boisterously to her in the same language, pointing at me. I heard "Fitz" in the jumble of syllables. After exchanging a few words, she came to me, apparently expecting the same intimacy. For a moment, I hesitated, then acquiesced, stroking her head, neck, and shoulders as she nuzzled my chest. More of that strange language flowed forth, an incomprehensible jumble of syllables ending with a heavily accented "Welcome Fitz."

Petchy spoke, "Her name is Stapleya. She says welcome to her home, and she will be very pleased to receive your boon, feed you, and teach you Language. Be on your best behavior, boy. Don't be provincial. These are civilized people, good folks, and we do not want to offend them. Your best behavior!"

My newfound friend took my hand and led me inside. We met quite a few individuals, obviously all females, and she seemed to be alternately introducing me and explaining to them who I was. Petch was greeted and variously nodded to and returned the greetings, but he got little of the attention they focused on me, suggesting he was already well-known here.

She kept eyeing me suggestively while chattering away as she led us deeper into the interior. Several times I caught her blatantly eyeing my crotch. I suppose, lacking her people's natural furry cloak, my exposed dangly bits do make an eye magnet. But hey! I didn't make the rules here. I am not dangling by choice! So, I steeled myself, squared my shoulders, looked her in the eye, and smiled.

Besides, I had stolen a few furtive glances at her furry curvaceousness; I guess fair was fair. So, I wasn't inclined to complain.

I tried to note and remember the people I met and remember their names. It was overwhelming. They all sported the same exquisite gray fur as my host, which made telling one from another difficult until I learned to distinguish faces and body forms. Their pelt also hindered estimating ages until I recognized subtle tell-tales in form, stride, posture, and fur texture. Nevertheless, I made a sincere effort to remember their names, repeating them while bowing slightly and making a mental note of any distinguishing characteristics.

Stapleya introduced a stooped, elderly male named Pugiya, or at least that's how I heard it; I dubbed him 'Grandpa' in my mind. Then she presented, with great emphasis, a seemingly pubescent female she introduced as Williya. I deduced that the entire clan shared the trailing syllable 'ya' like a surname. I resolved to ask Petch to clarify when we were not so distracted.

When presenting Williya, she stood with her arms around the girl for some time, chattering away; she gave the girl an extended endorsement. I deduced from her body language that this was her daughter. I tried to guess the girl's age, settled on equivalent to about fourteen to perhaps sixteen on my Earthly scale. I am terrible at guessing female ages, but clearly, she was young. In my mind, I dubbed her Lolita, a not inappropriate nickname, as I was to discover.

I did not know what she said, but I gathered the strong impression she meant it to be serious business. I nodded just as seriously as though I understood and bowed deeply, taking the girl's delicate fur-covered hand as if I were going to kiss it. I met her gaze squarely and solemnly responded in my best sensually masculine voice, "It is a very great pleasure to meet such a charming young lady." The gesture seemed to work as the girl broke into a broad smile and started chattering away, amplifying her introduction.

She surged into my arms and hugged me as if by an uncontrollable impulse, rubbing her budding breasts against my body. Taken aback, I responded by stroking her as I had seen Petch doing to the others. I was surprised and shocked when she escalated the greeting by hugging me even closer, gyrating suggestively. As she turned against my very being, I sensed an impending, unexpected, and manifestly unwanted expression of an ancient reflex. Suddenly, I was terrified at the prospect of embarrassing myself amongst strangers. An overwhelmingly female audience, no less! I pulled away from her slightly as I fought to retain control over the beast within. I covered by stroking her head and neck, thinking about ANYTHING other than this strange but extraordinarily young and nubile Lolita so enticingly nearby.

After several seconds, my impending tumescence receded, and I relaxed a little, though still flashing back to school days and those inopportune times the teacher might choose to call a young male to address the class. Here I had no textbooks to shield a rising semaphore. No doubt she had felt the oncoming stiffening heralding the imminent rise before I managed to break contact.

She seemed to have intended to elicit precisely that response. I wondered why she would try and so overtly embarrass a guest she had barely met. The only way she could have been more direct would have been to stroke it directly with her delicate furry hand.

Thank goodness she didn't go that far, a test I would have undoubtedly failed. Cultures may vary, but I suppose teenage girls everywhere instinctively humiliate the male in the never-ending mating dance. No doubt she was having a private little laugh at my discomfort. Would she have thought it funny had I failed to rein in my arousal? Probably! Hopefully, our host would not have been so insulted by such a display as to eject us into the gathering gloom, probably fatal if I take Petch's dire comments about nocturnal predators at face value.

I wished I had pants. Or a rucksack. Pants AND a rucksack. ANYTHING!

The greetings and introductions continued. Then, after perhaps a half-dozen more new faces and names, realization dawned that except for 'Grandpa,' Petchy, and me, everyone present was female. Petite bouncing furry boobies were everywhere I turned, with no other furry phallus evident. However, I had little time to ponder that observation as I struggled and failed to absorb names and faces.

Petch was busy with his greetings, hugging and caressing various eager furry friends as if greeting long-lost lovers. From time to time, he pitched words in my direction as if to clue me in, but I wasn't glocken his spiel. His words were neither helpful nor even understood, and my mind was reeling, trying to make sense of the cacophony. After I greeted Williya, I noticed her mother beaming as if I had pleased her, and Petch said sotto voce, "Good job, boy, you've got them eating out of your hand. She is eager!" No doubt clueless at how narrowly I had avoided disaster. I was puzzled but relieved.

Presently, we seemed to have been well greeted, and the multitude gathered in a 'great room' in the center of the house. The room was surprisingly well-lighted. High open windows let in the rapidly fading sunlight, providing air movement and ventilation. An absence of glass implied the climate was constant and thus no reason to close them. It also suggested perhaps they had not discovered window glass. The wall sported massive, high, elaborate wall sconces every few feet, sconces that flickered with actual fire. In the middle of the room hung the most massive chandelier I had ever seen: a real chandelier too, no electrically lighted imitation. An almost unbelievable array of real candles supplied the light, with polished reflectors directing it downwards. I did not take in all these details at once; I was in sensory overload from seeing so many furry, uh, faces, busily rethinking my initial skepticism about being on another planet.

Below the massive chandelier, a magnificent feast covered a vast polished stone table. Many of the dishes on display were unfamiliar, yet others would have been right at home on my grandmother's dining table. If I had a grandmother and she had a giant stone dining table, that is. The roast pig was a little odd but recognizably porcine. The turkey was a lot skinnier than a classic American Thanksgiving bird but still recognizably a turkey.

The table itself appeared to have been carved from a single massive block of marble, polished to a glossy smoothness and sheen that almost defied belief. It also bore the signs of great age and much use. Around the table, on all four sides, massive, matching stone benches provided seating.

In the corner of the great room was a raised area upon which stood what appeared to be a group of musicians. They confirmed my initial impression by pulling out a collection of simple instruments; they began to play. The Philharmonic they were not, and the music was unfamiliar, yet their effort was pleasant and professional.

The musicians played us to our seats. Stapleya invited me to sit next to her as her guest of honor, I presumed. Exquisitely beautiful, highly polished stoneware was loaded with food, and as the meal was about to begin, the musicians paused. Our hostess stood and clapped for attention.

I wished dearly I had known the language. The words may be lost to me, but I can recognize political speech-making when I hear it. Stapleya's cadence and timbre rose and fell as if she were telling a great tale. Her fur rhythmically undulated as she spoke and gestured. Her audience laughed on cue and applauded as she ended. I don't know what she said, but it seemed well received. Thankfully, the speech-making was short, and with a gesture and rising cadence, she ended with what could only be "Let's Eat!"

The musicians resumed their melody-making, and the crowd fell to with enthusiasm.

CHAPTER 7

FEAST

I was hungry enough not to care what I was eating. I was game, as long as it wasn't too hard to chew and wasn't staring back at me from the plate. The dinner conversation was boisterous and frequently punctuated with laughter but mostly lost to me. I began to pick up a few underlying themes. Some things rise above words alone. Sexuality, it seems, is a given, and a dirty joke is a dirty joke in any culture, and some gestures seem to be universal. My nearly all-female audience seemed rather raunchy, based on my limited interpretation of what was happening around me.

I realized my Lolita had joined me as she snuggled up to my side, her firm, rounded hips pressed firmly against mine. I had become the tube-steak in a three-person sandwich, Williya pressed tightly against me on one side and her mother on the other. She touched my shoulder and began chattering away, meaningless syllables to me, oblivious that I was missing every word. As I listened to more and more of the language, I fought to fit the sounds into a framework of meaning. I tried to judge when to nod or comment based on context, but it was difficult to know. A couple of times, I got quizzical looks, to which, not knowing what else to do, I shrugged. Other times I elicited enthusiastic agreement without the first clue to what I was agreeing.

The more she chattered, the more familiar she got. She pressed firmly against me and began to become outright handsy, softly touching again and again to emphasize her words. At first, she seemed captivated by my biceps, then slowly moved from relatively neutral touches of arm and shoulder to the knee, then thigh. She stroked my inner thigh a couple of times, and I discretely took her hand to redirect it away from her apparent target. Trying not to offend, each time, I gave her hand a discrete little squeeze, drawing it away from her obvious target to a more neutral area, trying not just rudely to push her hand away but to guide it gently to a safer zone. It only worked for a moment. Each time, within moments, she returned to explore the contested territory, becoming more aggressive on each thwarting. I began to worry that if this continued, I again risked the potentially disastrous embarrassment I had so narrowly avoided just minutes before. This girl knew what she wanted and had fixated on her mother's guest as her victim.

I made every possible effort to guide and redirect her explorations, yet despite my best efforts, she managed to reach her goal time and time again. I almost jumped from the table at her first success, and each time I hastily redirected her exploring hand and fought mightily to retain control. But despite all I could do, each touch she landed met a more turgid touchstone until I could no longer restrain my tortured flesh from its full pride.

I was sweating bullets and not due to the climate. I was sitting between the mother and daughter, feigning outward calm, trying to pretend everything was normal while sporting a raging turgidity just out of the line of sight below the table's edge. So, terrified her mother would twig to what was happening below, I struggled to avoid permitting the child to tease the object of her fascination further. This tiny, seemingly pubescent child was an unrelenting sexual aggressor, and I was her target.

This could not end well!

This situation persisted until her mother unaccountably came to my rescue, unaware, I think, of the disaster she was averting. She spoke softly to the child. Again, the syllables were mere noise to me, but her meaning seemed clear. She told the child to stop harassing her guest and let him eat in peace. At least I don't THINK the child's mother had noticed what was happening beneath the table since her manner remained calm, and her voice did not rise.

Without appearing notably chastised, the child turned to her platter and ate quietly for a while, allowing me to calm and recover. She still glanced knowingly at me between bites, eyes smoldering as if eagerly awaiting a planned assignation. Undoubtedly, she had more in mind. So what on Earth was I to do? Better scratch the 'on Earth,' I thought wryly.

I focused on my dinner and futilely concentrated on reigning in my throbbing, uncooperative tumescence. Finally, absent further stimulation, and by calmly focusing on the food and the language flow around me, the surging under the table waned.

Then it was time for the after-dinner entertainment. 'Grandpa' stood and quietly clapped for attention and began addressing the group, a canned speech he had given many times, judged by his manner. He spoke slowly and haltingly, his audience listening politely. He finished quickly to perfunctory applause. Our host then stood and spoke sprightly and enthusiastically as if introducing an honored guest and then handed the spotlight over to Petchy.

Petch stood to a massive round of applause. He was a bit of a celebrity among these people, or perhaps they were just really starved for entertaining after-dinner speakers. Petch clasped his hands over his head in a congratulatory manner, bowing slightly to his audience, and began to speak. First, he said in English, "Watch and learn, kid, watch and learn!" Then, lowering his hands and shifting to their incomprehensible language, he gave a Billy Sunday-style rousing speech like nothing I had seen outside of a church or political rally. The audience loved it. I don't know what he said, but whatever he was selling, they were buying in bulk!

Then he turned to me; syllable flowed after syllable. It seemed clear that he was telling them something about me; what, I had no clue. Finally, he paused, then quietly said, "You're on, boy. Doesn't matter much what you say, they won't understand English anyway; just say it with passion."

Hoping and praying the troublesome noodle had visibly subsided, I stood to face the audience. Sensing a welcome bit of floppiness, I dared not glance down as I prayed silently for calm and inner peace.

I had sensed Petch was about to toss the baton to me. From the moment he had stood to speak, I had been racking my brain for something, anything I could render from memory as performance art. I had once been active in the theater of a fashion, a few high-school plays, but that was long, long ago. I struggled to remember anything at all. Any lines I could deliver rote from memory. Finally, I settled on some lines, as best as I could pull them from my flailing brain, from a long-ago school rendition of Macbeth.

No doubt Petchy was cringing and crossing his fingers that I could pull something out of my, er, that I could think of something. Slowly I raised my hands, clasping them above my head and bowing as Petch had done, paused for effect, and then intoned in my best theatrical voice:

By the pricking of my Thumbs,

Something wicked this way comes:

Open Locks, who ever knocks.

I forgot what comes next! My brain went empty. Stuck for words, I dare not let them see my panic, so I bowed my head to hide my face, to gather my thoughts. The audience responded with tenuous applause. Easy crowd, I reflected. Or at least polite.

A few more lines came to me as my tortured brain began to move along a once long-ago familiar path. So, I raised my head to continue; the audience fell silent.

Round about the cauldron go;

In the poison'd entrails throw.

Toad, that under cold stone days and nights

has thirty-one Swelter'd venom sleeping got,

Boil thou first i' the charmed pot.

Double, double toil and trouble;

Fire burn, and cauldron bubble.

Fillet of a fenny snake,

In the cauldron boil and bake;

Eye of newt and toe of frog,

Wool of bat and tongue of dog,

Adder's fork and blind-worm's sting,

Lizard's leg and owlet's wing,

For a charm of powerful trouble,

Like a hell-broth boil and bubble.

Petch was beaming as the words began to flow from my panicked brain cells. Then, as the chorus came round again, he jumped up and joined in:

> **Double, double toil and trouble;**
>
> **Fire burn, and cauldron bubble.**

I continued with the next verse, growing more confident now as the lines began to flow.

> *Scale of dragon, tooth of wolf,*
>
> *Witches' mummy, maw and gulf*
>
> *Of the ravin'd salt-sea shark,*
>
> *Root of hemlock digg'd i' the dark,*
>
> *Liver of blaspheming Jew,*
>
> *Gall of goat, and slips of yew*
>
> *Silver'd in the moon's eclipse,*
>
> *Nose of Turk and Tartar's lips,*
>
> *Finger of birth-strangled babe*
>
> *Ditch-deliver'd by a drab,*
>
> *Make the gruel thick and slab:*
>
> *Add thereto a tiger's chaudron,*
>
> *For the ingredients of our cauldron.*

The chorus came round again, Petch waved, and the whole audience joined in, which shocked me into almost stopping.

Double, double toil and trouble;

Fire burn, and cauldron bubble.

Easy crowd. I decided to bring it to a close before I again found myself stuck for the lines.

Cool it with a baboon's blood,

Then the charm is firm and good.

I ended by resoundingly slapping the table before me. The audience went wild!!

Bowing to acknowledge their applause, I hoped desperately they didn't expect an encore. But unfortunately, I quickly realized that they obviously did.

Fighting, struggling as to how to proceed, I abandoned my fractured Macbeth and wracked my brain for ANYTHING I could recite from memory. If only I had Google for 30 seconds. Only one thing would come to mind, a song I used to sing at Youth Group campfires long ago. So, it would have to do.

I raised my head, held out my hands, and began again, singing *a capella*.

In a cavern, in a canyon,

Excavating for a mine,

Lived a miner, a forty-niner

And his daughter Clementine

As I started the chorus, I nodded at Petchy, and without missing a beat, he joined right in, loudly, with passion, slightly off-key. It didn't matter.

Oh my Darling, Oh my Darling,

Oh my Darling Clementine.

You are lost and gone forever,

Dreadful sorry, Clementine.

She was dainty, like a fairy,

And her shoes were number nine

Pretty boxes without topses

Sandals for my Clementine.

The next chorus came round, and Petch waved enthusiastically to the whole table, and though the language might be incomprehensible, the crowd joined in, mangling the words with enthusiasm. The orchestra picked up the rhythm and joined in, too, adding instrumental accompaniment.

Oh my Darling, Oh my Darling,

Oh my Darling Clementine.

You are lost and gone forever,

Dreadful sorry, Clementine.

On a roll now, I waved, jumped, and danced enthusiastically, not sure what any of my movements had to do with the song, but it didn't matter. Only theatrics counted. Next verse:

Drove she ducklings to the water

Every morning just at nine,

Stubbed her toe upon a sliver,

Fell into the foamy brine.

And again, the chorus comes round, and my furry audience attacks the (to them) unfamiliar syllables with gusto, ringing the rafters. Next verse:

Ruby lips above the water,

Blowing bubbles soft and fine,

But alas, I was no swimmer,

So I lost my Clementine.

The chorus comes round, and they are beginning to get the hang of the words. Next verse:

How I missed her! How I missed her!

How I missed my Clementine,

Till I kissed her little sister,

And forgot my Clementine.

Once more, the chorus comes round, and everyone is jumping and pounding the table, a fur-covered wave of enthusiasm. Next verse:

Then the miner, the forty-niner,

Soon began to peak and pine,

Thought he oughter join his daughter,

Now he's with his Clementine.

And again, the chorus comes round, and again my furry audience attacks the unfamiliar syllables with gusto, shaking the very walls with their enthusiasm. A critic might say their diction was flawed, pronunciation imperfect, words were mangled, but that didn't matter. Not in the least. Last verse:

In the church yard in the canyon

Where the myrtle doth entwine

There grows roses and other posies

Fertilized by Clementine.

In this final verse, I slowed and dropped my voice, lowered my hands, and bowed. The audience seemed to understand that the song was over; there was no more chorus. The last syllable died away, and silence befell the chamber for about two heartbeats. Then the audience exploded. I think my impromptu performance was a hit.

An easy audience, indeed. Thank God they were.

Please visit the Chromosome Quest Reviews Page and leave a nice review.

https://www.amazon.com/review/create-review?&asin=B00R8NXS56

If you're enjoying the story so far, why don't you help an author out by leaving a nice review on Amazon?

Chapter 8

TERROR

A fter my performance, our host stood, figuratively took the spotlight, and spoke briefly. Again, her words were meaningless, but her meaning was obvious. She was thanking the audience and winding up the evening's entertainment. Once she pointed to me and chattered enthusiastically. She waved me up, and I stood and bowed to the crowd, again receiving enthusiastic applause.

I resumed my seat, and she continued only a few brief moments, winding up the evening. As she ended, the audience stood and began milling about. Many of them drifted away.

But not my Lolita! She grabbed my arm and squeezed like a python as she squired me around the room, engaging the remaining residents in conversation, babbling incoherently. She was telling them something about me or her plans for me, but what; I had no clue. She never missed an opportunity to rub against me, so much like a cat, or so I imagined, except she was not merely content to strop my thigh. Again and again, she targeted my sensitive alter-ego. I was continuously on guard to twist and swerve as needed to avoid contact, to constrain her to safer territory. She seemed to take it as a personal challenge.

I tried to accost Petchy for guidance, but he was busy, insulated by a furry coterie of his own. I desperately needed help fending off this child. I like girls, and indeed it has been a long dry spell since my last serious relationship ended. Partly, that's why I am having so much difficulty with the inner beast. He's hungry — but I'm no child molester. If her mother wanted to play, I think I could well handle her, fur pelt and all! Mama is a delightfully curvy dish, but her pubescent child was just too scary.

Many a man has ruined his life over an attractive nymphette, and I do not need such trouble, especially on an alien planet!

That this was not Earth seemed evident. I suppose someone could have built the castle and all I had seen as an incredible stage in an intensely tropical uninhabited corner of the world, but it seemed unlikely. The park-like setting where I awoke, the exotic woods, the overpowering hot and humid climate, and the fur-people I had met with their unfamiliar language. Occam's Razor suggested I was indeed on an alien world, and I had accepted the premise. That I had arrived here by way of magic seemed wholly irrelevant. I suppose no law requires interplanetary travel to use spaceships.

When I first arrived, I had found the language of these people incomprehensible. I had been in a room full of native speakers for hours and had endless opportunities to point, ask, and hear nouns, pantomime verbs, and otherwise pick up bits and pieces here and there. In-between sexual assaults from my personal Lolita, I had picked up numerous words. Unfortunately, the word for the bathroom was not one of them, and I was unsure how this would play out. Likewise, I was uncertain about communicating my need by pantomime in polite company.

The culture here seemed to be decidedly non-technical, veritably stone-aged. So far, I have seen no evidence of anything my world would consider technological. No recording devices, not even the written word, were in evidence. Exquisite paintings adorned the walls, but they seemed very old. I had seen no paper, no books, little metal even. The prospect of finding American Standard plumbing seemed remote. I did not relish stone-age equivalents! With trepidation, I finally decided I must communicate more directly.

The party was winding down, and I was getting tired. It had been a very long day, and I had experienced a lot of activity. It was unclear what sleeping arrangements they planned, and I felt intense pressure to unload the day's burdens and rest my weary body. I caught my host's eye, pantomimed a yawn, and gave her my best questioning expression. She smiled and nodded in understanding, acknowledging the idea that it was getting late.

She clapped her hands for attention.

Her speech was short. As near as I could tell, she said, "Our guests are tired; it is late; let us seek our beds." Again, I had picked up numerous words, but I could only get the gist of her meaning at best.

That must have been close because the others quickly began filing out. Many came to me and bowed slightly, some shook my hand, and others hugged me suggestively, but they all immediately said goodnight and departed.

In scant moments we were alone. Stapleya, Williya, and I; Petchy had vanished sometime during the after-dinner mingling and was nowhere to be found. So, I was on my own, skydiving without a parachute!

The mother babbled something incoherent at me. I thought I recognized a word I had earlier interpreted as music. Its usage in this context was baffling. I gave her a questioning look, and she repeated much of what she had said and indicated Williya. I was open-mouthed, uncomprehending. Then without another word, she turned and left us alone. Stapleya entrusted me to this child. Or she to me.

Great! Just what I needed. I have been struggling all evening to avoid being put in a compromising position by this aggressive little piranha. Now her mother walks away, leaving the weasel in charge of the eggs.

I was uncertain which of us was the weasel!

Williya was delighted with the arrangement; of that, there was no doubt. She immediately hugged me and began sensually gyrating against my body. I gently pushed her away and motioned as if for us to go. That worked; that got us moving. She seemed eager to take me, well, somewhere. She grabbed my hand and led me out of the great room into a hall. We headed up some stairs and down a long corridor. We turned left, then right, traversed another hallway, climbed stairs again, and followed another hallway until we came to what could only be described as a sleeping room.

It seems the child had led me to her bedroom, although it appeared sparsely decorated for a girl's room. Perhaps it was not her room, but it seemed she intended to stay. However, as these people do not seem strongly inclined toward decorations, I could not judge.

As she showed me the room, one thing immediately grabbed my attention. These people might be essentially stone-aged in their culture, but they did understand plumbing. Almost conventional bathroom fixtures took up a corner of the room. Almost. No vitreous china or porcelain as we might expect, but highly polished marble served the same end. The first significant metal I saw was in the form of valves. The toilet bowl even incorporated a bidet. In an unclothed culture, a bidet makes sense.

It was the functional equivalent of plumbing I was used to, but it was off-putting that the fixtures were right out in the open.

I have seen plenty of ensuite bathrooms, but this was far more 'en' than 'suite.' They understand plumbing. Personal privacy? An unrelated concept.

Cue that awkward moment when you're first alone with someone you've just met.

My guide hugged me, unleashing a stream of bubbling vowels and consonants capped by a tiny squeal, then hurried over to the throne. Without prudishness or ceremony, Williya made the best use and washed up thoroughly as I looked on, bemused. Indeed, this was not the first time I had shared a toilet; but in my mind, such private moments belong to intimately involved couples, not those who have scarcely met.

I am experiencing an alien encounter!

As she finished washing, she looked at me quizzically. I did not wish an audience, but my need was urgent with no obvious alternative. Afterward, I tried to take a cue from her thorough washing example. I had been a little impressed, as we Earth humans usually seem not nearly so fastidious. Indeed, I don't know whether cleanliness is next to godliness as I was taught as a child, but even if not, it seemed a good idea in a culture that eschewed clothing. I heartily approved.

Our ablutions completed, she once again came into my arms and renewed her sexual assault. I pushed her away as gently as possible and pointed to the bed, pantomiming sleep. She seemed surprised and questioning, but she led me to the bed, and as I lay down, she jumped on top of me. Again, I pushed her away.

That's when things came wholly unstuck!

First, she slapped me, a roundhouse blow rattling my teeth and leaving me seeing stars. Then she teared up and began crying, babbling incomprehensibly. I tried to comfort her, but she pulled away and ran out of the room, apparently bawling for her mother. I was shocked, looking after her, wondering why she was so upset.

Moments later, I was still standing there, dumbstruck, when her mother came in, screaming, bawling, and ranting; her voice must have echoed over half the castle. I tried to communicate that I didn't understand, but she refused to buy it. Instead, she gave me a long tirade of venomous language at the top of her voice, culminating in spitting on the floor at my feet!

CHAPTER 9

SMILES

P etchy arrived at a dead run, appearing disheveled and
confused. He tried to talk to her, but she unleashed a stream
of invective that scorched his bald spot and curled his thinning
hair.

Before he could get in three words, she spat on the floor at HIS
feet and left in a huff, her venom echoing the halls as she stomped
away. Petchy stood staring after her, mouth opening and closing in
astonishment.

He turned to me in shock. "This is bad, very bad," he said. "If
she makes good on her threat to throw us out into the night, we
shall surely die." He sat glumly. "Hopefully, she will at least wait
until morning. If so, we have a fighting chance to hike to the next
residence before night falls and a chance to beg admittance."

"What the hell happened?" he asked. "These people are the
gentlest people I have ever met in all my travels. Though their race
is dying, and although they live a stone-age existence, I have never
seen them anything but kind and welcoming. I can't imagine what
could have been so monumental as to provoke such a reaction."

"I really have no clue. I had thought we were getting along fine. The little vixen was very determined, though; I did everything I could to control the situation."

He looked at me askance, suspicion in his eyes. Then, he said in an oddly lowered voice, "Tell me exactly what happened."

I told him how the pubescent child had assaulted me repeatedly throughout the evening, how I had deflected her advances, tried my best not to let her create a scene, and fought to resist responding to her aggression. As the tale progressed, he began to cloud up. Finally, when I got to what occurred in the bedroom, he exploded!

"You idiot!" he ejaculated. "You goddamned triple-plated FOOL!" Invective flowed from language to language, shifting in search of virgin profanity. Finally, he jumped up, gesticulating wildly, winding up for a real blow-up.

Deciding I had enough, I jumped up, grabbed his arm, holding him in place, and towering over him, leaning in to within an inch of his face, I shouted with all the force I could muster, "S-STOP IT RIGHT NOW!!!"

Pulling back slightly but still firmly holding his arm, I continued, "I have been d-dumped into a culture I do not understand and where I don't speak the language. I have been sexually assaulted in a manner that could have earned ME hard prison time in my own culture had I not used every skill I possessed to deflect a potentially disastrous misunderstanding. I have been cursed and insulted in a language I don't understand, spat upon, and given no chance to even know what is wrong, much less respond. And now you, my only friend on this whole goddamn planet, the only fellow human and earthman, attack me too, and again I have no clue what is wrong. S-Stop cursing me in languages I don't understand; tell me what is wrong and what I can do to fix it!"

With that, he collapsed, sitting down, shoulders slumped in submission, staring at the floor. I stood over him for another moment, then sat beside him, putting my head in my hands.

After a moment, he began to shake silently. For an instant, I thought he was sobbing; then, I realized he was laughing. His silent laughter became vocalized and grew into almost cartoonish guffaws. Not quite feeling his humor, I giggled slightly in sympathy as I waited for him to gather himself and explain.

Moments later, he wiped his eyes and shook his head. Then still suppressing laughter, he explained. "You're wrong on two counts. First, these people are as fully human as you and I. Don't let their lovely fur covering fool you; that is merely an insignificant genetic expression of genes all humans possess. A competent geneticist could tweak your genes and, in a week, cause you to grow a coat just as luxurious or tweak theirs and turn them hairless in a matter of days.

"Second," he continued, "I am not an earthman; I am not from your planet. But, yes, I have lived on Earth for a long time and studied your culture. Not well enough, apparently, however."

He sighed and clapped me on the back, "Boy, the fault is not yours; it is mine. I misjudged you and the culture from which you come, a culture I have studied extensively. I should have understood the position I was putting you in, yet I did not. Out of stupidity and hubris, I have committed a grievous error, and it is for me to fix things if I can.

"I often seem to fail at grasping taboos. I failed to comprehend the taboo you faced when confronting a very young lover. The concept of jailbait is very different, even nonexistent in other places. No mature culture condones harming children, of course. Only uncivilized, brutal savages would permit the kind of abuse you imagine, not that there are not a few of those around. Still, the boundary between what constitutes a child and what constitutes abuse can vary widely, and this one is a bit of an outlier, I admit, but she is more mature than you seem to think. Don't let their small stature fool you, she is no child. She is a grown woman on this world.

"I simply never considered that a man of your obvious virility and sexuality, so long without a sexual partner, would hesitate when with a very willing and attractive female, furred or not. That you would consider her a child and balk at violating your taboos was something I failed to anticipate. You did nothing wrong. Still, we are in quite a pickle."

I released a small ironic laugh. "She was indeed very willing and attractive. I think she would have had me right there at dinner. I exerted every ounce of self-control I could muster to avoid embarrassing myself with a massive erection in front of the entire dinner crowd.

"But what do you mean by that remark about how long it has been for me. We only met today. Or is today still today?"

"I suppose we did skip a few time zones. But no, I have been observing you your entire life. The present contretemps notwithstanding, I think I know you most ways better than you know yourself." My eyebrows shot up at that. He motioned me back. "Time enough to explain later; I promise I will tell all in due time if we survive.

"Trust me, son, had you not only aroused but blatantly pinned your Lolita against the table smack amid dinner, there would have been no shock or embarrassment in the audience. Resounding applause, most likely. Sex is a spectator sport here. Your taboos are not their taboos!"

At the expression on my face, he went on, "These people are dying. You no doubt noticed a paucity of males. And children. It has been over a decade since a child was born in this house. Their few remaining men no longer produce the Y-chromosome in any useful quantity. If they can make a baby at all, it is invariably female. They have not had a male child in this house in several decades. When we first met, Stapleya mentioned, and I translated, that she was delighted to receive your boon.

"That was no idle chatter.

"They desperately need babies, especially male babies with healthy heterogametic determinants. That is part of your mission here. Yes, Williya is very young, but she is a fully adult woman in her culture in every way that matters. More importantly, she is a fertile female, an extraordinarily crucial detail. She wants — desperately needs — your seed. She and as many of her sisters as you can manage. By denying her, you insulted her; you hurt her badly, not just her, but her entire people. I need to go see if I can repair that hurt."

Sitting in stunned silence, my mouth opening and closing soundlessly, "I had no idea...." I stammered.

He stood, put his hand on my shoulder, and looked me in the eye. "Do I have your word that if I can fix this, you will bang the living daylights out of every fertile female they make available?"

Glumly, I nodded. With that, Petchy left me alone. I sat in silence, contemplating. Then, somewhere in the distance, I heard screaming and shouting. Ominous language became louder and louder, becoming a virtual brawl. I don't know how long the altercation went on, but after a time, the noise subsided, and all was quiet. For a long, long time, things were very, very quiet.

Then Petch reappeared, bedraggled, sweaty, and spent.

"That woman would wear out a bronze statue!" he expostulated.
"I won't bore you with the details. I'm too whipped to do any more
boring right now. But your apology is accepted. Their desperate
need for your healthy Y-chromosome outweighs the hurt and
insult you unwittingly inflicted. So, we don't die this night!" He
seemed relieved.

Well, so was I; the commutation of a death sentence will work
wonders.

He added, "Your little Lolita is determined to have you to herself
tonight. She is already planning the coming birth. She will be here
as soon as she finishes bragging to her sisters.

"Tomorrow, they will be queued up outside your door, taking
numbers to stand in line for your seed. Talk about the labors of
Hercules; he got off easy. He only had to perform twelve! Oh, and
by the way, I explained the story of Lolita, and she likes the name.
You might call her that in the heat of passion."

With that parting shot and a wink, he left.

Chapter 10

TRAINING

I didn't sleep much that night, and while Petchy's comment about my suitors queuing up and taking numbers was hyperbole, it was only slightly so. They didn't draw numbers.

I soon learned I had other duties in between bouts of copulatory calisthenics. The topmost was learning the language. Or 'Language' as they think of it. Mostly, they have but little concept of other languages and thus zero incentive to give their own a special designation. Stapleya, to my surprise, was my teacher. I discovered that she already knew some English. Not much, a few words here and there, although I would later learn she had been playing possum. That woman is full of surprises. Petchy had been here many times over the years, and she had absorbed a lot through osmosis. Only much later would I learn that she was sandbagging and understood far more English than she admitted.

We soon began to communicate with the smidgen of Language I had picked up vocamotically and the modicum she admitted of English. By the end of the week, I had an elemental dictionary of basic terms and was starting to focus on pronunciation and syntax. I was surprised to recognize that the two years of Latin, one of French, and the year of German I had studied in school were all helpful. I resolved that I must ask Petch about possible cross-pollination between worlds.

Although, unlike any Earthly language I knew, theirs was recognizably a Romance language, seeming derived from the same common root as Latin. Learning it was difficult, but there was enough commonality to ease the process.

Along the way, I learned that they do have a written language. I had wondered about that. What they lacked were proper materials with which to construct books. She showed me the family library. Roughly two dozen immense volumes consist of thin sheets of copper with letters stamped on the surface and numerous linen scrolls with the letters burned into the fabric. They had a crude sort of paper that seemed made from vegetable matter but was fragile, delicate, and rapidly disintegrated when handled. They also had chiseled stone tablets; hundreds and hundreds of them. They did not have quality ink. They had carbon, some chalks, and a few pigments, which had permitted the paintings I had seen. Modern paper, proper inks, and other everyday bibliographic items were not abundant.

Theirs was indeed a stone-age culture, and mostly what they had to work with was stone. They had a lot of stone, precious little metal, mainly copper, and a minute amount of bronze. They understood the basics of metallurgy; what they lacked was raw materials. It seems this planet is incredibly parsimonious with her natural bounty.

Standing at stud and studying Language occupied my time. Fortunately, the two duties overlapped. In between, uh, practice sessions, I got to practice Language with my partner of the moment. These gals love to talk almost as much as they love to, well, never mind. We talked a lot! Especially in the first weeks, except for two hours in the morning and two hours in the afternoon. We devoted this time to physical training — I needed the rest.

If I had been shocked by what I had seen up until now, I was positively stupefied when I received my first lesson. Frankly, though, my shock circuits were in overload. I never had much practice doing so before, but now I regularly believe in the impossible. Some days I believed as many as six impossible things before breakfast!

I had noted before that Petchy was surprisingly muscular. I had no clue! It was the third morning of our sojourn on this 'Planet Oz' when Petchy introduced the next stage of our mission. Petchy had thus far declined to tell me the name of the planet or much of anything else. When I asked, he kept saying he would explain all in due time, but I should relax and take things one day at a time.

Petchy took me to a large clearing some distance from the residence and explained that this was my training field. The first goal, he stated, was strength training.

I said I was admittedly no jock, but I was trim and fit and had once had some formal strength training. So, despite a career path that kept me in front of a computer many long hours at a time, I felt I was in pretty good shape for a computer engineer.

He guffawed loudly at that!

I was, he explained, too sedentary in my lifestyle and lacked the proper nutrition. As a result, any strength I had developed on Earth would pale compared to what I was about to achieve. As he talked, we walked into the training field, and I was surprised to see some impressive barbells on display, ready for use. They were of polished stone, not metal, but serviceable.

He demonstrated his point by walking over to and hoisting a rather formidable weight. With slight visible strain, he casually picked it up with one hand and handed it to me. I reached out to take it and quickly regretted it. I belatedly realized this was far too heavy for me to hoist one-handed. I grabbed it with both hands and found, even then, I was overwhelmed. I lowered it to the ground with a loud grunt, overloaded muscles straining at the unaccustomed effort.

"Point taken," I conceded. "What sort of training do you have in mind. I know many athletes develop great strength by using anabolic steroids at a profound cost to their health. Is something like that what you're suggesting?"

He smiled, "Yes, and no. Yes, we shall augment your Earth-developed physique with a combination of nutrients and training, but the nutrients are natural to this world and have none of the harmful side effects of steroids. They are also much more effective. Steroids on steroids, it will seem."

"Really?" I asked. "Every drug I know has severe negative side effects."

"True! Of every drug you know. Perhaps it will help if you merely think of this as taking natural nutrients. Trust me, my boy, this is like Viagra for the Biceps. You're gonna love it!"

"So when do I start this vitamin regimen?" I asked.

"You already have," he answered. "The nutrients in question occur naturally in the soil and thus the vegetables. The meat, too, as the animals eat from the same soil. Meat and vegetables, especially the root vegetables and tubers. All you need to do is eat your veggies and work out."

"That doesn't sound too dramatic," I allowed. "What exercise regimen will yield all these results?"

"It will vary. For starters, you are going to do pushups. A lot of pushups. He pointed to a square stone pad before us and commanded, "Start now."

"How many?" I asked.

"Let's not set a number. Just start, and let's see how it goes."

And so it began...

That first session, he let me off with one hundred pushups. I was winded when I stopped. I was proud of being able to do it, although I found my muscles screaming in pain from the unaccustomed effort. I guess I had been somewhat sedentary of late. That afternoon he pulled out a crude hourglass and challenged me to do 100 pushups before all the sand fell through the hole. I made it to 90 and got chastised for being a sluggard.

Petch demonstrated what he expected by resetting the hourglass and then smartly counting out 250 pushups, with some grains of sand still to fall when he stopped. I was surprised and impressed. I thought of the earlier evening when I angrily got in his face. Perhaps I was close to death that night in more ways than one!

I realized that there is a rhythm at which pushups become much more manageable. Done slowly, you support your entire body weight on your arms for an extended time. Done quickly and rhythmically, you only give short, rapid pushes with your body's inertia doing the rest, and your arms recuperate between strokes.

Suddenly motivated, massaging my biceps, I fell to and gave my best shot at equaling his feat. Unfortunately, I failed, although I improved on my first try by a significant amount.

Not all our exercises were traditional, formal exercises with no purpose other than muscle-building. A stone-age society has endless jobs that are perfect for strength-training workouts. I had noticed how firmly muscled the fur-folk were at our first meeting. I had received a harsh lesson about just how strong a tiny girl can be. Lolita packs a mean right hook! I soon came to understand why. A primitive lifestyle is a lot of work!

The first exercise they introduced me to with a more practical bent than merely doing pushups was swinging a maul! Even in this hot tropical climate, a large household needs lots and lots of firewood. Heating water, cooking, cleaning, and so on require heat, which requires fuel. Without fossil fuels, fuel means wood, lots and lots of wood.

There is an art to swinging a maul, to splitting the wood just right. I came to love that satisfying thunk! But, of course, you must put your whole body into it to get it right.

The proper tool for splitting wood is not an ax, a common misconception. The appropriate tool is a maul! A maul is much larger, heavier, and has a broader head. Sharpness isn't a huge factor; you're not cutting wood or chopping it. You're splitting it! A maul ends in a point, but it need not be exceptionally sharp. Even if sharp, it will quickly dull, and if the edge is too thin, it will chip and break easily.

The challenge, then, is not to break it or damage the edge and keep it smooth and pointy.

Chopping wood is effective for muscle-building. First, you take a large piece of seasoned wood. If the wood is green, leave it for a few months. The fur-people had a massive stack of wood from trees previously felled, sitting in the sun to that end. Had, as in past tense, before we came here to train.

Trees are felled, cut into rounds, slices about 18 inches long, and left in the sun to dry. Then when they have become seasoned, these rounds are split into kitchen-stove-sized chunks.

You set your large piece of seasoned wood on a chopping block. You then position yourself such that your maul hits the wood right in the center when you swing with straight arms. Be careful not to miss; if you must miss, miss on the side closest to you. Missing on the far side risks breaking the handle. Better to hit dirt than to break the handle. The fur-people were miffed at me until I got the hang of it.

Swinging the maul takes practice to get right. First, make sure there is nothing nearby you might damage, especially humans and animals. Then, stand and face the wood, lift the maul straight over your head with both arms. Let the maul pull back behind your head as far as you can and still control it, and then swing it forward using the strong muscles of the upper back, bringing the shoulders and biceps into the act as it arcs over your head and descends, finally going lax as the maul impacts the wood.

Build up your speed and let the momentum and weight of the maul do the work, not your brute muscles. As the maul strikes the wood, relax your arms to dissipate the shock without carrying it up into your shoulders. Keeping your arms and muscles stiff and powering into the wood with your muscles adds little to the impact and is very stressful on your arms and shoulders. Limp muscles do not transmit the shock.

Do it right, and the wood splits with a roundly satisfying crack. Do it often, and you build tremendous strength in the shoulder and back muscles. I did it until the wood ran out.

Many other tasks of the stone-age household were similarly good exercise. Carrying water was a good stand-in for lifting weights. I also pulled a plow, which is a hilarious story in itself. I was shocked to learn there were no large draft animals on Planet Oz. Horses, oxen, and such are not available, the best draft animal being humans! It seems odd, but even on Earth, only a few large animals have been genuinely domesticated; sheep, goats, cows, pigs, horses, camels, llama and alpaca, donkey, reindeer, water buffalo, yak, etc. Even fewer have been essential to farming; cows, pigs, sheep, donkeys, and horses. The fur people have a type of cow and pigs, neither of which is suited to draft duty. Other mammals are scarce; lizards dominate their ecology. Although some serve as pets, lizards fare poorly as domestic creatures; hooking a deinonychus to a cart doesn't seem promising.

I spent the next several weeks in this manner, doing pushups, lifting weights, splitting wood, carrying water, learning Language, lifting more weights, and baby-making gymnastics. At least I hoped I was making babies. I would hate to think I was taxing my poor body so many times per day for nothing. Not precisely an onerous duty, I concede, and good exercise too. But still, it was an activity with a definite purpose, and I wanted to do it well.

During our first session, something most curious happened. One of the fur-people carrying a small drum appeared at the edge of our training field. She stopped at the end of the path and momentarily stood at attention as if waiting to be noticed or acknowledged, then began banging the drum and reciting something rhythmic that I did not then understand. Then she started reeling off a litany of pronouncements. Of course, this was, at the time, incomprehensible to me, and I looked to Petchy to translate.

Petchy explained that this was the 'Crier,' a person whose role was to keep the residents apprised of important news and activities. The stone-age society version of social media, I presumed. I realized that the Crier made regular rounds amongst all the areas where people would be working, coming around at least once a day, often twice, morning and afternoon. She would announce various news items, the menu for evening feast, the progress of crops, and anything the population needed to know. She would also carry personal messages, doubling as an ersatz postman. This society had seemingly not yet conceived the need for a postal service type of function, but the Crier was a close approximation, at least within the castle. Communication with other communities was another matter I would learn more about later.

During the coming months, I came to relish the Crier's visits. Along with the other workers, we would arrange to take a short break, absorb the news the Crier brought, and sometimes give the Crier a message to deliver to someone; I would frequently send brief messages to my Lolita.

By the end of six weeks, the progress was significant. I could quickly count out one thousand pushups with a 100-pound weight strapped to my back and hardly feel the strain. Also, I could easily do one-handed pushups with either arm, counting them out with speed and precision. I joked that the next challenge was to do so with the 'short-arm,' which got a hearty laugh from Petchy.

Once I had demonstrated mastery of pushups, we moved on to other, much more demanding strength-building exercises. Of course, we still did pushups by the thousands. Still, pushups became merely warm-up exercises to the more demanding regimen devoted to pushing the boundaries of my body's capability in muscular development.

I had no clue that I had such athletic potential. Were the 'nutritional supplements' paying such dividends? I had always had a good physique. Although as an engineer and computer guy, my lifestyle had been too sedentary to do much with it. I once joined a gym, pursued strength training, and made exceptional progress for a while. I suppose I have good genes for this sort of thing. It was, however, time-consuming and a lot of work.

After a few weeks, the demands of my job intruded, and I abandoned the gym membership. That may have been a grave mistake. I realized I had real potential at this, a physicality I had hitherto neglected.

Petchy's training was brutal, and my body responded faster and in ways I had never anticipated. At the six-week milestone, I equaled his strength in many ways and no longer found it challenging to keep up with him in many endeavors. At the eight-week juncture, I was exceeding his best on most benchmarks.

He had added rope climbing to the training. I discovered it exercised a whole different set of muscles, and I did poorly at it for a time. He kept telling me that the ability to go up a rope or down one might easily save my life. I persevered and, after a while, began to do better. I was never very good at it, but he darkly hinted that a predator at my heels would inspire me to excel. I took that to heart and worked harder at it.

I had become comfortable with Language, and quite a few bulging bellies attested to my competency in performing those 'short-arm' pushups. I was, however, a little surprised that more babies weren't on the way and worried whether I was producing sons. These poor people did not especially need more females.

Petch assured me that the medical exam I had endured confirmed that plenty of 'Y's' swam in my genetic alphabet. I was overwhelmingly prone to sons, expecting about a ten-to-one ratio or better. They had been looking for precisely that in their initial selection process, and they had further tweaked my hormones to augment the type and quantity of output. My tadpoles are rocket-powered, it seems.

But he told me, not only had their male fertility vanished, but their females were also in severe fertility decline. That was why they presented me with what I initially considered as 'jailbait,' only the young girls conceive quickly, and even then, it does not come so very quickly. Their waning fertility peaks soon after puberty and declines rapidly after that. That explained the low uptake. Many of my suitors seemed immune to even my Energizer-powered tadpoles.

He assured me that we had as many expectant mothers as we did was miraculous and a tribute to my virility. But unfortunately, these people were dying out, and even my virile contribution would only forestall the inevitable.

I didn't understand why the people were so fertility challenged, nor why Petchy's people weren't doing more to help them. It seemed evident that Petchy and his people must have advanced medical technology. Can't they help?

One day I put this to him bluntly. He stopped and sat on the bench beside me. He stared into the distance as if thinking hard before responding.

"My boy, there is a bigger picture here than I have shown you. A much bigger picture. I'm not intentionally keeping secrets, really. I am trying to ready you for what is to come. The survival, or not, of this stone-age culture on this backwater planet, while important to them, and to me too, I might add, is but one pixel in the larger picture. Our mission's success affects not only the long-term survival of these people but your home world and mine too. Honestly, we are not working and sweating here for whimsy or trivialities. More than you can possibly imagine is at stake. Trust me.

"Now quit jawing and get up that rope!"

Although I tried various tactics, I seldom elicited any helpful information from him. Instead, he would say, "All in due time, my boy, all in due time."

CHAPTER 11

TRANQUILITY

After a hard morning standing at stud and an even more demanding afternoon developing muscles, I spent my evenings with Williya, or as she now preferred to be called, Lolita. I guess, as the boss mother's privileged (fertile) daughter, she had claimed me for her own, though circumstances dictated she must share my seed with her sisters. We had grown close, but once she knew she bore my child, she insisted that any life force I could muster must find a fertile recipient. She would not allow me to waste my essence on her bounteous baby oven. That was okay with me as I was well spent anyway by the end of the day. I was sore and, at times, barely able to function. There are limits. I won't try to tell you how many of the castles' fair, fertile ladies I was boinking in a day. Frankly, you wouldn't believe me anyway.

Sex, whatever else it is, is an athletic skill. The more you practice, the more you can, the more you want to, the more you enjoy it, and the less it tires you. I will merely say that I was kept busy, and the veggies seemed to augment more than just my biceps. Maybe. Nor can we ignore the Coolidge Effect from the unending variety. Nevertheless, I was utterly exhausted by the time I had fulfilled my day's quota. Tough duty!

On our second night, seeing my exhaustion, she left me alone for a brief while, and when she returned, she brought me a special treat. She called it, loosely, 'Grow Juice,' as best as I can translate the idiom. Well, it tasted like fertilizer. But she assured me it would help me recover more quickly; bitter, foul-tasting stuff.

I can't honestly swear it helped; I might be experiencing a combination of the Placebo Effect and the Coolidge Effect, but it did seem beneficial.

Honestly, it seemed to help a lot, and I resolved one day, I would find a way to do a proper double-blind study to prove or disprove it. I asked Petchy about it, and he admitted it might help. He said he had once checked into it a little. It seemed harmless at least, being effectively a concentrated extract of the 'vegetable steroids' I was already eating in pursuit of physical development. He appeared confident there were no harmful effects in the natural dosage I would get from eating or the concentrated variety. I considered it a worthwhile supplement and made it part of my routine.

Though Lolita and I were not actively copulating now, we were intimate in other ways, and she was a pleasant bedmate. Not to imply that our relationship was non-sexual, more the opposite. She's an insufferable tease who, although not accepting my bounty unto herself, ensured I was primed and ready for my duties at stud each day.

Fun gal!

She did love to touch, hold, and fondle my landing gear. I had never met a female so fascinated by the penis in my life. I'm not sure whether she loved me or just my alter ego.

I think most of the other ladies felt much the same. A healthy penis had become quite a rarity in their eyes and thus an object of fascination. Frankly, they love a penis the way most guys enjoy boobs and can't stop looking, touching, squeezing. They can't get enough. Even when not overtly sexual, they will find any excuse to touch, even brushing against me in the hallway.

Lolita also permitted, or I should say demanded, that I pleasure her with whatever other methods I might bring to bear. She liked orgasms, big, boisterous, noisy ones. Her screams of pleasure doubtlessly echoed throughout the massive stone residence, which made me cringe. Well, as Petch had said, my taboos were not hers. On the contrary, she seemed proud of her orgasmic histrionics.

She also loved to talk, almost as much as she loved to massage my coupler and gave my budding skill with Language a real workout. I would frequently stop her and ask her to explain or teach me to pronounce something correctly. No doubt I was learning. I would learn to speak it too if only she let me get a word in edgewise. Perhaps I exaggerate. But if we were to be in a long-term relationship, I must find a way to rein in her loquacity. Her constant chatter could get old.

I was only mildly surprised to learn that the group dinner on our arrival was not exactly a special occasion just for us. They hadn't known we were coming; they put on a big, formal group feed every evening. This group meal was known as Evening Feast, being the main meal of the day and an essential part of their social structure. Sort of a traditional family dinner, but for a gigantic family.

True, they do not have naked aliens reciting morbid Shakespearean poetry and singing folk songs a capella in an incomprehensible language as after-dinner entertainment every night. Nonetheless, they eat communally, and after dinner, various family members present status, updates, or concerns in their areas of responsibility. The head gardener might present an update on the progress of the potatoes, for example. However, the after-dinner entertainment was usually dishwater dull compared to the day of our arrival.

They asked me to give several more performances over the coming months by improvising whatever new pieces I could pull from memory and repeating what I had done before. With Lolita's help, I even translated Clementine into Language and taught it to them.

Of course, I had to explain what a 'forty-niner' was. Not to mention, what 'excavating' means, what a mine is, and so on. I was a little surprised at that last; they seemed not to grasp it quickly. It took a few tries, but I think they got the flavor of it, and by the time a few weeks had passed, I would often hear Clementine being hummed or even sung by someone going about their daily labor.

I came to wonder about the consequences of such cross-cultural pollination. Not only was I leaving a massive quantity of my y-chromosomes here, but the leakage of concepts as might be embodied in that silly song could conceivably have a profound impact. For example, the concept of mining was foreign to them. The idea of digging into the planet for bounty, minerals, metals, and such had not occurred to them. It's no wonder this planet had seemed so parsimonious with her bounty. They had merely been, until now, content to pick up and use whatever was on the surface. I was unaware of the impact my simple song had until one evening at dinner when the newly minted 'Chief Excavator' stood to report on the progress of their first deep mine. I stared open-mouthed, wondering what I had unleashed on this innocent world.

I took my worries to Petchy. He smiled and then shook his head. "The truth is, son; it won't matter. Unless we succeed in our quest, this society, these people, are doomed, despite however many strong male babies you may sire here.

"The gift of your semen is merely the most valuable currency we can offer them for their help and support. These people do not understand the reason for our presence, only that we are on a quest, preparing for a great mission. They scarcely comprehend that their survival is at stake too.

"This household, this castle, is one of only a few outposts of humanity left on this planet. A hundred years ago, a great house like this existed every few miles all over this continent. There were thousands of communities like this, many much bigger, and all were thriving. A hundred years from now, they will be all gone."

I asked, "Why. What is this monstrous plague that has sapped their fertility? How can it be stopped?"

"It is not just them. I told you I am not from your Earth, but I have lived on Earth and studied your culture for a long time. The simple truth is that I have made the Earth my home these last many years because my home is already gone. I am the last surviving son of Krypton."

I don't know what I expected — this was not it! I almost laughed. Then I realized he was deadly serious. I pondered his words for a moment, the incredulity spreading.

"Krypton?" I asked with raised eyebrows.

He shrugged. "My little joke, an obvious paean to a popular comic book hero in Earth's cultural mythology. The actual name of my world wouldn't mean anything to you, and I don't want to get into the semantics of my language. Just as we have been calling this place Planet Oz, Krypton, or just 'Planet K' will do for my world. My former world.

"These people have no real concept of the multiplicity of worlds, of cosmology. They are, in fact, brilliant, but some things just haven't occurred to them yet. Like mining, for example."

He said, "Few of us remain who are old enough to have been born on our home world. Only one other survivor of my world is on our team, one other who was born there before the cataclysm. Fortunately, our peoples had spread to other planets long before, and our civilization survives, although our world is devoid of life.

We, and they, have been fighting since long before you were born to combat this. Not only for the sake of these stone-age people but also for all of humanity, all over the galaxy.

"You notice, their beautiful fur notwithstanding, how similar these people are to Earth humans." I nodded silently. "They may superficially resemble felines because of their fur, but they are human to the proverbial nineteen decimal places. So am I. Your race, my race, and their race can all freely interbreed, as can a variety of other human families scattered all over the galaxy. I can't tell you why this is so, although I might hazard a few guesses. For the moment, accept that it is true. There are many regional variations, such as their fur, stature, differences in melanin, the epicanthic fold, etc.

"I know these variations cause difficulties in many cultures under the general rubric of race, but in the larger reality, there is only one race, the human race. All humans everywhere are inter-fertile — present concerns notwithstanding.

"This plague is decimating humanity everywhere, every race, every culture. Earth's scientific press has carried numerous concerns for the last two decades, including articles on the declining sperm counts of men, and in general, women have been having fewer and fewer babies. Many couples resort to in vitro fertilization (IVF) and hormonal therapies to conceive at all. Many Earth societies are not reproducing at a rate to even sustain themselves. Only a few cultures remain fecund, and even they are noticeably declining in total numbers of offspring.

"Simply put, male fertility is falling, and the span of female fertility is shortening. Cultures that embrace young motherhood are still reproducing madly, but those who wait for more maturity find themselves increasingly challenged at this most basic of life's mandates.

"This is not new! The number one cause of the fall of human civilizations has always been uncontrolled depopulation. When the Romans conquered the ancient Greeks, the Grecians had already entered a period of significant population decline. When the Roman soldiers entered the Greek peninsula, they found cities virtually deserted, few present to resist the incursion. Roman soldiers did not even need to set up camps, as there were plentiful unoccupied houses they could move into. When the Romans asked the Greeks where everyone was, they answered that Greek families had merely stopped having children.

"The same thing happened to the Romans, too; by the time of Attila the Hun, few Roman families had more than two children. In the case of the Romans and the Greeks, some of the blame might fall on lead poisoning. The population drank wine stored and shipped in lead-lined casks, which leached lead into the wine. The Romans also built a massive public water system that extensively used lead piping. However, lead contamination of the water was minor because a thick calcium carbonate residue would have quickly built up. This layer effectively insulates the water from the lead, so there would still have been some contamination but far less than one would expect. Nonetheless, lead's well-documented effects on the human organism include reduced fertility, impaired cognition, and a host of other problems.

"Lead wasn't the only factor and isn't a factor in the current decline, of course, but affluence is. Not that wealthy people don't have babies too, but the effect of a rising standard of living on a population changes how various factors play out. In impoverished cultures without decent medical services, infant mortality is high. It is necessary to birth numerous babies for enough to survive to seed the next generation.

"Then there is the issue of providing for one's elder years. In a society without significant social safety nets, elders must be cared for by their children. As the community becomes wealthier and provides increasing services, the pressure decreases to raise many children to take care of the parents in their decline. Children no longer bring their elders into their own homes and care for them, and the parents do not wish to be a burden to their children. Thus, the state takes on the role of elder care, even though that itself is fraught with difficulties.

"Finally, wealthier people tend to wait until later in life to have children, something made easier by the advent of medical technologies that allow easy conception control. It is one of the great conundrums of life that the best age for childbearing, the period of youth and fecundity, is an awkward age for raising children, much more comfortable in the later years of greater maturity, wisdom, and wealth. When a society becomes wealthier, people tend to defer children, spending their youth on education, career-building, and other things instead of childrearing.

"That fertility declines rapidly later in life becomes a factor in lowering reproduction as a culture becomes more affluent. For example, a healthy young mother may easily give birth to a dozen children between ages 15 and 30, whereas the years between ages 30 and 45 are not nearly so fertile. Affluent people often wait until after age 30 and struggle to give birth to even two or three children.

"Much of that is cultural, of course. Affluent cultures wait until later to marry and have children, but there are additional factors today. Fertility is crashing on the Earth. Human fertility. Some Earthly societies are on an obvious path to extinction. Due to young motherhood, others are still thriving, but that will soon change as the decreasing fertility continues down the inexorable curve. As has already happened on this planet, even very young mothers will eventually struggle to bring babies into the world.

"Many factors have acted to reduce human populations; disease, warfare, natural disasters, etc. In typical situations, fertile peoples quickly replace the losses. However, recovery is not as straightforward or assured when catastrophe attacks fertility itself. For example, the Greeks and later the Romans lost significant fertility due to lead poisoning and became unable to replace their losses due to war and other diseases.

"Even the disease of affluence can deal a crippling blow to any society. Today, humanity's threat is artificial in nature, genetic in origin, and originated on my home planet. It is more deadly to humankind than lead contamination was to the Greeks and Romans.

"Earth scientists have not yet recognized the seriousness of this trend. The population is so high, the Earth so densely populated, that any slight decrease in fertility seems a good thing. Perhaps it would be if it were not the beginning of a long slide into extinction. Instead of celebrating the reduced fertility and worrying about the 'population bomb,' Earth should be worrying about opening new planets and new spaces for humans to live and grow.

"As populous as humans are, humans on Earth will be all but extinct in one thousand years. Probably much less, really. Once fertility falls below a certain point, the population crash will happen quickly. A dozen generations and your people, too, will be living a stone-aged existence, watching your race die.

"I cannot help but find it comical that so much of Western society is working itself into a frenzy over various perceived life-threatening 'end times' issues. Pollution, climate, diseases, overpopulation, and more, yet a genuine and in-your-face disaster is bearing down on humanity like a runaway freight train, completely unnoticed.

"Humans won't survive on the Earth long enough to cause the kinds of decimation forecast by some; a fertility failure is going to soon 'save the planet' from the ravages of Mankind unless we can successfully intervene.

"We must succeed; we must eliminate the threat, or else all humanity will soon perish. Not just here, not just on Earth. Everywhere!"

Chapter 12

WEAPONS

S trength training gave way to speed and agility. We marked
a trail through the woods, and I ran. And ran. I had never
been much of a runner, and the ever-present sweltering heat made
it especially tough. Nonetheless, I had been sold; I had gotten
religion. I had bought wholeheartedly into Petchy's doomsday
scenario and was determined to make the most of my contribution
to the quest. So, I ran. The veggies must have helped because I soon
found I could run ten miles in excellent time. Then I ran twenty.
I would have loved to have a useful stopwatch. Unfortunately,
all we had was a makeshift, poorly calibrated hourglass and some
grains of sand. Still, each day I got better and faster. Frankly, I
was continually amazed at my newfound athleticism. Once we
opened the door to my potential, I exploded in all directions. I was
developing from the stereotypical desk-bound computer nerd into
a super-jock at a stunning pace.

For weeks, my regimen consisted of pushups, lifting an assortment
of ever-bigger rock weights, and running. In the beginning, I had
mistakenly thought I was in pretty good shape, even though, at
first, I had struggled to perform even one hundred pushups. After
several weeks under Petchy's driving, I could do one thousand in
under an hour, non-stop. He insisted that the world record on
Earth was ten thousand non-stop pushups. A few months later,

I was routinely doing ten thousand non-stop, and once, on a bet with Petchy, I did one hundred thousand in 24 hours with only a few short breaks. That was a long day!

Then there was weapons training, which was tricky since we had no weapons. What we had was plenty of rocks. I switched from lifting them to throwing them. Next, I learned sword-fighting without a sword. Mock swords cut from tree branches. They have swords, but blades are rare and precious on a planet with little metal. They were not about to trust me with such a valuable artifact. Petchy nonetheless saw that I learned the basics of the art. He direly predicted I would one day need it.

Our hosts had made nearly all they had available to us. Coming to their stone-age culture from the technological age I knew was jarring, and I kept thinking of their society condescendingly. I should have cured myself of that foolishness by now. They might have little in the way of raw materials and nothing of what we would consider technology, but they were not precisely primitive. On the contrary, they had a way of doing more with less.

Several weapons I had instinctively discounted as primitive and ineffective in what I thought of as 'modern combat' were, in fact, available to us. I quickly learned that these 'primitive' weapons were hardly ineffective. On the contrary, they could be incredibly deadly in the right hands. However, not my hands, as great skill is necessary to use them effectively. Skills I profoundly lacked. That was what we were here to fix.

I said we threw rocks. True enough. I had never thought of simply throwing rocks as all that formidable, but merely throwing rocks is, in a way, the most elemental weapon. The eye-hand coordination required to throw rocks accurately also applies to other weapons. Earthly baseball pitchers routinely break 100 MPH. I have no idea what speed I hurled a rock, but I do believe that since I had devoted weeks to intense strength training, I was now in the same realm of speed as the best Earthly pitchers. Between the effects of the local nutrients and Petchy's aggressive training regimen, I had developed a pretty good arm.

Force equals mass times acceleration. Or, in the case of a rock hitting its target, deceleration! Rocks are heavier than baseballs. A baseball-sized rock, hurled with world-class musculature impacts with tremendous force. Hit any enemy squarely with that, and he is going down. The problem is one of accuracy. Most people can't hit a barn door 50 feet away with a baseball, and I was utterly like most people! We worked on that. I improved. Soon I was taking down small trees with a single rock. Then when I ran out of small trees, I started targeting bigger ones. Well, the cooks needed firewood. It wasn't a waste.

The next step up from hurling rocks is using a sling. Note, I did not say "Slingshot." We had no modern elastic materials with which to build a useful slingshot. We had slings. Very different.

The 'Book of Samuel' tells us how David slew Goliath using a sling. Unfortunately, many moderns mistakenly read that as slingshot purely from ignorance. They didn't have much in the way of elastic on Earth in 7 BC either.

A sling is a simple thing, merely a piece of leather or fabric forming a pocket and two pieces of rope. It is simple to use. Put the rock in the pocket, twirl it fiercely, release it at the proper time, and the missile flies toward the target with much more force than just hurling. I said it was simple to use. I didn't say it was easy. Hitting a target once with a sling can happen due to either luck or skill. Hitting the target twice requires skill. There isn't that much luck in the universe. In the hands of the unskilled, the safest place to stand is probably directly in front of the target.

I was profoundly unskilled. Worse, I seemed physically incapable of learning the skill. So when I first began with a sling, in front of the target was, by far, the safest place. I even managed to whack myself with the rock. Several times! It left a mark.

I practiced throwing rocks and then slinging them — a lot. I couldn't grok the sling. I persevered. Unfortunately, perseverance didn't help. It took days before I could make the release happen well enough to launch the rock into the same compass quadrant as the target. Though I practiced tirelessly, I never, ever hit the mark. I couldn't even get close. Sometimes no matter how much one perseveres, at some point, you must face the reality that you can't do it. Some things cannot be self-taught.

Petchy recruited a teacher. It turned out a young warrior I had already met a few times in my other profession was one of their most accomplished hunters, and her weapon of choice was the sling. She demonstrated. I capitulated. I no longer insisted it was impossible. She started giving me lessons. I rewarded her personal attention with some personal attention of my own. We worked for days and days, but finally, one afternoon, I nailed it. Then in celebration, I nailed her. I can't prove it, but I think that was the day she finally caught, as soon after that day, she started to swell. We had a twofer. We were both happy with the outcome.

After that moment, all that remained to master the sling was practice, and I worked at it for hours and hours. It took a long time and a lot of work, but I eventually became strikingly proficient. Finally, my teacher presented me with a sling she had made just for me, a virtual work of art, almost too beautiful to use. I thanked her profusely in a manner that would not seem wasteful in considering her growing tumescence. She was louder than even Lolita.

With the sling conquered, finally, we added archery to our repertoire even as I continued honing my skill. I began practicing against a target, and after several weeks of steady improvement, I learned to hit a stationary target reliably, as long as I had ample time to aim. But I never became proficient at archery. Unlike the sling,

I could hit something with an arrow from the beginning. But, like the sling, progressing beyond that basic level to proficiency required expert instruction.

I continued to practice with rocks and sling and ran miles and miles per day. I did endless pushups of both types. But my stud duties had slacked off, as I had by now serviced every ostensibly fertile female in the castle many times over. Those who were going to bear progeny were doing so. Those who had not yet conceived probably would not if Petchy's statements about diminished fertility were accurate, but I kept banging away at the task regardless.

Perseverance and all that!

With lessened demand for my stud-craft, I found I had more time for training. Petch added another hour in the morning and the evening. Now I was vigorously training for six whole hours every day. When I wasn't eating or sleeping, despite decreased demand, I was standing at stud servicing would-be mothers as rapidly as my poor tortured testes could manage. Then I began to recognize new faces.

Having exhausted the local pool of potential mothers, I discovered Stapleya sold my talents at auction to prospects from other castles. Candidates made an arduous and often dangerous journey to partake of my service. However, it would seem that my attentions were able to command a very high price in the market, and Stapleya was busily making bank for her family!

I was shocked when I first learned I was a prostitute, but once the surprise faded, I recognized she was an astute businesswoman. My taboos are not hers, and although I don't believe I would have thought of the idea, I decided it made sense. She controlled a valuable commodity that was in high demand. Why not? Good for her! Although the duty was not unpleasant, it was arduous.

These people had been unfailingly kind, polite, respectful, and yes, even loving to me, to both of us, as we imposed on them dreadfully, eating their food, taking their valuable time away from essential tasks. That I was able to compensate them with my precious essence, which cost me nothing, well, who was I to get all wrapped up in taboos? I tried hard not to equate this with prostitution and illegality in my mind. A fair exchange between private, consenting adults should not be something that a tribe should punish its citizens for, should it?

It turned out my sling-huntress friend had a sister who was equally proficient with bow and arrow and others who were master fletchers and whose services were available to us. So, we took advantage of them and what they could teach us. I use us because Petch was now as much the student here as I.

I was astonished to learn that almost everything I had known or thought I knew about archery was wrong. So very wrong on so many levels. I realized I had absorbed tremendous misinformation from old movies. Hollywood has propagated endless piles of archery-flavored bovine excrement in how they portrayed archery on screen. So many awful ideas have made their way into the modern sport itself, to the detriment of the art.

I came to understand that archery was once a highly skilled art, an art that had been virtually lost centuries ago on Earth. For example, the master archer does not draw her arrows from a quiver on her back, as usually shown in the movies. The back quiver is, in fact, a Hollywood myth and is useless if one needs to move quickly. It snags on tree branches and spills the arrows all too easily. Worse, drawing a hand from a back quiver and shooting it is unnecessarily complicated and inefficient.

Arrows are held in the hand while shooting. Not the hand that holds the bow, but in the draw hand, not just one or two. Although loading up the draw hand seems cumbersome and counterintuitive, it enables the archer to, in fact, draw and repeatedly fire in rapid succession, launching two or more arrows per second.

My teacher could fire at least ten arrows with machine-gun rapidity, seemingly under five seconds as I counted them off! Lesser fusillades are even faster; three arrows fly in an eye-blink. My teacher considered standing still and taking careful aim laughable. While targets may be stationary, living prey is not! My master archer can shoot quickly and accurately while running and jumping, while in mid-air, and while on the bounce. A classic Hollywood quiver would spill the arrows on the ground at the first bounce, leaving the archer defenseless. My teacher, a master archer far beyond any skill level I had imagined possible, did not use a quiver. Her arrows were always in her hand, ready to fire or firmly tucked at the waist. She wore a belt designed for just that purpose.

I had instinctively placed the arrow to the left of the bow and squinted with one eye to aim. More Hollywood tripe! Moving the missile to the left of the bow wastes motion and time. My master archer instead places her arrow on the right of the bow, a much more efficient action that allows for much more rapid-fire. The movement of the hand this way more nearly resembles throwing a ball, and like throwing a ball, aiming uses both eyes! As I had said, accurately pitching a ball is very similar to shooting an arrow and is a prerequisite.

It was necessary to unlearn what I thought I knew on the topic thoroughly! My practice at throwing rocks played directly into the skills I was learning once I realized all that I had been doing wrong.

Aiming an arrow is almost precisely the same motion sequence as aiming a ball. It requires intense practice to learn to do it properly, but the skill, once perfected, is spectacular in motion.

Modern archery on Earth is a joke, with elegant compound bows, elaborate quivers, and fancy aiming devices. But, of course, that is only practical standing still and shooting at fixed paper targets. My master archery instructor would have a boisterous laugh at anyone dumb enough to think such activity was archery!

The fletchers taught me the art of making my instruments from any suitable local materials, tree branches, vines for string, various vegetable fibers, strips of carefully cut leather, or even my hair if I must. I learned how to slightly char the tips of soft wooden arrows in a fire to make them harder and more deadly. I learned how to select and shape a branch into a mighty bow. At the end of my training, I could make a good bow and arrows with little more than a knife using basic materials readily found in the forest. If pressed, I could make do with a sharp rock! If I had some honest string, bowstring being the most challenging thing to make in the wild, I was golden!

I studied hard under these experts, taking every advantage to learn this surprisingly complex and skillful craft. Unsurprisingly, while I was taking advantage of them, they took advantage of me. I paid both the archer and the fletchers in the same coin, my highly prized seed. Both were in the thus-far failed-to-conceive group, and despite my very best extra-special attention, they remained so. I promised them all we would not give up. Despite the disappointment, I got individual one-on-one instruction in the art of archery. I gradually became passable at it, unlearning all the wrong ideas and relearning the proper way to do things.

Then after a great many additional hours of practice, I became more than merely passable. It took months, but I became a 'Master Archer' in my own right.

When I graduated from archery training, my dear furry friends surprised me one evening at the communal dinner with a ceremony marking my achievements. They formally presented me with the biggest, strongest, and heaviest bow I had ever seen on this planet or my own. Not just a bow, but also a double baker's dozen of the sturdiest, most deadly arrows to match it, arrows crafted of finely polished quebracho hardwood and tipped with precious brass!

This bow, they told me, was no ordinary hunter's bow! That much was evident from the intricacy of its craftsmanship. This was a true Heroes bow, one of a series of nine exquisitely crafted many years ago. As a Hero's weapon, she had a name. These people did not, as a rule, name their everyday weapons, but finely crafted works of art such as this deserved special recognition. Being the seventh bow in a series of nine identical masterpieces, she was dubbed The Lady Seven of Nine! I was left speechless by the extravagance of the gift. I was now a master archer in my own right, and the gift of such elegant weaponry was better and more meaningful than any diploma.

The strength of the archer's arm is paramount. My teacher was amazingly strong, especially for a female. Better scratch the disclaimer. She was surprisingly strong for anyone! The pull of her bow was immense; her bicep was like iron. Even so, I had the advantage on her and not a small one, thanks to endless pushups and Petchy's brutal training regimen.

I could pull even a much stronger bow with my newly developed muscles, and The Lady Seven fully qualified! But, unfortunately, the best archers of this world could not pull her draw; until presented to me, she had spent her entire existence as merely a beautiful work of art to be displayed, a wall-hanging too demanding for mere mortals to use.

But draw her I could, and soon, with my finely-honed skill, I was able to drive my arrows with a force and power unmatched by absolutely anyone! Petch was no slouch either, but I had him beat by several points! My bolts fairly exploded into their target, hitting with a degree of force only insignificantly less than smaller firearms might muster. The best conventional arrows were rarely reusable after hitting a solid target when I let loose. Even Lady Seven's special brass-tipped hardwood arrows took a severe beating. Better materials are the one area modern Earth archery bests these people. Application of advanced carbon fiber and high-strength polyethylene fiber technology to the ancient art as these people practice it would be fantastic!

We trained with spear, knife, and ax too. With metal scarce and valuable, our practice implements were of wood and polished stone, but they were still deadly. In my hands, they soon became deadlier. Having learned the value of experts with sling and bow, I asked for and received expert instruction in the art of spear-fighting and close-quarters knife combat. I learned that even the lowly stone ax was a deadly art form. I was getting the hang of this, becoming a highly proficient fighter. But it is not enough to practice against a tree or a rock. One must use these skills in the field against a life-form that can run, dodge, and even fight back.

Keeping a large family like this supplied with food is a massive operation. A large percentage of the family turns a hand to the continual food production. The vast bulk of their diet comes from starches, those ever-present root vegetables, supplemented with meat as they could provide, mainly deer and wild pigs. They farm, raise vegetables and keep some domestic animals, but they also hunt regularly. Petch arranged for me to join the hunt. I was to pit my skill against a living target. The idea made me queasy. I eat meat, and I know someone must kill it. I had become a trained killer, but I didn't want it to be me. I was a trained killer who had never actually killed and became slightly nauseous at the prospect.

A formal enemy faced squarely on the battlefield I thought I could handle. Bambi was another matter. Still, people must eat, the cycle of life and all that, and a stone-age existence does not lend itself well to vegetarianism. They get many of their calories from starches, those root vegetables, and some fruits. So, meat is a crucial part of their diet, providing nutrients they would not otherwise obtain from vegetables.

I hunted a dozen times and accompanied hunters on additional trips as merely an observer. Finally, I was able to take down a deer with a bow and arrow. The bow had become my default, go-to weapon of choice, though I became deadly with any instrument. Sling and even just throwing a rock lacked the element of surprise. They would hear me winding up to release and vanish. I hadn't expected that. I practiced my technique, whirling the sling from behind a tree, and stepping out to release. After several tries, I bagged a buck with the sling. Not easy; they are unexpectedly quick. Bow and arrow are much more practical. The spear was effective, and bare-arm rock-throwing was also deadly in my hands.

Other game had their quirks as well. Wild pigs were suckers for the sling if you were brave enough to stand your ground. If an angry sow is charging you, a miss could be fatal. If they were running away, they were easy pickings, if you were quick. The training was valuable, but I never learned to like it. I seriously contemplated turning vegetarian after that.

After endless months of fierce training and constant practice fine-tuning my skills, I sensed we were running out of new skills to learn and reaching the point where continued honing of my existing skills yielded diminishing returns.

We had plateaued in our training for some time now. I say "we" and "our" advisedly because while Petchy had started as my mentor, he and I were much more equal now. He was training just as hard as I. I had become stronger, faster, and more capable by every measure, but he adroitly comported despite being a lot older than I. He still refused to give his age but continually hinted it was more than I would believe. A few wrinkles and a balding pate belie a powerful man.

Then one morning after my stud duty, I approached the training area and realized we were not alone. Someone was with Petch. I don't mean one of the fur-people; female, tall, lean, muscular, voluptuous, with a flaming mop of waist-length crimson hair, and, of course, totally nude.

HER!

I dropped my bow. And tripped over it!

Chapter 13

MILADY

I picked myself up and continued to stroll into the training field, struggling to seem nonchalant. She had been sitting on a rock with Petch, apparently deep in conversation. If she noticed my nerdy clumsiness, she was polite enough not to mention it, although I imagined I saw her shoulders shake with mirth.

As I approached, they swiveled to face me. Petch waved me to join them. "My boy, our leader, our third member of our jolly band, has arrived. I believe you may have met briefly once before. I want to introduce you formally to our leader. Fitz, this is Athena. Milady, meet Fitz."

I've never believed in love at first sight; lust's passion is that which must first be served. It's a pity we can't be honest about simple desire. Love grows so much more slowly. But whether in love or lust, I was flustered, unsure how one greets a Goddess.

Shaking, I stood tall and bowed, nearly falling as my tilt light blinked. In response, Athena stood and reached out a hand as if to shake. I took her hand gently and leaned precariously forward, almost as if to kiss it, nearly falling in the process. Instead, I gave a slight squeeze, a tilt of my head, and said, "Pleased to meet you, Athena."

Somehow, the name fits.

"Call me Teena. Petch tells me you have done well here." A deep, sensual contralto with a faint accent, just as I had imagined. Yes, I think she was the masked doctor in that long ago exam room. Or a sister perhaps, difficult to be sure. She did not seem like a 'Teena.' A Teena should be petite, shy, retiring.

But then I once worked with a giant bear of a man known as 'Tiny,' and of course, there is the stooge-immortal Curly with his shaved head. Nicknames have always fascinated me. Commonly, nicknames may be a diminutive of the person's given name; Teena is undoubtedly a diminutive of Athena.

Nicknames may also describe a person's characteristics; a chubby person might be called 'Fatty,' for example. Or instead of accurately reflecting a characteristic, the nickname implies the opposite of a particular characteristic; so often, the term ironic nickname was coined to describe the usage. Calling this heroic goddess 'Teena' is most definitely an ironic nickname.

I did not process the psychology of her name at that moment, however. I was too busy inhaling the fragrance, the presence of this spectacular example of human physicality, trying to regain my composure and not melt down into a stammering, slobbering nerd.

That damn tilt light was still blinking.

Fighting for inner calm, I nodded. "I like to think so, but perhaps I lack objectivity. Petchy has pushed me beyond my utmost expectations."

"You will be pleased to learn your training's end approaches. But, unfortunately, the end of training means we will soon embark on a treacherous journey, travel far, infiltrate an impregnable stronghold, and defeat a terrible enemy. I have high hopes for our success, but the danger is great."

"I would like to ask some questions if I may. I understand Petchy's reasons, I think, but he has mostly kept me in the dark."

She smiled, and the sun brightened. My calm retreated. The tilt light no longer blinked; it was now solid. If I had not just come from my morning duties, I might have hoisted much more than a smile in response. Even so, I felt a stir I dare not acknowledge. I wondered where she stood concerning social taboos. Somehow, she didn't seem to be the type who would be easily intimidated or insulted by a gallant salute. Scratch the 'easily.' She looked much more like the type to do the intimidating.

Struggling to remain in control, I tried to guess her age. Petch had once hinted she was older than he. Well, he had said she would likely kill him if he revealed her actual age, and he considered her something of an old hag. Hyperbole, sure, I suppose. However, she didn't seem the least bit hag-like. Focusing purely on her face, she first appeared perhaps seventeen.

Letting my gaze descend, I upped the ante by about a decade. Mature, no hint of stretching or sagging. Never suckled. I concluded that she could not possibly be more than twenty-five, a seasoned, well-endowed twenty-five. Twenty-five, well trained, and with access to the same augmentative nutrition I had been consuming, or so I imagined. I realized with a sudden start that we were similar in build and musculature in many ways, though it wore better on her. She could pass for my sister. My younger sister! I was bigger and stronger, especially in the shoulders and biceps, but not by much. She was no delicate flower; instead, she was a well-endowed, well-muscled Amazon warrior, equal or nearly so to my newly developed physicality.

We took our seats on the convenient rocks as she continued, "You are welcome to ask any question you wish, and I will try to answer fully and truthfully. Before you do, however, let me clarify something you haven't asked.

"Petch has kept you relatively ignorant for excellent reasons. Knowledge can be dangerous. More dangerous than you suspect. Dangerous to yourself, as well as to us. We needed to know beyond doubt that you would meet the requirements for the job at hand, and if we chose not to use you, we wanted to be able to return you to Earth with as little detailed knowledge and as little impact as possible."

I nodded. "I surmised as much; Petch has been very evasive whenever I have asked questions and miserly with information."

She went on. "Until now, we could safely return you to your old life on Earth without much risk. True, you could, of course, tell others of your off-world experiences, but no one would believe you. You have massive gaps in knowledge and little with which to support the tale. Your stories would be thought pure science fiction from a fertile imagination, or perhaps less charitably, the lunatic ravings of a madman!

"That changes now. Today is a day of decision, both for you and us. This moment is the point of no return.

"You either go home, and we start over with a new candidate, or you fully commit to the mission and get the answers you seek.

"It's time to choose between the red or the blue pill.

"Unless you tell me now that you want to go home, that you are unwilling to continue, you are thoroughly committed. Once we commence the mission, we set in motion forces that no one can stop. If you do not give your utmost effort, your complete commitment from this point forward, you will; we all will surely die a horrible death, and so will many others along with us. So commit or bail right now. Are you in?"

I pondered the question. I decided another way to put it; am I a hero or a boob? If I am a boob, I go back home to forever remain ignorant despite being consumed with curiosity, desperate to know the motivations behind this mysterious quest. I intentionally decide to be a boob, but I would also be choosing to remain ignorant. To go back to battling a tight job market for a decent job in my field, to go back to my cramped sleeping room, and leave the fate of humanity in the hands of who? The second-best candidate?

Before I could answer, she continued speaking. "If you choose not to go forward with us, you will be paid well for your time and efforts. We will not send you back to earth penniless and destitute. You are a professional, recruited for your professional skills. We have taken months of your life, great quantities of your seed, and asked you to work prodigiously. We will reward you accordingly. You will go back with payment for your time commensurate with your efforts and risks, enough to be able to resume your old life in relative security."

That sounded somewhat better. Money helps, but money is seldom my primary motivation. Of course, I expect commensurate pay for my work. Any competent professional does! When I take a job, I do so because I am passionate about the task. However essential the money might be, I am far more concerned with the passion. I suppose that's one reason I am not wealthy.

Money was not a factor, I concluded. If I quit now, I would still be a boob. "If I choose to return to Earth and accept the money, what happens to the quest?"

"You are not our sole candidate. You have scored the most highly in our evaluation and come the farthest anyone has. That is why you are here at this juncture. If you elect not to continue, we will start over and do it all again with the next candidate. We also lose a lot of time, and our chances of success diminish, but we will still give our all."

"I see," I responded. "From what I understand, from what little Petch has shared, this quest is of supreme importance, and chances of success are poor enough as it is. So, let's not go with second best. However, I require one oath from you. If you can look me squarely in the eye and honestly tell me I am the best hope humanity has, then I'm in."

I was shocked when, slightly squealing, "Yes!" she jumped up and threw her arms around me in an enthusiastic bear hug! Better make that 'bare hug,' smothering me with her endowments. I embarrassed myself with an unintended physiological response!

After a few moments, she unwrapped herself, straightened her tresses, and sat back down. Whether being prodded by my sudden rising was a factor or not, I don't know; she ignored it. I tried to do likewise, although with difficulty. Petch was scanning the horizon, presumably for distant threats. On reflection, I presumed, for her, such prodding was probably not an uncommon experience; she does manifest an overwhelming presence, a virtually guaranteed woody for any man with a pulse. If she asked a man to cut off his head, he would hesitate only to ask to borrow a knife.

Again solemn, she said, "Ask away then; we will tell you all you want to know."

Taking a deep breath and trying to slow my pulse and otherwise reign in my throbbing physiology, I said, "I hardly know where to start. How did we get here from Earth, where are we relative to Earth, and what is the nature of the enemy we face? There is so much. Please, start at the beginning and tell me your story."

CHAPTER 14

PORTALS

She began, "As you know, we are not from Earth. Our home, our entire civilization, was destroyed by the same factors plaguing this world and yours to a lesser degree. Except in our case, it was much more direct, a much more frontal assault. Our planet was at the epicenter of the disaster that presently endangers all humanity. Yet, this world is scarcely on enemy radar. The extension of this threat into other worlds was less dramatic but still devastating.

"The origin of the threat is not a natural one. So, you see, I am ashamed to admit that we are, unintentionally, guilty of unleashing this plague upon the universe.

"Before I explain the source of the plague, though, let me digress and cover some more background, things you must understand to grasp the larger problem. Some of your physicists are beginning to play with new ideas in physics, and a construct called 'Hyper-dimensional Physics' is gaining a slight amount of credibility. Unfortunately, it is thus far out of the mainstream, and those giving it any attention find themselves mocked and their careers destroyed. But it will ultimately provide many answers, though that may be decades into the future. You know, of course, the general concept behind the Einstein-Rosen bridge, or as it is popularly known, a wormhole."

I nodded.

"You have doubtless heard it said that the universe is 'alive' in some metaphorical sense."

I nodded again, wondering where this was going.

She continued, "What you do not know is that although they have some of the underlying physics slightly wrong as yet, such portals as Earth's scientists imagine are not only possible but occur naturally. These portals link all human-inhabited worlds, naturally occurring gateways that allow humans, animals, and even plants to pass between worlds. Life as we know it has spread throughout the universe via these pathways. Creating such a portal using the energies at man's disposal is challenging. I will stop short of saying impossible, but the ability to do so lies far in the future for even the most advanced human civilization. The cosmos, however, routinely plays with naked energy on a scale far beyond that of humanity. We cannot make such portals on demand, but we can use those that the universe freely grants and sometimes even influence them.

"The universe is alive, in a manner of thought, and life has unique properties that function in association with the universe. The natural flow of energy and space-time intertwines with life itself. Therefore, life is sacred, not just in a metaphysical sense but holy to the very universe itself.

"It is unclear which is the original home-world of humans. Countless civilizations have risen and fallen; humanity has existed for millions of years. Civilizations rise and fall endlessly. Entire worlds have gone barren and then become repopulated by 'leakage' from other worlds. Adam and Eve style origin stories have occurred countless times when a few people cross through a portal and survive in some hitherto unknown and unpopulated world. Sometimes, an Adam and Eve from an advanced world intrude on a planet that already has a human population but is not nearly as sophisticated, the more advanced humans displacing the prior.

"Our Universe as we know it is nearly 15 billion years old. Humans have existed somewhere in our cosmos for a significant percentage of that time. We don't know how much or where they began, but humans have been around for millions of years, not just the paltry few thousand Earth science recognizes. We are not even confident that humans originated in the universe we know; there are fringe ideas that the human genome may have come from an entirely different universe, leaked via a portal much as we travel from world to world. Our understanding of portal physics does not constrain them only to our Universe. These ideas allow for the possibility that human life predates the universe itself, at least in some form.

"Portals come and go on natural cycles. Some pop up for five minutes once every thousand years. Some are almost constant, almost perfectly stable. Hyper-dimensional Physics gives us the tools to detect, model, and predict where and when they appear. My people have been studying and mapping them for a long time now."

I said, "That's how we got here then. Through a portal?"

She nodded, "Earth has many such portals. Some worlds have many, some very few, but all inhabited planets have at least one as far as we know. Traveling from world to world requires careful timing, knowing which worlds have portals and when they are open. There are also some tricks to passing through a portal. Many portals are delicate, sensitive things, popping like a soap bubble on the slightest stress, while others are much more robust. For example, most portals only permit life to pass, beings enclosed within a strong aura of life energy.

"Creatures strong in life-energy stress a portal the least, pass through most efficiently, while non-living, non-biological matter presents the highest burden. Non-living items, such as food, supplies, or weapons, naturally cannot pass through any but the most stable of portals. Attempting to enter most portals with anything non-living will cause the gateway immediately to evaporate. The more robust portals will recover and restore themselves quickly. Others may not return for a long time.

"A helpful analogy is to compare the portals to the children's toy plasma ball typical on earth. You have seen these, a six or eight-inch globe filled with noble gasses and excited by high-voltage electricity, displaying filaments of sparkling energy arcing within. Next, visualize the entire universe as a massive plasma ball, with the tendrils of flowing plasma energy as conduits between far-reaching points within the sphere. A striking, if a flawed, illustration of reality.

"You witnessed a transit that day in the plaza. I had exited a portal, mere feet from where you sat, and crossed to another one nearby. The two overlapped for only a few moments before both disappeared. That is what we term a '*Rapid Overlapping Transition.*' When two portals simultaneously appear in proximity, we can pass between them to transit to a third destination. Often pairs of portals are linked and follow a synchronized pattern.

"It can be challenging to make such crossings, especially in cities. I was, of course, worried that someone clothed would bump into my exit portal and cause it to disappear before I could make the transition, stranding me in the city. Or possibly worse, given the unclothed protests starting that day, someone might accidentally step through and find themselves elsewhere without the knowledge or ability to cope. One can easily be stranded in strange and often hostile lands by portals. Portals can be dangerous for the unwary.

"It happens more often than you might imagine. Think of all the mysterious disappearances. At least some of them are likely unfortunates who just stepped into a portal by accident. The fact that non-living materials do not readily transit an event horizon prevents most modern humans from passing accidentally, as a generality, thanks to the prevalence of clothing. Things might have been different in civilizations that did not have the same taboos, not to mention animals. Who especially notices when a dog or cat appears or disappears? Or even less remarked are the wild creatures. Deer, for example, are present on every inhabited planet. They seem to find transition particularly easy. Perhaps they are naturally drawn to the portals and strongly endowed with life energy.

"Extraordinarily stable portals allow non-living materials to transit. One factor in a portal's stability is the magnitude of energy flowing between the portal's endpoints. We always try and incorporate those long-lived, stable portals into a permanent base of operations. The building where we examined you is one such. That portal has been open and stable for over 500 years and is highly accessible. We have studied these phenomena extensively, trying to unravel why and how this is so. Even though we have been traversing portals for centuries, we are only beginning to formulate the theories that unlock them. It is a specialty of science to which advanced academics have devoted their entire lives.

"There are solutions to pass non-living matter through even the most delicate portals. One such solution to passing items through the most delicate portals is if they are inside a living being. For the sake of discussion, you could swallow a phone, walk through a portal, then regurgitate it on the other side. As long as the foreign object is less than about one percent of the mass of the living being and completely encased in living matter, it can transit almost any portal. However, one cannot simply make a 'meat bag' and send stuff through is if in a postal envelope. It must be a living being, not just so much dead flesh. Anything massing over a percent of the living being quickly becomes problematical, depending on how sensitive the portal is.

"This is not as strange as it seems. Consider a creature with freshly consumed undigested food in its system. If not for such tolerance, transitions would be much more difficult. We almost always have a chunk of non-living matter within our bodies, food, and other inanimate matter necessary, but not a living part of our body.

"This 'Planet Oz,' as you and Petch have called it, has two portals of immediate interest to us. The one we came through to get here, and one that opens to our destination, the world where we must attack the adversary and hopefully end this plague. That one is unusually sensitive and delicate."

"Sounds like a chancy way to travel, a good way to get yourself stranded somewhere hostile. So, what happens if you step through a portal, totally naked, from a hot tropical place such as this to something resembling Antarctica in winter?"

She grimaced and nodded but said nothing. I sighed, trying to collect my thoughts. "So that is why we came here to train and prepare?"

She nodded. "We could have done so elsewhere, but there are many strategic reasons why this was the best place. For one thing, the laws of physics here are ever-so-slightly different than on Earth. Subtle differences affect the flow of electrons and chemical reactions. You have undoubtedly wondered why these people have nothing you think of as technology, despite their apparent very high intelligence. Much of what you think of as technology does not work here. Numerous physics effects have eluded them for a good reason; they don't exist. Not here, anyway. Electronics won't work correctly because of subtle electron behaviors; even most explosives tend to fizzle, the reaction perturbed enough to blunt its forces.

"Our enemy is a technological enemy, entirely dependent on technology, so this world is largely veiled to the enemy. The enemy uses cyborg drones, tiny insect-like biological robots specially designed to pass through portals. Though crafted from living tissue, they are not alive and depend on technology to function. The drones falter and die when they enter this world and do not return to report home. That is a significant strategic advantage for us. We can work freely here without fear of discovery. We count on the enemy's belief that we cannot use it either."

"Then where is the portal to the enemy world, and how do we fight them when we get there?"

"The portal we must transit is more than five hundred miles away, across this continent. That is a huge challenge, a monumental feat. Crossing this hostile land and surviving to transit a portal and arrive in fighting shape on the other side is a serious challenge, one for which you have been training, one for which we have all been training. Once there, effectively fighting the enemy and winning is a different problem. I have been working on that problem with thousands of others for many decades. We must solve the first problem of getting there, and we must do it quickly."

I digested this information. Petchy had darkly stated that there were significant nocturnal predators here. That would make crossing five hundred miles of territory a challenge. I voiced this concern.

"Not challenging!" she stated bluntly. "Guaranteed fatal. There are three extraordinarily vicious creatures and a variety of less forbidding ones. They have kept human populations under threat of becoming lizard food for millennia. It is not for no reason that the people here live in massively large families in colossal stone castles. A more modest structure would not protect them.

"These predators and the intensely communal lifestyle they enforce is in some ways a serious detriment to individual creativity. The lone wolf, the social outcast who works alone in a private laboratory or garage tinkering at some idle pursuit, does not easily arise under these conditions. The concept of personal time or private enterprise does not grow easily in such a society. Those who do not turn an industrious hand at the communal wheel are turned away from the communal meal. A perfect work-or-don't-eat commune fighting for bare subsistence leaves scant room for individual creativity."

She sighed, "Fitz, this world still has dinosaurs! Big, mean, nocturnal ones! One of the most troubling is the tyrannosaurus rex. Or a close analog. They are big lumbering beasts, able to knock down almost any conventional structure. A sturdy log cabin is so much tissue paper to a raging T-Rex. Then there are the Velociraptors, or at least the next thing. Much smaller, think giant 50-pound chickens, but much faster, meaner, vicious, and crafty. If you have ever seen the viciousness of cockfighting, imagine cocks ten times their size, ten times more vicious, and ten times faster. T-Rex are rare, solitary, lumbering beasts. Velociraptors hunt in packs and are much more intelligent. An armed human might, and I say 'might' advisedly, barely survive an encounter with a single Velociraptor. They never travel alone. Packs or flocks of ten to twenty-five or more are commonplace. Killing one with a bow and arrow is improbable. Killing a flock is starkly impossible.

"Then there is the close cousin to Earth's deinonychus. Most people think of this satan's spawn as a velociraptor, primarily due to misinformation propagated by Hollywood movies. He is the velociraptor's much bigger and much more deadly cousin. Five times the size, this beast has an attitude and disposition that makes the velociraptor seem like a candidate for a cuddly domesticated household pet. They don't travel in packs like the velociraptors, but they congregate in pairs. Encountering any one of them is a quick journey to the afterlife. They are vicious and nearly invulnerable, too fast to outrun, and too hungry to face on any terms. So, humans must hide behind massive stone walls. Or die!

"There are a variety of smaller lizards, including flying pterosaur-like predators, some dangerous, not all nocturnal, none nearly so deadly as these three. Fortunately, the worst varieties of beasts found on this planet do not like the heat and sun of the daytime, so they only hunt at night. The pterosaurs are cathemeral instead of nocturnal, irregularly active at any time, day or night. They eat mainly fish. They are rarely seen and then mainly over bodies of water. This 'Planet Oz,' as you named it, is a nice enough world as long as you are behind massive stone walls before the sun goes down. Being out at night is not so nice, limiting our ability to travel to the distance we can cover in daylight and our pathways to straight lines between stone shelters."

I asked, "Are there sufficient shelters to hop-scotch from safe-haven to safe-haven and reach our goal?"

"There used to be," was the reply. "No doubt Petch has told you this world's peoples are experiencing a population crash. A few decades ago, we could reasonably count on it. Today we don't know. Many castles have been abandoned to nature and have fallen into ruin. Some castles we need have gone silent in recent years. If no one is living there, it may be because the lizards have breached their walls, or it may be that collapsing fertility meant that there were insufficient people to keep a family functioning. Some might be repairable if anyone wanted to; many may not.

"We run a serious risk of traveling as fast as we can for an entire day, only to find our intended haven for the night is not so safe. So, before we can plan our route, we must determine whether we can find viable shelters. So, we must send telegraph messages to other castles and learn their condition."

CHAPTER 15

TELEGRAPH

Telegraph, she had said! That gave me a pause; we must call ahead and make our reservations! With no technology, we are supposed to send wireless messages to far-distant castles. Neat trick. I wondered what stone-age technology might provide such messaging. Telegraph, she called it. That conjured up a specific set of preconceptions. Every day, I learn more about this supposedly primitive society and discover new ways in which they are more sophisticated than I imagined.

It turns out that without anything I would have previously considered technology, these simple stone-age people, in fact, do have a sophisticated telecommunications network. But, of course, it does not depend on electron flow in copper wires. I understand that that would not work even if they had the copper wire or the source of electrons to drive it. So they use the scorching tropical sun instead, reflecting it off polished metal mirrors.

They communicate over long distances technologically using reflected sunlight, but they also have an extensive relay network of runners who travel between nearby castles. These runners carry messages, goods for trade, and anything a young, athletic girl might easily bear. Any given runner can only reach the next castle, of course, and the necessity of being behind thick stone walls before darkness falls limits the distance a runner might travel; camping roadside is out of the question! Nonetheless, regular mail and commerce spirit along the trails and pathways.

There are no beasts of burden on Planet Oz! There are no horses or oxen. All cargo transport is via runners, either carrying packs or pulling lightweight two-wheelers. They use the buggies sparingly because they are much slower than a lightly encumbered runner, thus limiting the distance they can reach in a day. Nearby castles can easily trade cargo via rick-buggy, but the more distant ones rely solely on fleet-footed young girls and the small packs they can carry. Teams of runners take turns in the role of the draft animal. Carts come in different sizes, the larger ones requiring corresponding larger teams. A typical trade party might consist of two, four, to as many as eight runners, taking turns drawing a single cart. The heavier the cargo in the buggy and the vaster the distance, the more runners accompanying it.

It turns out that several of the ladies I had met while performing my copulatory duty are what we might designate on Earth as Communications Officers. They had told me their title and job function under less formal circumstances, but it was a meaningless noise to me at that time. Now that I had a clue, it suddenly made sense.

Their sole daytime job was to monitor the distant mountain peaks for flashes of light, messages sent from neighboring castles. They had great, polished mirrors crafted from the limited, scarce metal supplies they possessed. They used those mirrors to reflect the sun and cause light flashes on those peaks; they send and receive messages via encoded light flashes, not unlike Morse Code.

Direct communications were necessarily limited to routes between castles able to observe the same distant peaks and the time of day when the sun is at the optimum angle, which meant that wireless messaging was severely limited. They had developed an extensive and complex system of relays, whereby they bounce messages castle to castle, sun and visibility permitting. In some cases, castles are close enough to allow direct visibility. Great 'Watchtowers' on walls and roofs above the castle enable direct, line-of-sight communications between castles. Where wireless techniques fail, messages carried by runners bridge the gaps—vital communications flow across the entire continent in days.

I talked to the communications specialists at some length to learn how it all worked, and I must say I came away awed with how sophisticated their network is. Even though limited, it is efficient. The communications are necessarily slow and cumbersome but functional. As I understood it, the network functions much better than the first long-distance underwater telegraph cables Earth had built in the 19th century, even though we had the advantage of using electricity and copper wires. I was impressed!

It took many days to send the necessary messages, to have the communications relayed to distant castles, and then for answers to make their way back. I thanked the communications specialists with my usual exclusive personal attention, but they all placed in the 'not catching yet but still hopeful' category, and sadly, nothing changed. My unique currency was decreasing in value as it became more and more evident that only so many swelling bellies were to grow, no matter how many gametes I might provide. Still, they appreciated my ministrations, and I welcomed their messaging efforts. It was a win-win for us all.

I was pleased to report to Teena and Petch that we had a clear path and willing hosts for our entire route, except for one dead zone. Almost precisely in the middle of our course, one castle had not reported back. Their immediate neighbors confirmed they had heard nothing from them for quite some time. They had unaccountably gone dark.

It was routine to abandon a castle when its population fell below the numbers necessary to keep things running smoothly. Maintaining one of these households takes a lot of hands. When the headcount dropped too low, two castles would often combine their resources, leaving one abandoned. Sometimes, its neighbors would attempt to maintain an abandoned castle lest the forest reclaims it. We received reports that two of our needed refuges are uninhabited but intact. Their population had declined to the point that they could not maintain their society, and they had merged with a neighbor. They regularly visit the physical structure itself and keep it in repair after a fashion. There might be no one there to welcome us, but we could, we were assured, expect to shelter there safely.

This mysteriously unresponsive castle was a different matter. The inhabitants had not just abandoned the structure to combine with another, locking it up to keep out vermin. Instead, they had suddenly unaccountably gone dark and ceased communicating. The neighbors thought that some great disaster befell them, perhaps a plague, or even possibly their walls had been breached by a determined predator. But, because of the distance and risks, no one had investigated.

While I was busily sending and receiving telegraphs with the aid of my friends in the communications office, paying them for their services with my ever-welcome currency, Teena and Petch were equally busy planning our route and the impending assault.

Our training schedule continued unabated during this activity, with Teena now joining our sessions. I found myself driven to ever greater heights. My body cajoled into ever greater exertion, lest the intolerable possibility of being outperformed by a 'girl' should tilt my male ego off its precarious perch. But, of course, this spectacular example of Amazonian pulchritude was no girl.

Although she could not match my biceps, that was the only area where I had a significant and indisputable advantage.

She could equal or better me in many areas, especially archery, with accuracy, if not absolute power. An individual's draw length is their arm span, measured from the tips of the middle fingers, with arms fully extended and divided by 2.5, which determines the size of the bow one can adequately draw. The pull force comes from the 'archery muscles,' the large muscles of the upper back, the same muscles used to row a boat, for example. She merely lacked the span necessary to be physically able to pull The Lady Seven's massive draw. But with her own slightly less demanding bow, she was indeed fearsome, the equal or superior of any of the fur-people in strength, with near-equal skill.

Watching her perform did illuminate the hazard underlying the gruesome legends associated with the original Amazons of yore. Fortunately for them, the dedicated archers among the fur-people were not so endowed as to have that type of problem. On the other hand, Teena was indeed hindered by her natural assets, forced to use care when releasing her arrows. A moment's careless jiggle could spoil her aim with crippling pain as the side-effect, but she did not allow the prospect of a painful misfire to slow her down.

Running, especially, was another area she excelled at, bounding along with a rhythmic grace I could not begin to match. I could best her on pure speed and raw endurance, but she ran smoothly and gracefully in a way neither Petch nor I could equal.

Our route must zig-zag across the land, hop-scotching from castle to castle. Many days' journey would merely be a modest ten or twelve miles, but several covered more than twenty-five miles, and a few were much further. I could run ten miles in well under an hour and be confident my companions could keep up with anything I could manage. Twenty-five miles was more of a challenge but manageable. Earthly marathon runners run twenty-six miles in about two hours. I was in that range, but unlike runners in an Earthly sports contest, I had to carry a pack with all my worldly possessions, weapons, and necessary food and water and do so otherwise naked and in oppressive, smothering heat.

Despite exercise, conditioning, and supplemental nutrition, I could not run flat out at maximum speed on the longer runs, especially carrying the necessary packs. The longer the distance, the necessarily slower-paced our run. If every leg of the trip were ten miles or so, even up to twenty-five, we could manage the trip without difficulty. We must not only maintain an inhuman pace, but we also must carry our provisions and weapons. We must bear a significant burden, depending on what we ultimately settle on as necessary.

For the most part, with the nearby inhabited castles, we needed to carry little, as they would welcome our arrival and gladly feed us and supply anything we desired in exchange for my highly desired currency. However, we must carry our weapons lest we encounter something nasty on the road. Fortunately, in the more densely populated areas where castles are close together, dangers are few.

It seems my currency was always in high demand. Several insisted that we stay at least two nights to better compensate them for their efforts. Of course, we resented the delay, but their support was crucial, and we understood and sympathized with their need.

The problem was the two uninhabited castles and the one for which the status was unknown, which we had started referring to as the Dark Castle. Not only was there no friendly reception to be expected, no food to be provided, but they were also much further from their neighbors. One leg was over fifty miles, and another almost sixty. Traveling fifty or sixty miles, carrying food and weapons, was daunting enough. The Dark Castle was the worst. It sat squarely in the middle of a 150-mile span. Moreover, it had become relatively isolated over several years as its nearby neighbors had failed, and the extreme distance had prevented visitation. They had still communicated via telegraph and the occasional extraordinary runner until recently, then they unaccountably fell silent, the last runner failing to return.

We must cover some 75 miles within the boundaries of the vermin-free daylight hours. We must carry all the food and supplies we would need, not just the barely manageable quantity required for a single day's run, but the night and the second day's run. And then we must desperately hope that we would find the Dark Castle intact and serviceable as a shelter. If vermin had breached its walls, we might be profoundly disappointed and likely become Dino-dinner immediately after.

This daunting leg of the journey seemed to be barely within the range of human capability. Few Earthly athletes could run 75 miles in ten hours under optimum circumstances. The official 100 Kilometer (62 miles) race record is a bit over six hours, and the 100-mile record is eleven and a half. Then, to rest only one evening and do it again the following day profoundly pushes the ultimate human limits. Add the necessity of carrying the food and supplies needed for the entire trip, and it became even more daunting. We were betting our lives we could do this. One fall, one sprain, one injury, and we are Dino-dinner. And then we must survive the night in an unknown shelter that may not be vermin proof when we find it.

We decided to make a practice run to gauge the limits of our abilities. We marked off a trail through the woods, thru the fields and gardens, more-or-less following the Criers route, circumnavigating the entire settlement. We started with my old running path, connected to the various trails until, with multiple passes, we could run a sustained distance of just under eighty miles. We loaded ourselves with packs of food and other necessities and spent a day making the run, full-up.

I noted I was correct in my original assessment of my companions, especially Teena. She was an athlete, entirely up to anything I was. I was slightly faster and stronger, but not immensely so. I outweighed her, but I only had her bested by a few percentage points on most objective measures despite my greater strength and energy reserves. Watching her move was breathtaking. Despite her mammalian encumbrances, she could run with smooth grace and gazelle-like speed. Watching her run affected me on a visceral level I can hardly explain, and the three of us seemed well matched. Ten hours of hard running left us all equally spent. It also exposed the foolishness of our plans. We might be superhumanly competent, but even we have our limits.

We ran out of daylight in the first trial with almost ten miles remaining. Had this been the real thing, we unquestionably would have been Dino-dinner.

We lightened our packs and streamlined our load and tried again. Better, we nearly reached the 75-mile minimum, but with absolutely no margin for error, but we had not carried provisions for the next day's run. So we rethought, re-planned, and tried again. But, again, we could only barely make the trip.

We had zero error margin and no hope of effecting even the most uncomplicated repairs should our destination not be perfectly Dino-proof. If the door had been broken in, for example, or even just jammed, we might be able to effect repairs if we got there before sundown. But, with a deinonychus hungrily nipping at our heels, we might not have time even so much as to clean leaves from the threshold to secure the door.

We tried again and again. Every attempt at this simulated leg of the journey seemed to end in favor of the dinosaurs. Oh, we might get lucky. Sometimes the big predators sleep late and do not come out right at dusk. Sometimes. Do you want to bet your very life on a slug-a-bed T-Rex?

There just seemed to be no solution!

Our hosts are not especially privy to our daily plans and struggles; we had agreed not to burden them with the overall seriousness of our quest. But, on the other hand, I had spent many hours with our Communications Officers, crafting the messages sent to neighboring castles, paying them for their services in my unique way.

I think Lolita was becoming moderately annoyed with this. Making desperately needed babies was one thing, but the mere friendly exercise in exchange for rendered services bothered her. Most cultures frown on straightforward prostitution, and I suppose that was the case here. When the end goal is desperately needed babies, the fur-people held no qualms. Otherwise, it was less clear-cut. I faced a demanding bedmate who refused to accept less of my time and attention than I was giving her sisters.

The fur-people are very open sexually and do not seem to have many of the taboos in which my society wallows. But a simple swap of sexual favors for services when desperately needed progeny wasn't in the offing seemed to push even their boundaries. I collected several mild rebukes from Lolita over this, although she stopped short of severe condemnation.

I think she was just jealous.

As a result of our time together, the telegraph crew had come to develop an appreciation of what we were up to, and one of them suggested that perhaps we should share our problems with nearby castles and ask their advice. They might know a better approach we had not considered.

I talked her suggestion over with Teena and Petch, and they agreed. We were desperate enough to accept help from any quarter. We crafted our story carefully because we wanted to limit the information we shared about our plans and because the text we could send was shorter than a tweet. Brevity was paramount. After a few rough drafts, we surrendered our message to the telegraphers.

It took five days to transmit, relay around the community and return the replies. Surprisingly, the responses brought a new suggestion to explore, something we had never even considered — traveling the leg past the dark castle by water. We all felt slightly stupid once they pointed out the obvious. A sizable river ran not two miles east of our trail, more-or-less the direction we needed to go, from the last friendly castle before the Dark Castle, flowing right past the Dark Castle to the next friendly one.

We could hike a few miles, take to the water, and paddle vigorously downstream, right past the Dark Castle to our destination. A hundred and fifty miles this way seems possible. We thought making 15 miles per hour for ten hours on the water to a sure haven was a better bet than making 7.5 miles per hour on land with no assurance of shelter.

Without powered watercraft, we had not considered it as going upstream was impossible in the allotted time. But we only needed to go downstream. We are not coming back. With a favorable river current and furious paddling, it seemed reasonable to maintain the necessary pace.

Unfortunately, we had no way to test our paddling skills beforehand, and averaging 15 miles per hour over ten hours, even with a favorable current, was still demanding. It seemed chancy, but a better bet than the other option. Or so we judged, perhaps a bit too optimistically.

Returning to our place of origin only became relevant after completing our mission. True, we would have to address that problem if we succeeded, but it was not an obstacle to the more critical issue of the success of our quest. Thus, pushing the challenge of the Dark Castle and its risks into the possible future of a successful crusade was entirely acceptable.

Finally, we received confirmation that the other two 'gray' or uninhabited castles were in serviceable condition and habitable. Although they did not currently have permanent residents, we learned they had small caretaker parties living there. Not as a full-fledged family, but small groups determined not to let the semi-abandoned homes fall into ruin. They had agreed not only to support our mission, but fertile candidates would make it a point to journey there to assist our journey and eagerly receive my payment.

Only the Dark Castle remained unknown, and we had an alternative solution bypassing it entirely.

Our extended period of preparation, meticulous planning, and brutal, unrelenting physical training was at an end. We were ready!

Chapter 16

COMMENCEMENT

We were, as near as we could say, ready. However, there were still significant gaps in my understanding of our mission. The evening before we commenced, I sat with my companions and quizzed them on many concerns I felt I understood poorly. I came away from that conversation even less optimistic than when I started.

My first concern was when the portal we were to approach would be open. This goal turned out to be closer than I had thought. The date of the portal opening was precisely sixty days away. That gave us sixty days to traverse more than five hundred miles. On foot through very hostile territory and still spend many evenings with our hosts along the way, paying them with my sole currency for their help and support while recuperating from our exertions. That is a tight window, but one we cannot change, with no room for any revised plans along the way. Nevertheless, we had to hit that window!

I also learned that the portal would be open for slightly under twenty minutes, late in the afternoon of the sixtieth day, and then there would not be another opening for thirty years. So this opening was our one shot at making this transition!

There was, of course, a plan 'B' if we could not reach this portal, but Teena and Petch insisted this was the best hope and that the alternate promised a much lower probability of success.

The other factor was that we would be too distant from a safe harbor if we somehow missed the portal. If we were near the gateway but still on Planet Oz when the portal closed, we were Dino-Dinner. It would be much too late, even if we ran for all we were worth, unless the local Dinos were seriously slug-a-bed. Further, if our luck held and we reached the castle before being eaten, gaining admission after sundown was problematical. It was a hard and fast rule that castle gates were never opened after sunset, no matter what, and for a darn good reason!

We had already established that this was not one of the more forgiving portals. We could take no weapons, absolutely nothing but our muscles, skills, and very tender skin through the opening. Thus, we would arrive on the far side of the portal unarmed, naked, and vulnerable and face an implacable foe with powerful weapons and technology. This enemy understood the portals and not only knew that ours was opening but precisely when. We only hoped that they would not expect us since 'Planet Oz' was blind to the enemy. Our chances of popping through the portal undetected seemed slim at best.

Our mission was to reach the portal in time, pop through without attracting an instantly fatal attack, somehow find and commandeer weapons on the other side and then mount a frontal assault against one of the most well-protected fortresses in the known universe. Gee Teena, why didn't you tell me all this sooner? Piece of cake. Yeah!

The discussion that evening got heated. The more questions I asked, the more I doubted we could succeed. Then, finally, Petchy chimed in with a dark, somber tone.

"Son, I know the odds are against us. Athena and I have devoted our lives to this and vowed to give our all. I have explained before that all humanity is doomed unless we succeed here. The stakes are impossibly high, and the odds are extremely long, yet we do believe we can win. In one way or another, every complex plan depends on an element of luck. It will take all the skill we have, all the effort we can muster, and a bit of luck besides, and we must court and use that luck."

Teena put her hand on my arm. Then, in her softest, most sensual contralto, she said, "Fitz, we simply must do this!"

I wilted. "You said that we might find weapons there. Why do you think so? And what sort of weapons?" That seemed a logical question.

She said, "I have not told you the full scope of our efforts. This fight is a war fought continuously since long before you were born. We have assaulted that fortress many times with different approaches, strategies, and weapons. Corpses of the soldiers who have tried the frontal assault and lost litter the battlefield on the other side. I have told you that some more stable, more dependable portals permit the transport of non-living objects."

I nodded.

She continued, "I have also told you that objects buried inside living tissue can pass through less forgiving portals to varying degrees."

I nodded again.

"So you understand that by sending many different soldiers through various portals, with objects carried one way or another, we have built a small cache of weapons there; a weapons cache created at a tremendous cost, incredible difficulty.

"Many brave men and women have died vainly attacking that fortress and thereby left us a few weapons. Weapons we now intend to use.

"Unfortunately, those who carried those weapons died in the process. No one has ever returned from a direct assault on the enemy. Most of what we know stems from historical records before humans abandoned the planet. We have very little current intelligence about what it is like, what fortifications are intact, and what may be vulnerable. We do not know how successful they have been at placing weapons for us. We may find little or nothing. Or we may discover a great deal. No doubt discarded weapons and the corpses of our fallen litter the landscape but searching for them will be difficult or impossible with the enemy watching our every move. We must improvise with whatever we find and take weapons from the enemy when and where we can.

"The portal we intend to travel through from this world is a portal that has never before been the source of an attack, a gateway that the enemy, hopefully, believes safe. We have previously attacked via portals that will allow non-living material, notably weapons, to pass through. Emerging naked and unarmed into hostile territory is not a promising strategy, and the enemy understands this.

"This attack is a Hail Mary strategy, one so counterintuitive and illogical that, we hope, the enemy will be unprepared.

"The enemy has thus far focused on defending approaches it considers threatening, approaches through which we could bring weapons. They have done so successfully despite everything we have thrown at them.

"We hope to use the element of surprise, a surprise purchased at a horrific cost. That surprise is not only because we are coming at the enemy from a direction thought blind to them but also because other brave fighters are to charge in a virtual suicide mission from a wholly different, more conventional approach. We will emerge near a fortress that is under siege.

The fighting will not be near us but will hopefully draw the enemy's attention, resources, and especially the armed bots away from our location. Except for that, we would be swarmed immediately and have little chance.

"Wonderfully brave men and women willingly forfeit their lives in a charge against that fortress merely to draw the enemy's attention that we may sneak in the back door, as it were. We dare not waste their blood. There is almost no more blood left to spill. The cost of this mission is horrific, and if we fail, it will be a long time before our people can mount another. Our forces will have to mount the next offensive without us because we will be dead."

I didn't sleep well that night. A concerned, almost frightened Lolita kept asking me why and I couldn't tell her. I let her believe it was merely anxiety over the next day's travel. That was, strictly speaking, accurate, if not the entire story. I had become attached to this child and hoped I would see her again. I did not suggest to her otherwise.

The first day's trip was easy, a little under twenty miles through the woods to a trusted neighbor, then food, good cheer, and, of course, my much-sought-after unique compensation. We started early, though, the sun barely cresting the mountains.

In addition to our weaponry, we each carried heavy packs, not solely for our purpose alone. It is customary for any traveler making a trip between castles to take additional items and messages. Spices and personal gifts were a regular commodity, for example. Sometimes they carry scrolls containing valuable documents, even individual letters.

And although not a physical burden, we also carried private verbal messages memorized by rote. Lolita, for example, had given me a personal note to her counterpart, a cousin, the youngest adult daughter of that clan's leader. I almost feared to deliver it, as it was rather explicit and downright scatological in flavor. Lolita considers me something of a prude.

Perhaps I am, by her standards.

Because the castles are relatively close, commerce between them is plentiful, and the family had queued many small items for transport. Two members of Lolita's family also accompanied us, also carrying enormous burdens of their own, for the same purpose. They would travel with us today and return the next day laden with items to bring home, a common practice for the nearer castles. Thus, despite the hazards of the great lizards, quite a lot of commerce flows among the castles, resulting in considerable traffic on the roads connecting them.

Our big day started early, with our hosts' early celebratory breakfast send-off and an extra special send-off by my dear Lolita, her bulging belly failing to inhibit her enthusiasm. She was due soon. Privately, I wondered whether I would see her again or ever see my son. Hers was not the only delivery nearing term, but she and her son were the closest to a real family to me. I will miss her.

The five of us set out shortly after dawn. We set a pace somewhere between a fast jog and a slow run. We had plenty of time and food. We could stop for a rest and eat mid-way and planned to do precisely that. Our packs were somewhat more burdensome than we would have liked, but we accepted it was for a good cause, and we're always glad to do our hosts a favor.

Our traveling companions were young girls, athletic, and fleet of foot. As we might categorize them, they were professional runners who made this trip regularly. Like all their peoples, they were much smaller in stature than we and, being very young, smaller still, but their packs were nearly as large as ours. Thus, their proportional burden was much more burdensome than ours relative to their body weight. They could not maintain our speed with such a load, and we quickly realized we must let them set the pace. No matter, today's walk was an easy one.

We let them take the lead and set the pace while we followed behind. Teena took our lead immediately behind our furry companions, then Petch, and finally, I brought up the rear. They endlessly assured me that there was no danger here in the daytime, but I kept a sharp lookout anyway. Ever since I had learned this world had an active dinosaur population, I worried. My head was on a swivel, and my bow carried at the ready, arrows in my draw hand. We were all armed, but I kept my bow in hand and at the ready.

I was not only bringing up the rear to be on the lookout for possible threats; I wanted desperately to think about what I had learned about our greater mission. But, unfortunately, following Teena's bounding curvaceousness too closely was detrimental to cognition!

The first leg of the trip was entirely uneventful. We jogged along smoothly. With our moderate pace, we had plenty of breath for conversation. I told a few raunchy jokes in Language for the benefit of our companions, unleashing gales of tinkling laughter. They responded with a few even more raunchy than I had dared; we all laughed. After a time, I shifted to English and started quizzing my fellow adventurers.

Teena was hesitant to talk further about the ultimate threat. Petch had been positively zip-lipped. She had once before admitted that somehow, they had unleashed the enemy, accidentally, unintentionally, but had not elaborated.

I poked and prodded, begged and pleaded, and gradually, in bits and pieces, the story emerged. I did not get the whole story that morning or that day. Or even that week. It was a painful extraction that occurred over our entire journey.

The enemy, I learned, was something almost straight out of a Hollywood screenplay. Not precisely, and I am grossly oversimplifying, but in essence, it was Frankenstein run amok. Endless prophets of doom since Mary Shelley herself had warned us against the perils of technological irresponsibility. Frankenstein, Monsters from the Id, Gray Goo Ecophagy, and the Terminators all were stories that entertained and cautioned us.

Perhaps their world did not have a Mary Shelley to sound the alarm. Or maybe, like the fictional Krell of Altair IV, in their arrogance, they ignored the risks, confident they could control their creations. In any case, their civilization died at their own hands. Their genetic contagion has 'leaked' via the portals into every human-populated world to threaten the known human universe.

The exact mechanism of that doom is still not well understood. Theories abounded that perhaps genetic contamination had been carried by a mosquito-borne virus or by prions in animals and consumed in their meat. Or possibly human beings themselves had been an unwitting vector. Had Petchy himself carried the lethal contamination to these gentle people? He had admitted coming here for a long time and spending many happy nights among the furry friendlies. Or, more likely, the infestation occurred long before; perhaps a predecessor of Petchy's had supplied the vector.

Our mission, then, was to poison and kill the Artificial Intelligence behind the threat and extract its research database for analysis. Even if we succeed in destroying the AI and yet fail to return with the data, there is no assurance humanity will survive. Unless we recover the strategic information for the scientists capable of interpreting it, they may not discover the key to ending the plague and restoring human fertility in time to save life as we know it. They needed to unravel the precise mechanism whereby fertility had been decimated and devise a repair that could be propagated, hopefully without inducing more terrible unintended consequences.

Such was the nightmare I was poking at, trying to wrap my head around, when we called a momentary halt to our hike. We had traveled almost two hours and had covered about half of the distance before us. Ten miles in two hours was a brisk pace, loaded as we were, and it would be unwise to wear ourselves out so early in the quest. We could have run the whole distance in far less time unburdened. But unfortunately, a large pack slows one down.

So, we stopped for lunch!

We unpacked our provisions and passed them around. The rest would be a short one. We would eat, drink, and perhaps share another ribald story or two and then hit the road again after no more than a half-hour. The more demanding segments of our journey will not permit such luxuries.

After our break, we again hit the trail. Fortunately, we found the second leg of the trip as uneventful as the first. My archery skills were entirely unneeded, and in due course, we arrived at our first new castle to meet an enthusiastic welcome.

CHAPTER 17

NEW CASTLE

We arrived at our destination still relatively early in the day. Despite our burdens and my fears, the trip had been uneventful and not especially strenuous. We were welcomed enthusiastically by our hosts.

They wasted no time at all demanding payment. I suppose it is only to be expected; after all, we had but a few hours here, and they had pinned a lot of hopes on some virile male babies soon a-birthing.

In fact, they had several gestating already, thanks to Stapleya's business acumen. Many of this Castle's fertile females had already visited with me, paying the steep price commanded by our host. Our visit now gave them a shot at getting still more progeny in progress and lowering the average cost of the next generation.

Our host met us at the door with a coterie of very young, nubile charges under her wing. The obligatory hugs and greetings and then I was quickly hustled off to an inner room to render my duty. Unlike that first, long-ago evening in this strange land, I was no longer troubled by taboos or jailbait phobias. I was now merely a competent workman doing a job that all parties had agreed to for our mutual benefit. In many ways, not so different from a medical practitioner, at least in that I was a professional, delivering a professional service.

Consider, for example, the case of the practicing male doctor. No matter how much he might appreciate the female anatomy in his private life, he doubtless fails to find the same pleasure in his professional life's endless stream of that same anatomy. However, much I might enjoy my time with Lolita or fantasize about some particularly well-endowed Amazon, which I won't mention, this was merely a professional duty. One that I must discharge competently and professionally with the skill that nature and long practice have granted me.

Noting the collection of eager pledges imposed upon me, I laughed privately, wondering just what sort of Superman our host thought I was. Even if there were three of me, it would be a Herculean task to do them all justice in a single afternoon. Nonetheless, I applied myself to the job.

We passed several hours in enthusiastic congress, the girls giggling and gabbing incessantly, comparing notes on my performance as if I were not even present, and speculating about the babies they hoped to raise. Frankly, this duty was, in some ways, much more demanding on the body and on the ego than the twenty-mile hike to get here.

They had been entirely serious about keeping me focused on my appointed duties. Moreover, they had well-supplied our room with comestibles so that we might continuously refresh ourselves and not have to break when the rest of the family gathered in the great room for the Evening Feast. Nonetheless, when the gong sounded announcing dinner later that evening, I insisted we take a break. I needed an excuse to rest my worn appurtenance, and I had very much come to enjoy the communal feasts with the entertainment and cultural insights they provided. Moreover, I liked the social atmosphere!

At first, they objected. Pleading exhaustion and needing a break, the girls finally agreed, and after some playful washing and freshening up, we headed en masse to the communal hall.

I was delighted when one of my hosts stood and began singing 'Clementine' after dinner, with the whole group joining in and pounding the table in enthusiasm. I continued to be amazed at the popularity of that silly song. Of course, Clementine was not alone; they had several similar of their own, but still, I seemed to have started a trend, and many contributors had since added a variety of new verses.

Suddenly they were clamoring for another song by me. Over recent months I had managed to pull several such campfire songs from my brain cells. I had recently pulled together one that I had not yet shared with my furry friends, and it seemed now was the right time.

I stood, and they cheered for me to perform. I raised my hands, paused for quiet, and then began in a high falsetto, then dropping to my best basso profundo when appropriate.

Who's that knocking at my door,
Who's that knocking at my door,
Who's that knocking at my door,
Cried the fair young maiden.

It's me and my crew and we've come for a screw
said Barnacle Bill the sailor
It's me and my crew and we've come for a screw
said Barnacle Bill the sailor

Are you young and handsome sir,
Are you young and handsome sir,
Are you young and Handsome sir,
Cried the fair young maiden

I'm old and rough and dirty and tough
said Barnacle Bill the Sailor
I'm old and rough and dirty and tough
said Barnacle Bill the Sailor

And on and on I went, singing the verses in English, then repeating some of the lines in Language. Of course, I gave them the more ribald folk-song version rather than the carefully sanitized American version. Knowing their propensity for blue humor, I figured they would appreciate the more scurrilous lyrics.

Boy! Was I right!

They howled, screamed, and pounded the table. I had another hit. If I lost my baby-making talents, I still could make a living here as an entertainer! My tired old folk and campfire songs were fresh and new here.

Soon, singing done, my entourage demanded we return to our lounge and resume their project. We spent the rest of the evening carrying out the agreed-upon procreational duties. I had learned that happiness sometimes consists in getting enough sleep. Though I got little sleep, I did manage to give each candidate a portion of my seed. I wished them all healthy sons.

The following day we again hit the road; today, a twenty-two-mile hike lay before us. This time our burden was lighter as there was little commerce, and we had no native runners accompanying us. So, we chose to put our hearts into the run and set a mean pace. We thought we could make the trip in about or a little more than two hours, and for a while, we made progress consistent with that goal, pounding out mile after mile, bounding along in silence. Petch was in the lead, setting the pace with Teena in the middle, and I brought up the rear. I enjoyed watching her form as she glided along with a grace and smoothness that was as difficult to believe as it was hypnotic to watch.

I pondered how she managed to run so hard yet so smooth. I presumed that without the support of a sports bra, a woman marathoner must necessarily learn to run gracefully, whereas I had more freedom to blunder along like the clumsy ox I am.

I wondered how this culture had not developed as simple a garment as the bra. True, the fur-girls are not as voluptuous as our Amazon and have not as great a need. Teena did not have a lot of such a need despite her entrancing avoirdupois. She is as naturally well supported as she was naturally endowed. Still, it seemed a logical development and one they had thus far overlooked, or perhaps, due to the heat, had merely decided the benefit did not outweigh the complications. Doubtless, such a garment would become sweat-soaked and uncomfortably warm. I believe I have mentioned the hot climate and the importance of efficient perspiration.

I wondered when my own culture had invented the bra. Was it a recent affectation, or had even prehistoric women used such supporting appliances? I resolved to Google it when I got back to Earth. But unfortunately, this was but one of the many occasions when I profoundly missed my computers!

I think the fur-folk had not felt the lack merely because they had not invented clothes and had no general need for them. Their natural fur, the constant and exceedingly hot climate, and their very active lifestyle had never inspired them to such adaptation. Their tight-knit social conformance would probably discourage innovation, too, to a degree. In idle moments I wondered about society and conformance instincts. Should a pop star of their community adopt such a garment, would they be openly ridiculed or slavishly followed? I decided it was a silly question. They don't have pop stars. Possibly if Stapleya, as the Castle's mother, fostered such a trend, it might catch on.

We were moving too fast for easy conversation, which was good as it gave me quiet time to think. As we ran, mentally, I replayed the various bits and pieces I had absorbed about our mission, pondering each stage and how we would accomplish the tasks before us. It occurred to me there was still a significant gap in my understanding of how we were to invade the enemy fortress.

She had said we were to poison the AI and retrieve its database. As far as I knew, and I was a computer jock who should know, this requires technology. Inserting malware, a virus, or its logical equivalent into any system requires bringing something containing said virus with us. Typing source code from memory, compiling, and deploying it in the time window described seemed impractical. If I understand the threat correctly, there must be millions, if not billions, of individual server pods or their logical equivalent, and shutting down a few will not accomplish much.

We needed a sophisticated, self-replicating worm that would deploy itself throughout the entire system. It must do so without being detected and then irretrievably wipe all the servers so it cannot fix itself and return to service. A logical equivalent to the old 'Format C:' command, else the system will restore the damaged nodes from backup and resume functioning. Thus, we must render them utterly incapable of functioning at the most elementary level.

I imagined that retrieving a massive database required we bring some form of storage back with us. But how was this to be accomplished? Did she have a flash drive or an equivalent secreted in her body somewhere? If so, how was it to be used?

We were about ninety-five minutes into the morning's run, not very far from our destination, and I was still busily pondering this and various other questions when it happened. We were bounding along smoothly; Teena was in the middle when she came a cropper, spectacularly swan-diving into the ground without a hint of her usual grace and smoothness.

I was close behind her and only narrowly avoided falling myself, nearly tripping over her sprawling body. I barely managed to leap over her, landing in front of where she came to an ignominious halt.

Petch was well in the lead, several paces out front, and for several seconds he continued, unaware; realizing what happened, he halted and came jogging back when he heard us both cursing.

I recovered my balance after the unplanned jump, stopped, whirled around, and returned to see if she was hurt and was helping her to her feet when he reached us. She was scuffed, scraped, and bruised, but she initially seemed uninjured aside from a minor cut above her left eye. She checked herself over, slightly stiff and sore but could stand and walk. We looked to see what she had tripped over.

We scoured the path for several minutes, finding nothing at first. Then something moved in the grass beside the trail, and a rabbit-sized, unfamiliar armored lizard crawled gingerly out, made a noise, and then disappeared into the brush with tremendous speed. As near as we could determine, there was nothing else she could have fallen over, so we surmised that the critter had burst from the brush just in time to collide with her foot at the perfect point in her stride to inflict a disastrous fall.

Teena seemed little worse for the wear, so we set out once again after collecting ourselves. Furthermore, we let Teena take the lead and set the pace. She was noticeably slower at first, but she began to pick up the pace after about a mile. Soon we were back to nearly full speed, but the incident had shaken our confidence. Very many miles from a haven, a severe fall or injury could only too readily be fatal. How many miles could I carry Teena, should she become incapacitated, and how quickly? Worse, what if Petch or I should become injured?

Fortunately, we were not far from our destination when the fall happened, and even with the lost time, we arrived ahead of schedule and still early in the day. I noticed that Teena was slightly but visibly limping the last half a mile or so. She had not noticeably slowed but was apparently in some discomfort. I was concerned.

Please visit the Chromosome Quest Reviews Page and leave a nice review.

https://www.amazon.com/review/create-review?&asin=B00R8NXS56

If you're enjoying the story so far, why don't you help an author out by leaving a nice review on Amazon?

CHAPTER 18

HEALING

O ur new hosts eagerly welcomed our arrival. Once again, the castle mother had my afternoon's work laid out in the form of a bevy of eager recipients of my boon. Proximately the same events of our previous afternoon repeated themselves as I spread my wisdom amongst the eager padawans. Like the evening before, I gave them a boisterous after-dinner rendition of Clementine and Barnacle Bill to rousing applause.

It soon became apparent that we would stay another day which delighted our hosts but worried me. The prospect of resting another day was welcome, but the reason was decidedly not. Teena was limping, not severely, but enough to be worrisome. As near as we could tell, she did not have a material injury, just overstressed tendons, but a strenuous run on an abused and tender ankle seemed ill-advised. We talked it over and agreed to another day's rest.

We feared that resuming the trek too soon might result in even longer delays. We hoped that if Teena kept off her feet and kept her foot elevated for a day, she might recover sufficiently to resume our trip. I had initially suggested she soak it in cold water, at which point she sharply reminded me that in this climate, this culture had little concept of cold. The best they could do was 'not heated.'

The room temperature was a long way from 'cold' here. I suggested trying hot water then, and she did for a while, but it didn't help. So, we settled for elevation and massage, with some healing crème the fur-people claimed to be effective.

While massaging and wrapping her foot, I was suddenly taken aback. Shockingly, I noticed that she has six toes on each foot! Polydactylism is not unknown. However, such supernumerary digits are often malformed, sometimes causing the bearer challenges and needing surgical intervention. Not so, in her case. Each foot is perfectly formed and symmetrical. Is this a natural human mutation or some artifact of her claimed alien origins? If so, why doesn't she have six fingers? I wanted to ask but decided it was none of my business; I opted to ignore it, pretending I had not noticed, though I did later look closely at her hands.

With an unplanned day of idleness to spend, I resumed my professional duties; a not an entirely unpleasant way to pass an extra day, and I am confident our host appreciated my efforts. But oh! My aching loins! When I return to Earth, I must contact The Guinness Book of Records!

The following morning, Teena seemed limp-free, so we set out for the next castle after due consideration. This one was a more extended run, a grueling forty miles. The length of this leg was precisely why we had opted to give Teena's foot another day of rest, and even so, I worried that she would have difficulty.

For this day's outing, we carried a minimal burden. We each sported a pack with water and food, fritters colloquially referred to as 'Journey Cake,' and nothing else save our weapons. We needed to make rapid time, not even stopping for lunch, just slow and eat on a jog, then resume the pace. We only need an average above four miles per hour, hardly a run, more like a brisk walk. However, that slow pace meant ten hours on the road, stretching the limits of the safe daylight hours. We could do it in much less if Teena's foot were able. Petch and I could probably do it between four and five hours or so, closer to four, I'd guess.

Teena's foot was the worrisome unknown. Again, we set out with her in the lead, letting her set the pace. We had a plan, should she begin to feel any stress or pain within the first five miles, we would call a halt and turn back. With my best dominant male stance, I took her arm, peered directly into her face, and emphatically told her not to try and push through, not to ignore any pain. We will abort if there is any distress within the first five miles. If she were stress-free, then we would push on to the destination.

She agreed. I wished I had trusted her! The last thing I wanted was to aggravate her injury at this stage. There would be time enough to play Wonder Woman later. I worried she might endanger the mission rather than admit weakness. We still had time and needed to conserve our resources wisely. She could be fiercely determined, and I feared she might not recognize when to back off.

We set out, Teena in the lead and me immediately behind her. This time I had no interest in watching her fluidly rhythmic movements. Well, not for THAT reason.

Or not only.

I positioned myself to spot any sign of stress that might mean trouble, and Petch brought up the rear. He argued about that, but he relented when I took him aside and told him why I wanted to be close behind her.

He was as protective as I.

It seemed odd, but Petch and Athena were more and more frequently deferring to me on operational tactics. More and more, I seemed to be becoming the leader of our band, at least in small things, or so it seemed. I was seriously wondering about that and the implications.

Teena set the pace and started briskly. Not a full-on run, but close to it. Well above the four MPH minimum we needed to maintain. She seemed to move smoothly, fluidly, with no sign of a limp or perhaps only the most infinitesimal trace. I carefully watched her stride for any hint of a reason to abort.

I didn't see one.

After a couple of miles, she picked up the pace. We were making a good run now. Beating that ten-hour deadline — a word with more than symbolic meaning — was assured if we kept this up. A few more miles, and she again accelerated. We were now close to our best speed. I could keep this up for hours; I had often done so in training. We were probably making ten miles per hour, perhaps even slightly more, and would soon annihilate the forty-mile span.

After two hours at this intense pace, I called a halt. Our original intent had been to merely slow to a jog, consume the rough carbohydrate while still moving, and then resume speed. I changed tactics. I decreed that we should take a short break, eat, sit, and rest. All told, we were making exceptional time; no need to kill ourselves.

We merely parked our posteriors on the trail. The trails these people used through the woods were well-maintained, smooth, and comfortable to walk barefooted. We were blocking the path, but there was naught in the way of traffic. Although runners indeed pass between castles regularly, if someone were to come along, they would likely stop and join us for lunch anyway. So, we rested on the trail, consumed our allotment of journey cake and water, lay back and relaxed for a few brief moments, then post respite, gathered our supplies, repositioned our packs, and readied ourselves to continue.

Shortly we resumed our trek. Again, Teena set the pace. As before, she started relatively slowly, and, as before, I watched her stride for any hint of distress. As before, she soon accelerated to full speed, and we fairly flew through the woods. I began to relax a little, the near disaster of the previous day's run was behind us, or so it seemed.

I thought hard about why I was so solicitous of Teena's well-being. Was it because she was the female? I can't deny that there was a protective male animal within my soul. I am accustomed to the woman as the smaller, weaker, slower, etc. Perhaps that had often been the case, but not here. This woman was an Amazon Warrior, the equal of any two ordinary men.

I'd guess that of the squishy type of nerdy, soft, city-dwelling man I used to be; she was the equal of any FOUR. I am no longer that sort of man. While bounding along behind Teena and Petch, I had time to think and marvel at the changes of the last few months. Not just my newfound muscles but my personality, too, as I have become confident, open, and outgoing in ways never imagined. The nerd still resides somewhere deep inside, but he is no longer in charge.

No, I convinced myself that I was extra cautious because she was, at least in my mind, our 'tech officer,' the one with the specialized tools and training to penetrate and defeat our enemy. That Petch was perhaps also competent, I did not doubt.

But all the signs argued that SHE was the one member of our team who was genuinely indispensable. I'm not entirely sure why I thought so, but I had come to take it as an article of faith that the other two could complete the mission if Petch or I became injured. But, on the other hand, I believed that if she became disabled, we could not continue. So, rightly or wrongly, I felt it my duty to protect her as much as possible.

I kept telling myself my only concern was the success of the mission. I was not becoming captivated by Teena's undeniable pulchritude. I insisted I was not falling in love. I repeated that mantra over and over to myself. I certainly was not lacking for sex. I spent every night with a whole room full of the lustiest, bawdiest, horniest females in the known universe, banging myself into oblivion.

All in a good cause, I keep telling myself, all in a good cause, and a man should enjoy his work.

Every night, I was doing my damnedest to plant my seed in every household we visited, determined to leave a little Fitz behind, or several, to carry on my legend. Yet I found myself endlessly fantasizing about the bouncing Amazonian booty I was chasing fruitlessly, mile upon endless mile across this dinosaur-cursed landscape.

CHAPTER 19

RIVER

I had come to love running through the woods. Not only was following Teena entrancing, and no doubt I was getting an endorphin runner's high, but in addition to those details, I enjoyed having alone time to think. I could, after a fashion, place my body on autopilot and let my mind go its own way. I suppose that was my problem, too much time to think with gracefully bounding Amazonian pulchritude little more than inches away. I found myself wondering what life might bring after our mission.

The next several legs of our journey went smoothly and were uneventful. Nobody fell, nobody was injured. Twice, we spotted easy prey near the end of our day's run and loosed an arrow or two to bring our hosts a gift of fresh meat. The longer routes left us spent and exhausted and required a second day's stay to recoup, much to our hosts' delight. Twenty-five miles was a piece of cake. Forty miles we could do with moderate difficulty. Those few legs of fifty-plus miles were dramatically worse. The arduousness seemed to increase exponentially with distance, especially anything over forty-five or fifty miles.

We must run more slowly, the greater the distance; I can run ten miles in under an hour without feeling stressed. I can make twenty-five in a little over two hours without being utterly spent.

Forty miles requires a full four and a half hours, possibly more, and leaves me well worn. By the time you're talking fifty, we are into the range of six hours plus with utter exhaustion at the end, and it gets rapidly worse from there.

We humans just 'run out of gas' as time and distance increase. Our bodies only have so much reserve fuel! Carrying a burden worsens things considerably. Every pound slows us, adds to the time required for a given distance, and increases the consumption of our metabolical reserves. Extended runs demand fuel. Running as we were, someone of my size can burn more than two thousand calories per hour. A five-hour run leaves us with a ten thousand calorie deficit, if not more.

We must carry food and water, especially water in the heat of this climate, on anything more than a short run. The weight of that food and water slows us down and causes us to burn even more calories. A single pound adds ten or more calories per hour to the fuel requirement. A fifty-pound pack means an extra two to three thousand calories on a five-hour run.

Not only must we run these tremendously long distances, as a matter of course, we must then rest but briefly and do it all over again the next day. We cannot often afford to spend more than one night recovering from a day's run. Earthly marathon runners might run these distances, but they typically have weeks to recover between events. We don't.

We had run up to about eighty miles in our practice runs under controlled conditions. In the real world, sixty miles nearly broke us. We elected to spend two nights at the destination castle after any day of fifty miles or more. We needed the recovery time. No matter how lavish Evening Feast might be, replenishing somewhere between ten and fifteen thousand expended calories in a single evening meal is just not possible.

Even with the consumption of journey cake along the way, after such an effort, replenishment and recovery demand time, conveniently ignoring the physical activity I was engaging in each evening to pay our way. Anything over forty to fifty miles per day is more than even our genetically enhanced and finely honed bodies can sustain.

We were mighty glad we were not going to tackle the back-to-back 75-mile runs we had contemplated for the Dark Castle leg. I think we all agreed such an attempt would have been a disaster; two such days back-to-back with little rest between seemed beyond even our capability. Perhaps the adrenalin of being chased by a T-Rex might give us a second wind, but the simple reality was that we were already dead if we found ourselves still on the road when lizards began to prowl.

Endless days of running. Hundreds of miles passed beneath our flying feet. Nights of massive feasts, trying to consume the calories we had expended each day, food and shelter bought and paid for with labor of my loins. Those busy nights were demanding enough without running all day too. As much as I appreciated our hosts and their charms, I would often have loved a good night's sleep even more.

We had covered over three hundred miles of our journey when we reached the castle closest to the Dark Castle. We had telegraphed ahead and arranged for a pirogue to be available for the water journey. The boat, paddles, supplies, and more were ready when we arrived.

Athena, Petch, and I gathered that evening after dinner. I had given choice service to my duties, sang 'Clementine' and 'Barnacle Bill' for them, and eaten my fill. Now, however, we needed planning time.

We studied our schedule and the remaining distance we must cover and discussed our task ahead. Then, consulting my companions, we decided that we were too tired to continue immediately. The last two legs had been arduous, and we were all feeling spent. True, we would be sitting in a boat in the next segment, but we would not be resting. Instead, we would be paddling furiously. We had to sustain a much faster pace on the water than we had ever made on land, and we had to maintain it much longer. We had a few minutes over ten hours between Dino-bedtime when the sun rises and the evening when the Dino-Rooster crows.

We must run from this castle to the river at top speed, about four miles from here. Then put our pirogue in the water and paddle fiercely, making our way one hundred and fifty miles downstream, beach our craft, then run a little over three miles to the welcoming castle before they closed their doors for the evening.

We were confident we could do it. We were brutally mistaken!

Fifteen miles per hour on the water seemed simple enough between the river's current and our motivated paddling. But, on the other hand, we had never done anything like this before. How much time would we lose getting the hang of it?

The good news is using a boat simplified carrying a burden. Our boat could comfortably hold a great deal of cargo. Far more than we could have reasonably carried, food, water, and freight to be delivered to the destination residence would sit in the boat between us.

I decided we would take tomorrow and do a dry run. Or is that a 'wet run?' In any case, we would arise early, do a full-up rehearsal of running to the river, loading, and launching the boat, and put in some time practicing our paddling, learning how the loaded pirogue will handle. Then we would return to this castle and get a good night's rest before doing it for real the following morning.

Again, our hosts were overjoyed at the prospect of having an extra day to collect my highly sought-after boon. The den mother of this castle presented a fresh collection of her youngest and most nubile fertile candidates. I fell to my procreational duties with alacrity once again.

It was well that we practiced. Our first attempt at loading the pirogue and getting it into the water was downright comical. I dearly wished I had a smartphone or even an old film camera. I suggested we must re-enact this on earth for the benefit of video. If this were for real, it could have been disastrous. Fortunately, it wasn't, and rather than a few relaxed hours doing a simple dry run, we spent most of the day laughing at our ineptitude and figuring out what we were doing wrong.

Launching the pirogue turned out to require more skill than we expected. Not that it wasn't readily learnable, but it took time and effort. The first time I managed to fall flat on my face, and Petch and Teena lost their footing, falling comically on the slippery bank. Then we capsized the boat while trying to climb aboard. We practiced that several times before we became coordinated well enough to smoothly launch the craft and hop aboard without making fools of ourselves.

By late afternoon we had the kinks worked out.

I concluded that loading the boat with provisions the morning of the trip was foolish and wasteful of precious time. Instead, we must prepare the pirogue and have it ready to launch the day before. We would place everything in the boat except the food, all strapped down and ready to float. Food, naturally, would attract wildlife, and we dare not leave it out. The craft would be positioned near the shore so that a quick motion could have it in the water.

Hopefully, nothing would disturb it during the night, though this was a calculated risk. Wildlife and weather could be unpredictable and destructive; these people never left their boats out at night. They don't leave anything out at night!

Finally, confident we could get underway without problems, we returned to the castle for another night of merry-making and hopefully fruitful copulation. At least I was making the two-backed beast with endless, eager partners; I am unsure what Teena and Petch were doing. Petch seemed to collect a clique at every stop. I know Petch was not shy about availing himself of the good times to be had, although it is not clear to me that he was leaving any progeny behind. The fur-people are remarkably uninhibited about such things, always ready to share pleasure.

But as for Teena, I had no clue how she spent the evenings. And I did wonder!

CHAPTER 20

DARK CASTLE

The morning of our launch, we started very early, so much so that we were taking a risk that a lizard or two could still be awake. We had listened carefully from the castle for any noises that might indicate vermin nearby. We had often heard them at night, especially the T-Rex, which is known to vocalize a deep, bone-rattling basso profondo when chasing a meal; or when copulating. I would love to see that! Dangerous spectator sport, though. I understand they do it much like dogs. Thirty-ton dogs. Unimaginable! I added witnessing that to my bucket list!

Near the bottom!

Anyway, the forest was quiet when we left the castle in the morning dampness. We stepped outside, listening intently. Hearing no threatening noises, we began moving along the path toward the water, trying to be as silent but as quickly as possible. The lizards should be asleep by dawn, but you never know if an insomniac might still be wandering about looking for a last snack before retiring. They avoided the day's heat, but it was not so scorching yet. Well, not for Planet Oz, anyway, only roughly like a steam sauna dialed up to twelve-point-five.

We reached the boat without incident, then quickly loading our food packs, we pushed off and were in the water. We grabbed our paddles and began to stroke energetically.

At first, we moved slowly despite furious paddling, but then we reached the current and accelerated with the flow. Soon we were skimming along rapidly, seemingly making excellent time.

Our hosts had a massive, centuries-old stone map of the river, which illustrates various landmarks along the way: various prominent bluffs, patches of white water, remarkable rock formations, caves, and more. We had studied it intently, memorizing details to better judge how we were progressing. I was also interested in knowing when we reached the closest approach to the Dark Castle, especially when we approached our intended destination. I studied the landmarks around that area most carefully, committing every divot in the landscape to memory. We positively must not overshoot and miss our only safe harbor.

I had considered scouting out the Dark Castle if time allowed. Depending on how rapidly we progressed, if we arrived there ahead of schedule, I imagined beaching our craft, making a quick run to the castle, and giving it a once-over to see if it was intact. I estimated we could do so at the cost of about an hour or less. My thinking was that as the water route would not work for us on the return trip since we could not make nearly enough speed against the current, we must brave that brutal, inhuman run we had avoided this time. But, of course, I refused to accept that we would not return. Knowing the condition of the Dark Castle beforehand was key to any hope of success on our hypothetical return trip.

When I studied the big stone map, I mentally divided the downstream course into six segments, with prominent landmarks denoting each portion. By noting the position of the sun and our progress against these landmarks, I hoped to be able to judge our speed. We were betting our lives on being able to maintain the necessary pace. If we are falling behind, I need to know!

Our first landmark was a particularly spectacular granite bluff towering above the water. We should see it about an hour into the trip if we achieve our intended pace. I watched the sun intently, trying to estimate when an hour had passed. I wished I had an hourglass. I wished I had a lot of things. Sunscreen would be nice — we had covered ourselves with some foul-smelling cooking oil for just that reason. It helped a lot!

I concluded an hour had passed, and no bluff was in sight. I waited several minutes, then asked Teena if she thought we were an hour into our day. She assessed the sun's position and decided it had not quite been an hour. I disagreed but deferred to her judgment. Finally, I looked to Petch, and he merely shrugged.

A half-hour or so later, we saw the bluff. I was becoming frantic. Our pace over the water seemed rapid, but I sensed we were falling behind our schedule. I put my all into each stroke and encouraged my mates to stroke faster.

There was no longer any doubt we were in serious trouble at the three-hour mark. The stone map had noted a patch of whitewater in the river. We had not expected any trouble with it, which turned out to be a miscalculation. When we came within sight of the roiling waters, I knew we had a problem. We had expected something between a class 1 and a class 2 level of turmoil in the water, easy enough for even novice boatsmen. What we faced, we quickly realized, was nearly a class 4 rating, with several sharp drops and requiring advanced paddling skills. We lacked advanced paddling skills. Stark raving terror gripped my throat as we passed the point of no return, committed to rough water above our skill level.

It could have been worse. We took on some water, and Petchy fell overboard, but we didn't capsize. Teena and I remained in control of our craft. That is, if by being in control, you mean screaming in terror and hanging on for dear life while trying to maneuver away from visible rocks with paddles that seemed to have little effect. Given all the water swamping the boat, it would have been impossible to detect that anyone had voided a bladder in terror. That was a good thing.

Petchy got wet and probably swallowed some river water but was otherwise unhurt. He probably needed a bath anyway. Thankfully, Petch is a powerful swimmer, and once we had cleared the rapids, we were able to bring him back aboard without difficulty. We paddled to the shore, dumped out the excess water, checked our cargo, and resumed our trek.

The whitewater was our marker, and we were well over an hour behind schedule when we reached it. The additional delay in clearing the excess water from our boat added to that. Unless we could somehow increase our pace significantly, we were Dino-dinner. We were already stroking our paddles furiously. We stroked harder, at our very physical limits, without noticeable improvement. We could see it was insufficient.

I was in a full-on panic. After we cleared the whitewater, I voiced my concern to my companions. They had already realized we were not making the progress we should. It seems a pirogue, being essentially flat-bottomed, did not glide thru the water the way a more sophisticated form might. Finally, we faced the reality that our only hope of surviving the day was to put in at the closest point to the Dark Castle and pray we could safely overnight there. We had no clue whether even the castle walls stood, but it was our only hope.

We had fatally misjudged the difficulty of our water trip, under-estimated our aquatic abilities, and stood to pay the ultimate price for our failure. Not only were our own lives forfeit, but those of the others depending on us. We had no means of calling off the assault on the enemy stronghold. If we did not survive this night, their pending sacrifice would be for nothing, and our entire mission would go down the tubes. Humanity itself will pay the price for our hubris.

We arrived at the closest approach to the Dark Castle more than six hours after the morning's launching. We were seriously late. My original plans had been to be here at least two hours earlier. We quickly pulled the boat onto the shore, unloaded our essentials, and headed on a dead run to the castle. We had several hours before sunset but might need every minute to effect repairs to our proposed shelter. We wasted little time securing the boat. If we did not find refuge, we would not need it again. Hopefully, it will be where we dropped it. We grabbed our food packs and ran toward the castle.

We arrived at the castle in minutes and quickly confirmed that lizards had indeed breached the fortress. The great door stood open, and dung, debris, and remains inside told the tale. Fortunately, the structure was intact, and with a bit of work, we could fix the door. We scouted the castle and soon deduced what must have happened. The residents had violated the most elementary rule of survival in Dino-country. They had opened the door after dark! Either that or a lizard had been out in the daytime, which seemed less likely.

Why they might do so is unclear. The residents thoroughly understood the risks and ordinarily would not open even for someone caught outside. Stone-age life can be brutal! The rules of their society often sacrificed individuals to protect the more substantial number. Perhaps a citizen had become trapped, and they honestly thought they could open to let her in, only to be overpowered by a beast.

Once they breached the door, velociraptors would have charged through en mass. They hunt in packs and are crafty. They are a lot like monstrous, blood-thirsty meat-eating chickens in many ways. Chickens that were six feet long with tails, three feet high and weighing over 50 pounds, and with a vicious attack-dog personality; I'd much rather face an attack-dog than these abominations. Anyone with experience with chickens might suspect the magnitude of the threat they represent. Even ordinary roosters are often far more intelligent and vicious than a city boy is likely to understand. It is not for nothing that cockfighting is a favorite sport. These giant ersatz chickens were far more dangerous than any earthly cock. A flock gaining entry would have made short work of the residents.

We only had to close the great door and secure the latch. But first, we had to clean out the mess. The place stank heavily of Dino feces, and although any actual bodies were long gone, copious bones, many recognizably human, plus many from other critters, were in evidence.

I noted the presence of many bones of animals. Athena was observing the residents' fate and speculating how they might have come to violate a fundamental rule in such a manner when a thought struck me.

Suddenly I shushed Athena and waved to Petch to likewise be very quiet. They shot me questioning looks. Then, motioning them closer, I very softly asked, "Where do nocturnal dinosaurs sleep in the daytime?" For about two heartbeats, they both stared blankly at me. Then suddenly, her eyes went round, and her lips formed an 'O.' Petch stood open-mouthed and silently slapped his forehead.

Tiptoeing in silence, we carefully scouted the castle. Dino signs were everywhere, as was their stench. We quickly realized the smell was not only from the remains of their meals and their droppings. Glancing into one of the larger rooms, we discovered a flock of velociraptors nesting, calmly sleeping away the day. Fortunately, they were blissfully unaware of our presence. We desperately hoped we could keep it that way.

Withdrawing, we quickly scouted the rest of the residence. Thankfully, no other vermin were evident. Fortunately, velociraptors don't like to share. Then, working as quietly as possible, we tackled the big front door, finished clearing the threshold of debris, repairing the latch, and ensuring that we could securely close the door.

Then we returned to the urgent question of what to do about our resident flock. Killing the creatures seemed improbable. On the other hand, remaining indoors with them seemed unwise. Out-of-doors was entirely out of the question. Whatever solution we were going to develop had better develop quickly. It was getting late, and they would soon be waking up!

We found a rope and a few tools while scouting the residence. We contrived a mechanism by which we could remotely shut the great door and latch it without betraying our presence to the predators. We weighted a lever against the door so that it would naturally close and then propped it open with a convenient rod. A quick tug and the door swung shut reliably, and the latch fell. We tested it several times, and it seemed to work as we hoped.

We worried about persuading the flock to leave. The lizards would not depart if they sensed that we were present. Being inherently hospitable beasts, they would insist on having us for dinner.

As unthinkable as that seemed, staying in the castle after the sunset was our only option. If we could hide undetected somewhere until our unwelcome guests departed in the evening, we might then be able to close the front door and take possession of the place. So, I turned to my companions.

"Is there any place that would be Dino-proof and undetectable by the beasts that we could hide until they leave?" Athena shrugged. Petchy thought for a moment. Then he brightened. "The Queen's Safe!" he whispered.

I looked at him questioningly. Finally, Athena's face lit up as she realized what he meant.

He went on. "I have occasionally been invited into the inner chambers of the castle's mother. The Queen's Safe is my whimsical name; they do not use titles, particularly of royalty. So calling the castle head 'Mother' is as royal as they get. But the head of the family has very nice chambers, with a protected inner chamber for valuables. So, if they haven't breached it, we should be safe enough."

"Are you sure?" I asked. "If they even smell us, they won't leave. They can't smell us or hear us. They can't even suspect we are here. Once they detect us, we are dead; they will wait no matter how long it takes. Inside, they will not retreat from the sun's heat. They will sleep by whatever door we are behind until we are all long dead from starvation."

"I don't know," he responded, "but it undoubtedly has a high window. So, hopefully, if we close the doors, our aroma will waft out the window, and they won't smell us, or if they do, it will be wafting in roundabout from outside, which would work in our favor."

Athena nodded and added her agreement. "Yes, that will work."

"It is our only shot. Show me where it is."

He led us up the stairs to the top of the castle. We passed through several sturdy doors, which we closed behind us. Someone had already secured those on the upper level. I relaxed somewhat as I saw that the vermin had not breached the top level. From what we could tell, when they had invaded the main level, everyone rushed to try and repel the invaders. Without powerful weapons, humans will not overpower a flock of velociraptors. That math does not work. Anything less than an M2 Browning would be the same as unarmed. I wished for an M2. Or not, as I understand it might not work here.

Nonetheless, I knew even with the Lady Seven and an unlimited supply of arrows, I was equally unarmed against this threat. No matter the specifics, no one was on the upper levels to attract them, and someone had closed the doors. I began to have some hope we might pull this off. The predators had no reason to suspect fresh food would have moved in upstairs.

Carefully closing the doors behind us, we inspected the Queen's Safe, as Petch had dubbed it. We lucked out. There was not only a high opening for ventilation, but it was almost directly above the front door, near enough anyway.

Quickly grabbing the rope, we dropped one end out the window. Then Petch tiptoed back down and tied it to the lever propping the door open.

We had no time to test our contrivance. It was getting late; the light was failing fast. Our guests would be soon waking up, and they would be hungry. Hungry enough, we prayed to go hunting immediately. We hoped to watch through the window until we saw them leave. Petch returned just in time, and I directed him quickly to help us dampen some towels, rugs, anything we could find, and we used them to block all the cracks around the doors separating us from the flock, lest our scent should manage to waft their way. We were plenty scentful between our natural odor from physical exertions and our ersatz sunscreen. They would not need a keen nose to track us!

Mere minutes later, we heard a T-Rex bellow somewhere in the woods. He was up early! We sensed a stirring below and some noisy distant rejoinders to the big boy. From that sound, perhaps food was not the first thing on his mind. I briefly wondered whether the fertility crisis affecting humans impacted the dinosaurs. One should hope, though I doubted it.

We waited, watching quietly, hardly daring to breathe. Athena crouched high on the window ledge, staring down at the door. I was below her, ready to pull the rope and close the door. Under less trying circumstances, I would appreciate our relative positions and the enticing view afforded, but abject fear for one's very life will curtail mundane drives. Even so, I found myself repeatedly stealing glances upward. Some instincts are deeply ingrained; what can I say?

Presently she whispered, "How many do you think there were?" I shrugged. "How should I know. I was too busy retreating when I saw them to bother with counting noses. Or beaks!" I turned to Petch. He whispered, "I think there were eight, maybe nine. I wasn't counting noses either."

Teena focused on the door. Not being able to focus on the door, I concentrated on Teena. Presently she whispered, "One has come out. It is walking around, probing and sniffing around the door. It knows we were there."

We could hear shuffling around downstairs. We guessed the beastie must be checking out where we had been. A few more came out. Teena silently held up four fingers. They continued sniffing at our sign. Several more minutes, and she added a fifth finger. No more came out for a good long while. We dare not spring our trap; there were potentially as many as four still inside. We waited. We waited some more.

I began to think the rest were going to stay inside. We were doomed, if so. I glanced around the room we were in, searching for something, anything I could use. I noticed a polished stoneware container of fragrant oil, not that different from what we had used for sunscreen. Hmm.

Grabbing the container, I climbed up on the ledge beside Teena, squeezing in beside her. Despite the very tight space, I balanced myself precariously with one hand and gave the oil a hearty toss, in the process firmly smacking Teena across her boobs with my arm as I hurled. I mouthed a silent apology. Well, they did kinda stick out. I honestly had not intended to commit sexual assault and felt intense embarrassment. Hopefully, she would not hold my clumsiness against me.

Despite the precarious position, tight quarters, and unintentional assault, the oil flew straight, sailing out into the gathering gloom, smashing itself to bits on a conveniently placed rock well out in front of the castle.

It worked. We could smell the splattered oil from here. The noise and the smell drew the vermin out; there were not eight or nine. There were fifteen! I shuddered to think of the disaster had we tripped our door on seeing nine outside. I was about to jerk the rope when I heard another noise downstairs, and another sleepy squatter appeared in the doorway. A Deinonychus! Where had THAT been hiding! I hope he didn't have any relatives! Where's its mate? There should be two of them.

The velociraptors had headed off on their hunt, and the chicken's larger cousin sniffed the air as he walked back and forth in front of the door a few times. Then, finally, he let out a screeching, blood-curdling bellow or two and strolled out into the woods. I wondered where its mate was once again, as they usually travel in pairs.

Do I dare close the door now? Or might there be another toothy guest still in the house? I cocked an eyebrow at Teena and Petch. They shrugged. If we tripped it too soon, there might be another nightmare inside. But waiting might also be a problem, as it was evident from the horrific remains that our guests often grabbed their dinner at the drive-thru and headed home to dine in. One or more might return at any time.

Teena stayed on her perch, intently watching as we debated the idea. Suddenly she hissed, "CLOSE IT!" and I gave the rope a firm tug. For a horrifying second, nothing happened. Then we heard the big door slam shut. We prayed the latch had clicked!

CHAPTER 21

QUEEN'S CHAMBERS

W e watched as our deinonychus walked around outside, pecking at the now-closed door. We prayed it would not open if the beast were to push against it. We watched frozen for several minutes until he decided to head back to the woods in search of more accessible prey. I had considered wasting an arrow on him, but the angle from my perch in the window of the Queen's Safe was less than ideal, and I was not confident in my ability to kill it with an arrow anyway! Even though driven by the tremendous draw of my magnificent Lady Seven, penetrating a dinosaur's hide was a tall order, and hitting a vital organ was still more challenging. Dinosaurs are indestructible beasts. Besides, a corpse near our front door would draw more deadly predators to the scene, precisely the opposite of what we wanted. Finally, when the beastie decided to head into the woods, we heaved a collective sigh of relief. We climbed down and cautiously descended to the main entry and checked the door.

Fortunately, the latch had worked as hoped, and the door was secure. Moving quickly, we added the additional braces customarily used at night. With these in place, the thick stone door is impervious to the lesser beasts such as the Velociraptor and Deinonychus and too small to attract a T-Rex's interest. Once we secured the door, we turned to the mess inside. Unfortunately, as the sun had set and the light was fading fast, the castle inside was getting dark. With no candles in the chandelier and nothing to push back the gloom, we decided we could do nothing about the cleaning, but we wanted to secure the building.

Scrounging around, we found some single candles, and with the small amount of light they yielded, we began a room-by-room inspection, bows at the ready, closing and securing every room against future intrusion. There was no way we could close off every space, and a lot of the interior doors were not very secure, being of comparatively light wood rather than stone. Nonetheless, we closed every door possible.

The vermin had missed invading a lot of the rooms. Their doors were closed, and I guess there had been nothing to attract them, scent-wise. Even though the lizards could easily smash a light wooden interior door, with nothing on the other side to draw them, they just hadn't bothered. On the other hand, they had smashed many doors, and the debris and remains in the space within told the gruesome tale. Wooden interior doors offer little protection from determined deinonychuses.

A thick stone door resists the vermin but offers no better protection in the long term if the lizards can smell you within. Indoors and protected from the sun, they merely camp at the door and wait until the prey emerges. So, your options soon boil down to choosing whether to starve safely behind the cold stone or to open up and be eaten. We found some who had chosen starvation. I supposed I might, too, given the circumstances.

After our inspection tour, we retired to the Queen's Chambers, as Petch had dubbed them, and scrounged up a few more candles and our meager food supply; we decided it would be best to securely close every interior door and sleep together in one room. Despite our efforts, we still did not know that the castle was 100% vermin-free, and whatever barriers we could place between ourselves and potential nocturnal danger seemed a good idea.

A few minutes later, we were safely ensconced in the relatively luxurious quarters of the head of the household with our meager food supplies. The gravity-fed plumbing still worked, and we had water, but with no family in residence to maintain things, it probably would not last long, I feared. In addition, a stone-age lifestyle requires the constant work of many hands to keep things running smoothly. I suppose so does a modern lifestyle; it's just not always as obvious. But at least we could wash and otherwise take care of our physical needs this night.

We were exhausted. The tension and adrenalin of dealing with the predators had taken a toll. We ate our meager meal and arranged ourselves to sleep. The communal sleeping arrangement was not unsatisfactory. It was the norm in our hosts' society, and while we might prefer more privacy, we had long since adapted. The native residents tended to sleep in collective groups; often, a mother would share a bedroom with her children, frequently even adult ones. With dinosaurs prowling about, sleeping alone seemed less than desirable anyway. There were plenty of beds available. Teena took the larger bed, the Queen's bed, we joked. Petch settled for a smaller bed against the far wall.

Another wall had a very satisfactory bed, roughly equivalent to a 'full sized' bed back home, smaller than Teena's, larger than Petch's. I quipped that it was the 'Goldilocks' bed, eliciting a faint giggle from Teena and a mock scowl from Petch. I perched there, turned my face to the wall, and promptly left the day behind. Well, I suppose I oversimplify. Sleep did not come as quickly as all that. We had been entirely too keyed up by the nearness of our deaths that day. Nevertheless, I quietly lay as though I had gone to sleep, eventually drifting away. I presume my companions did likewise.

It seemed almost a relief to have a night with no furry concubines. You'd think my poor abused anatomy should be grateful for the rest. Still, I had maintained a prodigious pace. The evening's sudden absence of demand left me in a strange state, almost like an engine heavily loaded only to rev out of control upon sudden unburdening. Partly, I guessed, I was missing a familiar furry snuggle with my Lolita. I wondered yet once more whether I would ever see her again.

As was often the case, the nighttime came with rain and weather. The climate of Planet Oz is tropical, with lots of rainfall. It tends to rain every night, and often there will be a brief shower or even two, sometimes three in the daytime. A light rain shower is quite welcome during our prodigious runs, bringing, as it does, cooling relief and a welcome dousing. This evening was unusual; we were treated to a spectacular weather display, much more of a storm than was typical. As a rule, the frequent rains are gentle and short-lived. This storm was more nearly an old-fashioned midwestern thunder-boomer, and it poured very hard for hours. No doubt the weather tumult impacted our sleep too.

Sometime during the night, I sensed Teena moving, making soft noises. I first thought she was having a nightmare. I turned toward her. She had left a small candle burning in the corner, and in the low light, I could see she was awake and crying. Petch, facing the wall, seemed dead to the world.

She saw me and saw that I was awake and watching her, and to my shock and surprise, she silently, wordlessly came to my bed and snuggled against me, making a spoon against my lap. I squarely confronted the sudden realization that something I had often fantasized about was happening this instant. I certainly wasn't lacking for companions and partners on this world, but that which is thought unattainable is always sought over that which is readily at hand; such is human nature.

Faced with the warm reality of her body pressed firmly against mine, I was suddenly terrified. Was this incredible super-woman really in my bed? I wanted to pinch myself. But instead, I put my arms around her. Somehow the cast-iron Amazon was as soft and warm as any I had ever held, and her breasts fit my hands so marvelously I never wanted to release my clasp. I inhaled her natural fragrance, and it hit me like a narcotic, overpoweringly feminine, lustful, and with her in my arms, I suddenly found I had no care in the world. Sex seemed superfluous.

I debated the meaning of this unexpected development with my inner voice, then my single-minded alter-ego awoke and immediately telegraphed his more practical ideas. His message reached its recipient without delay, and the reply was instantly forthcoming. I expected rejection; I had supposed she merely wanted comfort and a cuddle and expected only that, but rather than pull away, she pressed closer, grinding her hips slightly. Then, very quietly, she whispered, "Don't wake Petchy." The white noise of the ferocious rainstorm provided a welcome acoustic cover.

Sometime later, she sighed softly and whispered, apparently to herself, "If I were only even a hundred years younger!" and then we slept.

When I awoke, it was still dark, but the rain had stopped, and the sky I could see through the window was growing lighter. Teena had returned to her bed, and the tiny candle had nearly burned to a nub, sputtering on the verge of extinguishing. Petchy was still facing the wall, apparently oblivious. I hoped he remained unaware of our night music. I expected he would disapprove, and I did not want friction in our group. Too much was at stake to permit strife or jealousy in our band. As much as I fantasized about it, as much as I wanted it, I resolved not to let that happen again.

Sadly, I reflected that my resolve is notoriously unreliable in such matters.

As the sky lightened, I contemplated packing our stuff and getting ready to head to the riverbank where we had cached the boat, but it was much too early to venture outside. That bellowing T-Rex had been much too close last night, and no doubt the 'chickens' would soon come home to roost and be at the door any minute. We preferred to avoid breakfast with them. It would take them some time to accept that their home had been repossessed and to decide to relocate to more regular quarters. We wanted to give them all the time they needed.

Hopefully, they would not decide to sleep huddled against the door. That seemed unlikely, though, as the nocturnal lizards usually sought refuge from the sun, and the area around the door would not be to their liking.

No, depending on that toothy flock, we could not go to the boat for at least an hour or perhaps more like two. Assuming the boat survived undamaged! If we can get into the water within two hours, we should be able to reach the next stop about six hours later, based on yesterday's progress.

I lay watching Teena sleep. Soon I saw she was not asleep but was watching me as I was her. She smiled a knowing smile and pressed a finger to her lips. I was somewhat puzzled but resolved to keep what happened to myself for now. I decided to get her alone to talk at the first opportunity. What did she mean by that strange comment if only she were younger? Was she, in fact, well over a hundred? It seemed impossible; I couldn't see how that could be the case. Petch had indeed dropped several hints that he was much older than I'd believe. But at least he appeared much older than I, even if not nearly as old as he implied. She did not; she seemed much, much younger than he, in fact, a few years younger than I, like a younger sister, I supposed, recognizing our slight familial resemblance from a fresh perspective I had not fully acknowledged before.

And what of any possible romantic connection. Was Teena merely feeling an adrenaline crash after our near demise and needing some comforting? Or was she, like I had been a few months ago, feeling a long dry spell and needing essential human touch. My mind was in turmoil. Had this just been a random, meaningless coupling? Or something deeper. I already have experienced plenty of meaningless; I have little interest in meaningless.

CHAPTER 22

MUDDY WATER

About an hour passed, and Petch awoke. We began talking, planning our day, keeping our voices low lest some of the nightmarish predators might still lurk nearby. Just because they couldn't get to us did not mean we thought advertising our presence to them was a good idea. Petch didn't have much to say, and I thought he gave me several funny looks in the gloom. Had he been awake after all, and quiet as we had been, nonetheless heard our midnight jam session; or was he merely in a grumpy mood. Or was it just my guilty conscience bothering me? I resolved not to talk to him about it unless he broached the topic. Or she did. I, for one, was determined to keep the confidence; to the death, if need be. I did wonder how long that would last, though. Secrets, especially on that topic, seldom endure.

Finally, we arose and gathered the remnants of our supplies. We carefully peered outside via the high window of the 'Queen's Safe' and verified no predators were lurking around the castle. That was a relief. With their return to the castle nest thwarted, we decided they had sought an otherwise more usual perch for the day. Listening carefully, we opened the doors and, again arrows nocked, descended the stairs to the main level, securely re-closing every interior door.

Cautiously we opened the front door and peeked out. Sighing with relief at the peaceful, bucolic view, we arranged the front door latch so that it was secure yet accessible from outside. Typically, someone already inside must open the front door. As a precaution, we also suspended the rope from the upper story, providing access of last resort by climbing up the line into the Queen's Safe. We wanted to use this castle again and hoped another clan would decide to repossess it. Keeping the vermin out was necessary to both ends.

With the castle secured and future safe access provided for, we finally headed to the river. Our pirogue had been disturbed but was unharmed. It appeared as if it had been pushed around by the night denizens. They had clawed at some of the packs, too. Perhaps it had been windblown in the storm, as well. We speculated that they possibly sensed a slight scent of the food we had carried but gave up when they couldn't find anything.

Our pirogue was serviceable, though we did have to re-tie most of the packs. Nevertheless, we wasted little time getting into the water and underway. Soon we were in the center of the river and paddling vigorously downstream, determined to make our destination long before nightfall.

The storm had significantly affected the river; it must have been something! The river was swollen, muddy, and roiling; to our pleasant surprise, it seemed that the current was carrying our pirogue along much quicker today than yesterday. So I suspected we might make better progress today and make the trip in less time than first expected.

We paddled vigorously for two hours when I began watching for our first landmark. It appeared almost precisely on schedule. We seemed to be making excellent progress. Noon came, and it seemed apparent that we were on track to reach our destination well ahead of the six hours we had allotted. Nonetheless, I still worried as I had come to suspect the big stone map we had studied was not perfectly accurate.

At five and a half hours, we began watching intently for our landing. By six hours, we were starting to worry. We were hoping we hadn't missed it. By six and a half hours, we were in a panic. We didn't believe we could have passed it, but we almost certainly had. We debated turning around and going back upstream, knowing that we were dead if we had indeed missed our landing. Unfortunately, making any significant progress against the swollen current was unlikely, so if we had passed our destination, there wasn't much else we could do, though we would indeed die fighting.

When we hit the seven-hour mark, I recognized a distinctive rock formation. That we weren't lost was the good news. The bad news was that the rocky outcropping was too distinct to be mistaken, and it was well past our destination point. We had missed our landing, obliviously floating right past it. Turning around and paddling upstream was impossible in the time remaining before sundown, especially with the storm-swollen current. There was no question now; we had less than three hours to live!

Our only hope was to beach our craft and run back in the direction we had come, attempting to reach our destination castle overland. In theory, we should make faster progress on land than upstream against the current. However, the flaw in that plan was that while we might quickly run the miles to the castle on a regular forest trail, we were far from any manicured path and would have to cross overland through the rough forest terrain. Even a few miles could take far longer than the time remaining, assuming we did not get lost.

We briefly debated our options and agreed that we had zero chance on the water. On land, we had a slim chance at best. Hurriedly paddling into shore, we beached our craft. We did not take any supplies except for a small amount of water, not even our minuscule remaining journey cake. We were in no danger of starving! I also grabbed a small bag I routinely carried and my weapon, not that the Lady Seven could help us much. As the last act before leaving the pirogue, I threw the bag with our tiny amount of remaining food in it away from the boat. Perhaps the various night creatures would leave the craft alone with no food present, and the fur-people might later find it and recover the cargo we carried. Even that seemed unlikely.

We headed along the shoreline, back in the direction whence we had come, hopefully in the direction of our safe harbor.

We scrambled along the shoreline for about a mile, making reasonably good time over the harsh and uneven rocks. We noted several caves along the way, some small, some much larger. We speculated about what might inhabit those dark recesses in the stony landscape. We surmised that slumbering dinosaurs might well repose within, awaiting the disappearance of the afternoon sun to emerge.

Soon the stone gave way to soft earth and dense vegetation. We struggled with the undergrowth as it became increasingly dense. A pair of good machetes would seem highly desirable, but the result would be the same even if we had such tools. We soon came to a halt against the impenetrable forest. A crew with strong arms wielding fierce machetes for a month could doubtless penetrate the growth with relative ease.

We had bare hands and mere hours.

Reluctantly admitting defeat, we retreated along our path. We needed shelter and soon. I considered again taking to the water in hopes that we might pass the evening hours on the water, that the predators might not find us there. Teena vetoed that idea! Deinonychus swim, as do Velociraptors, and the big guy does not need to if the water is shallow enough. Well, how was I to know? I am no paleontologist! The middle of the river offers no refuge, we all agreed.

It seems we have no other option than to explore the caves. We assume that nocturnal predators sleep somewhere during the day, and caves seem like good candidates. Perhaps we could appropriate a cave and defend it against the beasts. Challenging, definitely, but our only possible option.

Retracing our footsteps to the caves we had passed, we cautiously approached the grottos as we eyed the sun in the sky. Unfortunately, our remaining daylight was fast disappearing. We needed a cave with a single portal small enough to quickly block the opening with rocks and the cavern itself small enough that we could definitively declare it unoccupied.

Selecting a suitable candidate opening at random, we entered the cavern slowly, ears tuned for the slightest sound and weapons at the ready. Unfortunately, we quickly noticed a strong airflow from deep within the cave. About fifty feet inside, we determined it was much too large to explore successfully and far too likely to have vermin deeper inside.

We did note one small chamber inside the cavern that might serve our purpose. It was just large enough that we could huddle inside, the interior space being about the size of a modest interior castle room, and it had a single tiny opening through which we could barely crawl. Decidedly claustrophobic! We debated crawling inside and blocking the entrance with rocks. After a moment, we rejected it as problematical since being inside the cave and thus sheltered from the sun; the apparent risk was that a beast would smell us and make camp at the entrance trapping us inside until we starved or suffocated.

Retreating to the out-of-doors, we again assessed the sun's position and moved on to another possible cavern. This one, too, suffered from being too large, most likely connecting deep underground with the previous cave. We rejected the second cave more quickly and hastily moved to another candidate without wasting time. The sun was getting very low, and we were almost out of time.

The third cave was a bust too. It was apparent that all the caves in this area were interconnected and ran deep underground. Finding one that met all our requirements was looking unlikely, and we had no time to explore further. Deciding a terrible choice was better than certain death, we raced back to the underground chamber.

We grabbed large rocks from the rock-strewn landscape and carried them into the cave. Petch and I quickly ran back outside and collected handfuls of smaller stones and some bits of driftwood. Then, crawling into the chamber, we blocked the entry as securely as possible, chinking the large boulders with smaller rocks, stones, and small pieces of driftwood. We hoped the beasts did not sense our presence, as even though the barrier was thick, it would not stand a determined assault by the vermin.

The sun was almost down, and we were sequestered in total darkness, in a tightly enclosed space, with no ventilation and no way to know what was happening outside. We had no way to know when dawn might come, no way to mark the time. With no ventilation, we risked suffocating as well. Our situation in this underground chamber was dire, but outside would be far worse.

Initially, I had left one small opening positioned so I could look out into the cavern. As a result, we could see reflected sunlight penetrating the outer cavern. The tiny opening would allow us some minute ventilation and permit visual and auditory perception of the enormous underground space. Within minutes the slight amount of reflected sunlight disappeared, and moments later, we heard faint sounds of creatures stirring within the cavern.

I quickly plugged the opening, daring to hope that our presence might go undetected.

After months of acclimating to the exceedingly hot climate of the planet, the cold, damp darkness of the cavern was uncomfortably chilly at first. With the blockage of airflow, our body heat began to warm the space, and for a time, despite being in total darkness, we became reasonably comfortable. At one point, I felt a soft hand on my body. Still tortured over the previous night's events, guiltily resolving not to let such things happen again, I reached down and took the hand and very quietly whispered a soft "no," intending that only she might hear. We held hands in the dark, but I permitted no further encroachment. I could feel that my semaphore had risen to half-mast, but I steeled myself against any possibility. Marauding predators or not, this cannot be allowed; how I wished otherwise. How can a man endure such torture?

I do not think we slept. Perhaps we did, but if so, it was fitful and uneasy, and I awoke frequently. Then, several hours into our enforced entombment, I became aware that my breathing had deepened. Carbon dioxide was building up in our confined space; suffocation was softly approaching.

Quietly as possible, I removed a chink from our barrier. A little fresh air intruded, but it was insignificant relief without cross-ventilation. Hearing no sounds and seeing nothing through the hole, I removed another chink from the opposite side. Much better. Still not as effective as actual cross ventilation, but some air was flowing. It helped.

I placed myself against the barrier, ears on high alert for any sign of our monstrous innkeepers. As I concentrated on every tiny sound in the quiet, I could hear my companions breathing; I could listen to the blood pumping in my veins. I could even hear the blood pumping through Teena's veins. Humans rarely experience silence such as this. Nor such darkness. My eyes became exquisitely tuned for the faintest ray of sunlight outside. I do not know how long we stayed in this position, myself huddled against our rock barrier, lovingly holding Teena's hand in the darkness, with Petch a few feet away near the far wall. None of us seemed to be sleeping; judging from the breathing sounds, we were all on high alert.

Hours passed. How many, I do not know. Once I heard faintly in the distance the bellow of a Tyrannosaurus. Then, I heard other more violent noises, closer at hand. It appears our hosts had found prey. Hopefully, they would all have a successful hunt and come to bed with bellies full, horrible appetites sated for a time, prepared to sleep the day away, oblivious to our intrusion into their home.

Finally, I perceived rather than saw a faint lightening of the space beyond our rocks. From the outside, I heard the tell-tale sounds of movement. As quickly and quietly as I could, I replaced those chinks. It was positively hot in the chamber now, but hot confinement in underground stone was preferable to the same in a beast's belly. I'll take stone any day.

I listened at our rocky portal, trying to sense when the beasts had settled for the day. Finally, I risked a peek outside. Carefully removing a chink, I could see hints of bright sunlight intruding into the cave entrance. I listened intently for several minutes.

Deciding that the beasts had settled, I began dismantling our barrier slowly and quietly. Placing one boulder so that Teena and Petch could quickly drive it back into the opening if need be, I cautioned them to do so if necessary, even if it meant stranding me on the other side. Then, with all possible precautions taken, I grabbed my weapon and crawled out into the cavern.

Moving slowly, ears on swivels and letting my eyes adjust carefully, I crawled into the cavern and stood, The Lady Seven nocked up. Daylight streamed in through the entrance, and there was no sign of our carnivorous hosts. It appears they make their home much deeper inside the caverns. After carefully surveying our surroundings, I whispered to Petchy and Teena to come on out. Moments later, we stood on the rocky bluff in the bright morning sunshine, the only known humans to have ever survived a night outside a castle on this reptile cursed planet. Not something I was eager to attempt anew, nor an experience I would recommend to others.

Taking a few deep breaths while shuddering in relief at surviving the night, I signaled my companions. What next? Traveling overland seems ill-advised, given the thickness of the forest. We decided that our best approach was to return to the pirogue. If it, too, had survived the night, our best option was to take to the water again and make our best progress upstream against the current and hope to discover where we had missed our landing. It would take some time, but we had a whole day to correct our error.

Our pirogue was intact, though not precisely where we had left it. The beasts, or possibly a storm, had moved it nearly two hundred feet from where we had abandoned it. Our cargo was intact, but we had no food. Today would be a hungry day.

I was already hungry. I felt a tizzy of light-headedness as we took to the water and felt my stomach writhing in protest at the motion. But I still had my weapon. We could, I suppose, take the time to kill a deer, or even one of those beautifully colorful squirrels, make a fire, and eat. However, that would take time, time which we did not have.

Hunting was just not on our schedule. We dared not attempt to survive another night as we had. We had been fortunate to endure such a misstep once. We must find our castle first, then eat. If we don't reach our destination, eating will be irrelevant.

The fierce flow of the day before had decreased significantly; the river was back to near normal. Sticking close to the shore and avoiding the strong current in the center, paddling upstream was sluggish but not too difficult.

Even so, a distance that had taken us less than an hour downstream in yesterday's strong current took us over four hours to traverse in the reverse direction. We suspected we must be close to our target but could not spot any sign of the trail nor any marker. It is astounding how much one spot of unmanicured forest looks like any other without distinctive landmarks.

We were debating landing our craft and exploring on foot in hopes of discovering a trail. However, if we did not find our target soon, we again faced the same difficulty we had faced yesterday, only now weak with hunger. Retreating to the caves for another night was an unthinkable option, but we might have to start thinking about it unless we soon found our target.

Just as we debated the dire choice, suddenly Teena let out a yell and started waving at the shore. There to welcome us was a gathering of our newest furry friends, the most welcome sight we could have imagined.

We quickly paddled ashore and were enthusiastically swamped by friendly fur folk. It was good to be back on land and among friends.

Our hosts worried that we might overshoot the destination landing and had gathered the first afternoon to watch for us, lest we glide by without spotting the landing. They had feared the worst when we did not appear that day but had correctly guessed that we might have spent the night in the Dark Castle. They had gathered again yesterday, but somehow, we had missed them. We later concluded that we had passed by the landing spot just minutes before they had gathered to greet us, thanks to the powerful current carrying us along faster than anyone had anticipated.

Fearful of the worst, yet hopeful we would yet appear, they had gathered again today, just in time to aid our landing. Our friends had just walked to the shore and were almost instantly overjoyed to see our pirogue on the water. Five minutes earlier, we may well have missed the landing a second time.

They greeted our harrowing tale of spending the night deep in the belly of the beast's cave with stark incredulity. I suspect they did not believe us, preferring to think we had survived via some unknown, mystical method known only to smoothies rather than accept our improbable tale at face value. As a result, they virtually refused even to discuss it.

We explained to them what had happened to the inhabitants of the Dark Castle, and they were appropriately horrified. There was a lot of chatter about the necessity of being safely inside before the lizards came out. They were speculating as to whether the inhabitants had opened the door after sundown or whether possibly a lizard had ventured out to hunt at an unusually early time, catching them off guard before sunset.

They talked about this for hours, and the next day we overheard them talking about routinely closing the doors earlier than usual as a precaution. We surmised that they would be much more vigilant in the future, lest the same fate comes their way. Vigilance is good. Of course, there was no way to know what happened, whether a lizard had appeared and invaded the castle before sunset, or the inhabitants had foolishly opened the door after sundown.

They were glad to hear that the castle was intact and now safe and could be occupied again and were soon making plans to contact other families and organize a group to clean and repair the fortress. I thought that was a good idea since they will need the living space if we succeed in our mission and the population rebounds. Many such abandoned castles had fallen into ruin and were now uninhabitable, so rescuing and preserving one safe harbor from that fate seemed like a clear win. We only hope they do need it someday.

I wondered again about the origins of the castles. From all I could see, the structures dated into antiquity. One must wonder which came first, the castle or the T-Rex. Without the safe refuge of a castle, early humans would not have been able to escape the ravages of the giant lizards, and without a threat of that nature, humans would have had little incentive to create such structures. Further, the castles would take years and years to build and the labor of hundreds, if not thousands. Carrying on such a project with active dinosaurs in the area and no other safe refuge seemed questionable. I wondered if they originally built the castles for different reasons, and T-Rex was a relatively late arrival.

I asked Petch and Teena about this. They agreed that there was a serious possibility that the giant lizards had arrived via a portal sometime after humanity had begun building castles. The fact that there were so few lizard species argued they had potentially developed elsewhere. Despite the reasonableness of the theory, no one knew. Perhaps after we succeed in our mission, genuine scientists will find the subject worth studying.

After being thoroughly greeted by the group, we all headed for the castle, where we partied, dined, and entertained similarly to that at all the other fortresses we had visited. The ladies especially loved the bawdy rendition of Barnacle Bill, shouting and pounding the table. After that, however, Macbeth, Clementine, and Barnacle Bill, yet the ladies were still demanding more, another encore. So, complying, I gave them a few incredibly bawdy limericks as a final encore:

> There was a young lady named Lou
> who said as the parson withdrew--
> "Now the Vicar is quicker,

And thicker, and slicker,
And two inches longer than you.

That was a cute little rhyme
Sing us another one, do—oo--

Here's to old king Montezuma
For fun he buggered a puma
The puma one day
Bit both balls away
An example of animal humor.

That was a cute little rhyme
Sing us another one, do—oo--

There was a young gal name of Sally
Who loved an occasional dally.
She sat on the lap
Of a well-endowed chap
Crying, "Gee, your ****k
is right up my alley!"

On and on it went until, out of ideas, bereft of rhymes, the girls let me bow for the very last time. Retire for the evening you think, I know, straight to bed, both yes and no, you conceive. Abed, I did go, but rest was so, elusive.

While I was busily fulfilling my chromosomal commitment to the nubile daughters of the clan, I found myself wondering what Teena was doing, how she was spending the evening.

Chapter 23

GREAT RUN

The following several segments went smoothly. After our serial near-death experiences in the Dark Castle and the dinosaur caves, we encountered a string of easy runs, several of no more than ten or twelve miles. The universe owed us a break! Of course, we paid for our food and shelter in the usual manner, but even so, the short runs gave us ample time for needed rest, and even with my chromosome commitment, I found myself getting sleep. Two different nights, after I had discharged my duties, Teena came silently to my bed, exacerbating my internal conflict. I tried to ask her about possible objections on the part of Petch. For all I knew, they might be married. I confronted the reality that I knew nothing whatsoever of this strange couple. I knew little enough about Petch, even less about her. She dismissed my concern without comment and declined to reveal anything that would salve my tortured conscience.

Mostly we just cuddled, but not only. Still, I tried to reserve my seed for those who genuinely needed it. I could tell that Teena's needs fell into a different category. In these moments, she seemed to bear the weight of the world.

Maybe she did. Or rather, more like the weight of the universe.

In any case, Teena had admitted she was not fertile, so I focused on giving her comfort and release and did not particularly care about my own. I wasn't exactly lacking. We had visited a great many castles and families therein, scattering my boon freely. Hopefully, there will soon be many new, fertile babies on our Planet Oz. Even if that is true, Petchy had darkly claimed that it would make little difference in the long run. My gametes would provide but a brief respite in their spiral toward oblivion.

Finally, we approached the end of our journey. We faced one more gargantuan run, our longest yet, nearly sixty-five miles, bringing us to the castle closest to the portal. None too soon, as it seems we had but three days before the gateway opened.

We must make the grueling sixty-five-mile run the first day; then, we get to allow ourselves a day of rest and recovery before we face a final run of merely thirty-five miles which then places us at the portal on the day of opening. We will arrive at the portal about noon or soon after with luck. The gateway is to open some thirty-five minutes before dusk. That would give us several hours to precisely locate the opening, rest, and prepare for our battle; we had cut it close. We could really, seriously use another day for resting and preparation for the fight.

I had been wracking my brain for days in anticipation of this run. I knew it was very near the physical limits of our endurance. We need to make the run within the allotted time — the available daylight hours — and conserve our energy as much as possible. We had to be in fighting trim immediately after. Even with a full day of rest after this leg of the trip, we were pushing it. It was excruciatingly demanding, taxing every iota of strength we could muster.

I hatched a crazy scheme that I imagined could help. The problem is two-fold. The more significant part is the sheer number of miles we must cover. We cannot change that; however, another good-sized chunk of the puzzle is the payload we must carry, the food and water. Every pound tires us faster, contributing to the exponential 'cliff' we must face as the miles increase. If we could somehow significantly reduce the load we must carry, we could make the run less grueling.

In hindsight, the answer seemed so simple. We cannot reduce the amount of fuel, food, and water our bodies need. The water, especially, is heavy. But we can have someone else carry it. Not the whole way, of course, but they can help us partway. Every mile we do not tote those packs conserves our bodies' caloric reserves.

The idea was simple. We ask the best and fastest runners from this house to accompany us part way, carrying as much of our necessary cargo as they can. They need not attempt to run our entire grueling run, only about one-third of it. They accompany us the first twenty or so miles. They carry our food and water; we run free and unburdened, conserving our strength. We will have consumed a significant portion of the supplies by the end of twenty miles. They hand off the rest to us and return to their home, carrying only the minimum for their return trip. They run about forty miles, the last half largely unburdened, and wind up at their home base, where they can freely rest and recover.

We can then continue the trip with the reduced load of food and water, finishing the entire sixty-five miles but only carrying the supplies for slightly more than forty. Hopefully, by reducing our burden by this amount, we will be better able to complete the journey.

I discussed it with the local runners, then with Petch and Teena, and finally, the house mother. Everyone thought it should work.

I had first thought we would need three of their runners, one to carry the cargo of each of us. We did the math. The problem, it turns out, is that their runners are young girls, much smaller in stature than we, and, although competent runners, less able at carrying cargo. They needed to bring both ours and theirs. Strictly speaking, if we each had three support runners, there would be more than ample cargo capacity, and each of them could carry an easy load. Unfortunately, the house mother was unwilling to spare nine runners. That was all she had, and as they would return home exhausted and need several days of rest, there would be no one available to meet her needs.

After some back and forth consultation, we settled for two runners for each of us, plus one more, a seventh runner who was only to carry extra water, which we would divide among us all.

We had a plan. We were going to be quite a party. There would be ten runners departing as early in the morning as we dared consider safe enough. We desperately hoped no insomniacs were still wandering about but kept our bows nocked, however useless that might seem.

There would be the three of us and the seven support runners. We would run entirely unburdened; save for a small amount of water we would quickly consume. We would then take the burden from them at about the twenty-mile marker. We would eat and drink and then shoulder the remaining supplies, and while they turned back toward home, we would carry on alone, now burdened, but not as heavily, and not nearly as spent as we would have been otherwise, had we carried this load ourselves from the beginning.

The day dawned bright and cloudless, and our support team hit the road the instant they opened the castle door. We would be hot on their heels in mere moments, giving them but a slight head start. Since they carried heavy burdens relative to us, they could not run at maximum speed, so we let them get out in front of us. The difference was not significant, but they would have ample time to rest after they had unburdened their cargo to us and before they must start the return trip home. Thus, they could expend their energy more frivolously early on. We would soon catch them but did not feel the need to dog their heels.

The trip started uneventfully, with Petch in the lead, Teena in the middle, and me bringing up the rear. I noticed some contention, with Petch and Teena seemingly arguing about who would go first. I paid it little mind at first, but then as we were running, I thought about it and realized there had been numerous occasions where some touch of irritation or disagreement had been evident between them. I started worrying about friction in our group and any possible impact it might have on our mission, feeling guilty that I might have contributed to it.

As we tended to do, we started comparatively slowly, then soon accelerated to our top speed as our bodies warmed up and acclimated to the pace. Since we had a long run, we did not even try to reach our maximum speed, but soon we were flying through the woods quite nicely. A little more than an hour into the run, we began to hear the sounds of our support team ahead of us. Again, not wishing to dog their heels, we slacked off slightly, reducing the rate at which we were overhauling them.

Soon nonetheless, we were close on their heels. I decided it was an excellent time to take on some water. Water is the Achilles heel of the long-distance runner in any climate, but especially so in the heat of Planet Oz. I motioned for the runner carrying only water to slow and join us. We all slowed to an easy jog and passed the water bladder around. We drank our fill, careful not to overload ourselves. Too much water can do as much harm as too little. Then we fell back into position and resumed our pace, still a significant distance behind our support team. However, that was not a problem as they were tiring and slowing. We quickly dogged their heels once again. We kept it up for another half-hour, perhaps a little more, and then our support team slowed and halted.

We had come twenty-two miles precisely, as indicated by the mile-marker stone beside the road. I have often wondered how the fur-people came to reckon distance in the same measure as an Earth culture so far removed. Did they get it from us, or did we get it from them, or did we both get it from a common origin? All good questions for which there were no answers and a greenfield to study. I envy the researcher who has the time and resources to unravel the puzzle.

We paused, took our cargo from our friends, hastily scarfed our mid-morning allotment of journey cake, and imbibed our water ration. Then with hugs and farewells, we bid our support team adieu, wishing them a safe and pleasant journey home.

According to our best estimate, we had forty-three miles to go. We were still relatively fresh, and although we now carried significant packs of food and water, it was manageable, almost light compared to what we would have had to tote had we traveled the entire trip alone without their support. This plan was starting to seem like a terrific idea.

I made a mental note to use this technique again and recommend it to our friends. Then, of course, we would do so when we faced that terrible seventy-mile run to the Dark Castle on the return leg. Assuming we survive to make it. I felt that we could manage that awful, demanding journey with this approach, and the fur-people could likewise make their runs to the Dark Castle more bearable.

The next forty-three miles went smoothly, and we arrived at our destination some five hours later and in good order. Having a support team accompany us part way made a huge difference. It made the journey much, much more practical. It had probably shaved almost an hour off the total trip time, and we were far less exhausted than we would have otherwise been.

Arriving at our destination in good order, we were welcomed and feted much as we had been at every other home we visited and sang, danced, and made Shakespeare's two-backed beast much as every other stop along the road. Though I again wondered how Teena was spending her evening, the trip had unquestionably been an overwhelming success.

CHAPTER 24

BATTLE BRIEFING

It was heavenly to sleep late the following day, and although I would have loved to indulge further, I still had chromosomal commitments. A long line of maternity hopefuls had greeted us last night, and an even longer queue awaited me this morning. Nevertheless, I fell to my appointed duties with zeal. I wondered what it would be like to go back to routine, everyday existence. How would my poor prostate cope once no longer called upon for such prodigious duty?

It would not be correct to refer to what I was doing as making love. It was a mechanical act, artificial insemination without the benefit of a medical intermediary, performed out of the necessity to grant these ladies a desperately needed conception, thereby delaying their entire race's demise. It was a payment rendered to compensate them for our much-needed support and shelter and the food and supplies we received. I barely got the name of each would-be mother. Although I tried to learn their names and memorize something about each, it was too much for human retention. I found myself wishing for my old Droid to take a picture of them and record their names. I tried hard to do right by them, as nearly as circumstances allowed, but conditions were what they were.

Late mid-morning, Teena and Petch appeared, announcing it was time to prep for the coming battle. I excused myself from my furry companions, and we adjourned to a private room where we could talk freely.

The scope and nature of our mission were a secret from our furry friends and honestly beyond their comprehension. How do you explain things like an AI run amok, WiFi, Bluetooth, Flash drives, and technological warfare to a Stone Age culture? I suppose it would not be impossible, but it would take valuable time and energy and would accomplish nothing toward our goals. But they knew we were on a quest and desperately needed their help. More than that helped no one, and we didn't have the time anyway.

I am not entirely sure how it came to be, but after a fashion, I had become the tactical leader of our group. Oh, no question Athena and Petchy had skills and expertise, experience and knowledge I did not, indeed could not hope to acquire without decades and decades of hard work. I was only a child beside them in many aspects of our venture, merely hired muscle. Yet, despite that, I had earned a great deal of respect for my talents and abilities by coming up with essential strategies and solutions.

The runner support team concept, the Battle of the Dark Castle, the Boat Trip, the dinosaur cave, and many more minor incidents along our arduous journey had earned me a position of respect and leadership. Even my unexpected prowess at song and improv comedy and entertaining our hosts was a factor in the leadership role I had assumed. Reflecting on this, I concluded that leadership was an elusive quantity. A cyberpunk-nerd does not usually aspire so high.

A leader, I concluded, did not need to be the smartest or most able on a team, indeed not the most senior. A leader focused and directed the team but was not necessarily its greatest fighter or even its best planner and strategist. What defines a leader is more subtle than that, in some ways, more important.

I was the most junior member of the team and the youngest, or so it seemed, yet I had somehow exhibited the necessary qualities to lead. I was in charge, but at the same time, I knew without a doubt that if I failed to lead in the direction Teena or Petch wanted to go, I would be ousted very quickly.

They controlled our strategic direction while I made tactical decisions, but they would overthrow me instantly should I depart from the core mission.

As the de facto leader of our group, I determined it was time I knew more about what we should expect to find once we went through that portal. Until now, when I had asked questions, they responded that my concern was to get to the portal and be ready to fight. On the other side, the fight was Teena's responsibility, and Petch and I were merely the muscle. We were near the portal and would be going through it tomorrow. So, I now demanded a full briefing and no more nonsense.

Teena began hesitatingly, "The world we will see when we exit the portal will be what's left of my home world, mine and Petchy's. It is a ruined world. We truly cannot survive there for long. The air is seriously foul; it has high radiation levels and is inhumanly hot. Partly we chose this world as a training ground because of the climate. The place we are going to is hotter and a lot more hostile. Quite aside from the dangers from the enemy, we would die there within a few hours."

I cringed but nodded acceptingly. Teena went on.

"We will come through the portal into a battle. Our brothers-at-arms will have assaulted the citadel from another direction, drawing the enemy's weapons and attention. We hope the enemy will be distracted away from our egress point. We hope. The best case is we skate through undetected. The worst case is they spot us instantly and open fire. Reality will likely be somewhere in between.

"Once we are on the other side, we will run. Run for our very lives, away from the portal and toward a small cave that we hope the enemy has not discovered. If we avoid the enemy fire, find the cave, and its contents are as hoped, we get to fight. If not, we get to die. There is no third option."

Swallowing hard at that, I asked, "What about Dinos or other indigenous dangers?"

She shook her head, "There are no dinosaurs. There is virtually no life there. It is a dead world. There are many indigenous dangers, but they are all non-living and will kill us. Even without facing the enemy or destroying it, we will die if we remain there long. So, we must get in, accomplish our mission, and get out in a very few hours.

Our mission is two-fold. The first part consists of killing the machine intelligence that controls the world. Once it dies, the battle soon ends, although it will not quickly fail, even if we successfully inject our digital poison. The second part is extracting the data for our study. Unless we can return with the database, humanity still loses. We must unravel the mechanism that threatens human fertility. It is not enough to destroy the machine. We must get that data!"

I nodded. "Ok, much of that I had inferred from earlier comments. What I am uncertain of is the devil in the details. Assuming we reach the cave, arm ourselves, and are able, how do we assault the citadel as you called it. You have painted a picture of an impregnable fortress. How do we penetrate it?"

Petch took the lead on this one. "The enemy is a machine. It is a very, very big and very complex machine. In our first conversation on this topic, you referenced the fictional 'Krell of Altair IV' and the 'Monsters from the Id.' That is not a bad analogy. Although reality differs in fine detail from the scenario painted in George Pal's excellent movie, it captures the essence. A planet-wide network of mighty machines run amok, mindlessly doing the misguided bidding of people long dead."

I nodded, recalling the massive underground complex, the enormous corridors depicted in the movie. "How did your people come to build such a machine?"

He gave a wry laugh. "We didn't, or at least didn't set out to do so. But pointedly, Earth is already well along the path to doing precisely the same thing!"

Now that got my attention! "What do you mean? As far as I am aware, we are not building anything like what you describe!"

Now he positively cackled. "But you are, not only are you doing so, but you've also used it every day, many times per day, for years. You have even wished for it here a few times!"

I began to realize what he meant. "What? Do you mean Google? You're saying Google is the evil that is destroying the universe?"

"Not Google specifically, massively interconnected global knowledge systems, yes. Machines of that ilk carried to the ultimate conclusion. You have many of them, constituting millions of servers worldwide. No one specific brand has arisen to anywhere near a level that could represent a threat on this scale, but your people are busily building them, improving them, and making them smarter and faster. Google isn't alone. Multiple brands compete against each other to be better, faster, and more intelligent. That is the path that leads to an intelligent, world-sized array of massively interconnected machines.

"Some of Earth's scientists have coined the term 'Singularity' to describe an Artificial Intelligence that exceeds the intelligence of its creators and then turns on those who built it, deciding they are superfluous. Fortunately, that view has not thus far proven precisely accurate. Canned knowledge, no matter how massive, does not equate to sentience.

"These systems are beneficial, extending the power of the human mind. It is not precisely my intent to repeat the parable of Mary Shelley's cautionary tale of technology run amok. That was not the point of Shelley's original story at all. Instead, Hollywood took a far more innocent tale and morphed it into an anti-technological tirade. That was not the story she wrote, not at all.

"Nonetheless, things can and do go wrong. Just as Hollywood has often depicted that in a moment of extreme carelessness, a locomotive might escape its driver and run away, tearing down the track uncontrolled with dangerous cargo in tow, so might any technology. We always need pessimists who will pay attention to the risks and ensure proper controls, overrides, and safeguards.

"Shelley's tale was more about careless and irresponsible parenting than an anti-technology tirade, and the battle we face tomorrow likewise more nearly resembles her original story. Shelly's monster was an innocent creation, abused and mistreated by society. It is not the technology that is the flaw; it is the creators' lack of oversight or parenting.

"We had entrusted our global knowledge system to manage various genetic research initiatives. From our genetically extended lifespan to Teena's genetically enhanced beauty, it produced many great things. But unfortunately, along with greatly enhanced lifespans, it also resulted in reduced fertility to compensate. It got too enthusiastic with that part of the process somewhere along the way. By the time we recognized the grave danger we had faced, the technology had 'escaped' not only our laboratories but our very world."

I must have seemed puzzled by this. Petch went on to explain further. "Earth's geneticists have tinkered with modifying food crops for various traits, improved resistance to insects, and better nutrition. Specially engineered varieties of both corn and rice have significantly changed agriculture. But, despite the most careful controls, both have had those enhancements leak out into more general crops and began propagating their new traits in the wild. Some pessimists have expended considerable effort to save the more natural plants in a seed bank against the day some terrible contamination should propagate that way.

The gain of function research that produced COVID-19 is another example. Life always finds a way, man's hubris and most stringent controls notwithstanding.

"That is, in a nutshell, is what has happened here. We intended fertility to decline in proportion to increased natural longevity to limit population growth. It was never to go to zero. But unfortunately, the plan went awry, fertility decreased much more rapidly than lifespans improved, and those traits leaked across the portals to infect all humanity; it took a long time to notice anything was amiss.

"The global knowledge system was designed to protect itself. When we discovered what had gone wrong and attempted to regain control, that defense became aggressive, and well, here we are. The system protected itself by destroying the planet.

"Earlier, we had talked about it being an AI. That is only somewhat accurate. Or rather, it is highly accurate but misdirects as to precisely what is meant by the term AI. Even the best, most sophisticated AI machinery of Earth, my planet, or any other world is not truly intelligent. By that, I mean it is not sentient, not self-aware. Some might say it has no soul, but I will forego the supernatural connotations. But, again, we are not dealing with religion but the realm of creation.

"Like the Great and Powerful Oz, which has served as our namesake for this pretty world, there is always an Oscar Zoroaster Phadrig Isaac Norman Henkle Emmanuel Ambroise Diggs a.k.a. 'Professor Marvel' behind the curtain pulling the levers. Any AI system's intelligence is always the result of human beings operating behind that curtain. Even the most autonomous system is only autonomous within its parameters.

"Not to suggest that there are no real concerns with the concept of a machine intelligence singularity. The capabilities of machines absolutely can exceed human ability to control, with disastrous consequences. Nonetheless, actual machine sentience is a myth! Fear of Terminators systematically destroying humanity is misguided. The risks of runaway machinery and unintended consequences are genuine.

"Some time back, there was a lot of publicity about a machine which roundly beat human contestants on a popular game show."

I nodded, remembering the contest he mentioned. It was an awe-inspiring feat.

"That machine does not know it won a game show. It has no awareness that it was even in a contest, any more than a sophisticated locomotive of my prior analogy 'knows' it is pulling a hundred freight cars, despite having all the data about torque and fuel consumption.

"Some of Earth's press and even some scientists who really should know better have been pontificating lately about the dangers of AI and prattling on how a superior intelligence to man will emerge and decide man had become unnecessary. Many movies depict a world in which machines intentionally eradicate humankind. That is not a realistic fear!"

I thought for a moment, then asked, "If it isn't intelligent, how is it resolutely destroying all of mankind?"

"It isn't. Or at least it is not 'resolutely' doing anything. These are not Terminators coldly calculating humanity's demise. A more apt analogy is a runaway locomotive, unstoppable in a headlong plunge while hauling hazardous cargo, one that will kill a great many people while carrying out its prime directive, which is nothing more 'resolute' than moving down that track at speed.

The only difference is that, unlike the runaway train of the analogy, this AI is not merely going to kill many at a future point when it crashes. Instead, this AI is killing in massive numbers merely by rolling down the track and will continue to do so until stopped or there is no one left to die.

"It is killing not by violence and brutal death, not by poisoning or wanton destruction, but by the simple expedient of preventing reproduction, blocking the very creation of lives. We can argue the semantics of whether preventing a birth equates to causing death, but the result is the same, a race, a culture, a civilization, a very planet dies. The imperative of all life is reproduction. Interfering with that must always be done carefully, as the future survival of life itself is dependent on new life continually growing and adapting. True sentient life depends on a steady influx of new brains to carry that sentience forward. Tread but lightly on these grounds, a commandment we should have heeded."

He said, "Our project then is to get inside the citadel and bring online a small storage unit, a 'jump drive' equivalent, which carries an exceedingly complex, carefully crafted chunk of software called Nematode. You are undoubtedly aware of how the Stuxnet malware shut down a rogue nation's nuclear research program." I nodded.

He continued, "That's what we are to do here. We have our own special Stuxnet analog."

I interrupted, "I get that. I had already well figured that out long ago. So where is this Nematode? Where is this jump drive? And what do we have to do to install it?"

He pointed at Teena. "She carries the data within her body. It is a storage device; a tiny jump drive secreted within her abdominal cavity." I digested that carefully.

"So, how do we get it out?"

The answer came back, "We don't, hopefully. You are familiar with WiFi and Bluetooth-connected devices. This device connects similarly. We merely need to get her body to the correct location and fend off the system's defenses; we buy time as she interfaces to the system and uploads our 'Stuxnet' equivalent. It uses faint vibrations to communicate status, with various patterns having meaning. This way, she can know when it is connected, when the upload is complete, et cetera. Otherwise, it is entirely automatic, a tiny packet of AI on its own. Much like the biological phylum used to kill various pests, our Nematode will automatically infiltrate and destroy this runaway system. Once inserted into the system, the overall system will begin to shut down. We are confident it has no defenses against Nematode. Once it is in the machine, it will propagate from server to server and, once spread, will begin issuing shutdown commands.

"It only takes time for it to die as Nematode propagates throughout the system and invades pod after pod. Nematode will spread itself throughout the system before taking any action that would draw attention to itself, and once it begins to shut down the pods, the impact will spread rapidly.

"We must deliver a two-part, one-two punch to win. Once we've uploaded the attack to the machine, the next stage is to download the main neural net genetic database. That happens very much the same way, except we have to penetrate a different location, and it is a huge amount of data and will take a long time to retrieve. We will have some time to move to the second location and retrieve the database. Once we insert the Nematode, it will take the machine a while to become seriously impaired. That unfortunately also means that the machine's defenses will still be dangerous until it finally dies."

Teena laid her hand on my arm. Petch gave her a dirty look. Then, she said, "There is one more thing you must understand. If I should be killed or seriously injured, you STILL must get my body or the data capsule within it to the proper locations to insert the virus and retrieve the database. The process is pre-programmed and automatic, but I, or more correctly, my cargo within me, must be in the right location at the right time.

"Remember, a dead body cannot transit a portal. Therefore, should I be killed outright and not merely injured, you must return the device to someone able to use it. As a practical matter, that means you must cut into my body, with whatever tool you can use, bare fingernails and teeth if nothing else, remove the device, and transport it back within your own body. Meaning you must cut it out of me, swallow it, and then get thru the portal by any means possible."

"What portal?" I asked.

"Any portal," she replied.

She continued, "We have several possible exits. One, the preferred choice, takes us back where we started, back to a portal near Castle Stapleya. Petchy knows precisely, but another portal opens almost four hours after our portal deposits us there. We had not specifically told you, but coming back here after the battle was never the plan. We never expected to retrace our steps across this continent. Do you remember I described a Rapid Overlapping Transition: two portals synchronized to appear together?"

I nodded. I had already concluded this, so it was not a surprise.

She said, "This is a related phenomenon known as the Rapid Non-Overlapping Transition. Two RNOT portals are synchronized and appear one after another so that it is possible to walk from one to the other. They are not, however, overlapping. One consistently follows the other in a fixed amount of time. The portal we are going through will take us from this world, this location, to Planet K, the machine world. Its companion portal will take us from there and dump us back to that little park-like glen where you first awoke. The only catch is that it will be very late in the day. We must instantly run for all we are worth to the castle. It will be tight; not a second to lose.

"There is a strong likelihood we will instead have to use another portal, and there are several to choose from. Petchy and I have them all stored in our heads. Unfortunately, there is no good way to give you that knowledge; you have to depend on one of us. Safe Portal travel requires massive amounts of data about portal locations and destinations. We have tools and tricks to help us with that, but even so, it is challenging. All of the portals in that area and timeframe will take us somewhere better than there." She shrugged as if to emphasize.

She said, "Worst case scenario, take any portal you can see. You know the markers and know how to spot an open portal. Friendly operatives will find us no matter where we land."

"So, we get in, get your abdomen, living or dead, within Bluetooth range of two computers, one at a time, wait a minute, and then get out. We have a total of four hours. That sounds simple enough. What about defenses?" I asked.

"Once inside the citadel itself, there are roving security bots. They would seem almost comical if they weren't so deadly — sort of like oversized upright robot vacuum cleaners with weapons. Or perhaps a little like one of Davros' fictional creations. Like the Doctor's nemesis, they kill anything human or animal on sight, although they don't screech 'Exterminate!' They are relatively slow-moving and easily disarmed if you are quick and determined. If you move fast, you can knock one out and take its weapon. They are dangerous but can be dealt with. They usually depend upon overwhelming invaders by sheer numbers, but we expect most of them to be elsewhere, drawn to the more overt invasion our brothers are mounting. Some strategic locations have cameras and automatic weapons. Otherwise, there is little in the way of defense inside.

"Outside, the same sort of camera-guided automatic weapons guard every possible entry and will shoot anything that moves."

I asked the obvious, "How do we get in then?"

"The entire complex is planet-wide and extends for miles beneath the surface. Power for the billions of interconnected pods comes from geothermal heat deep in the planet's bowels and is effectively impossible to shut down with any resources we can muster. There are many openings where air, wastewater, and so on flow. Several openings lead directly into the interior."

She grimaced and shook her head for emphasis, then continued, "Security grates block them and are supposedly impassible, but we have to find a way to gain entrance. There are multiple ways we might do that.

"For one thing, the device I carry is programmed with the wireless access codes of the security system. It is programmed to open any security gates automatically. If we are in luck, all we need to do is stand in front of the entrance, which will open. However, it may not stay open long if the system detects it and closes it again. If we are lucky enough to have a gate opened for us, we must dart through it quickly. Further, the system will adapt if it detects us. We may make it through several protected gates before being caught, but that capability will cease to work once detected.

"Our armies have assaulted the Citadel many times, often at a significant loss of life. We have inflicted much damage, and though the system does repair itself, some things might not work depending on the scope and location of the damage. We have a few possible sites where we think the damage has left an unsealed vulnerability.

"Finally, our weapons cache should have a small supply of explosives. If necessary, we blast 'em open!"

CHAPTER 25

K-DAY

The morning of our date with the machines of Petch's ersatz Krypton dawned with heavy overcast and rain. Rain at dawn is unusual on Planet Oz, or at least it has been in the months I have been here. Overnight rains and mid-afternoon showers were frequent, sometimes twice or even three per day, but dawn had invariably been sunny and welcoming. Not today! Some might take it as an omen, but our hosts paid it no mind.

Perhaps it was more normal than I understood. Even so, the incident once again reminded me of an observation I had meditated on before. Time and again, I had noted some happenstance that Earth's peoples had built complex superstitions around, only to observe that the friendly and practical inhabitants of 'Planet Oz' just accepted it and made no effort to seek magical explanations. They seemed not to need supernatural forces and gods to worship.

I worried about why that might be.

Perhaps they already have real gods, gods that appear magically, walk openly among them, perform miracles, and then disappear just as mysteriously. Gods they refer to as 'The Smooth Ones' in whispers when they think we are not aware. I concluded there was much I did not understand concerning the relationship between Petchy's people and the fur-people of Planet Oz. Their influence on this Stone Age culture seems far more profound than I had imagined. That caused me to wonder what effect they exerted on Earth.

Omen or not, rain is not a hardship, not on this planet. The inhabitants supremely welcome rain, and given the oppressive heat, any rain provides we runners a most welcome cooling and refreshment. The clouds mitigate the sun's heat even though we mainly tended to run under a leafy canopy; there were enough stretches where we ran under an open sky that clouds, overcast, and rain are always welcome. The idea of avoiding rain, aborting a trip, or stopping in the middle of a journey to wait out an inconvenient rainfall was ludicrous. On the contrary, running naked in the warm tropical rain was a delicious, sensual pleasure to be appreciated.

Clouds and precipitation notwithstanding, we hit the road as early as possible. Given the weather, we were again taking the risk of being out of doors dangerously near sunup. It was not entirely unreasonable that, given the dark overcast, a fierce meat-eater might miss the siren call of Dino-bedtime and still be on the prowl. Fortunately, they tend to be noisy beasts. We listened for ominous forest noises before leaving the safety of stone walls.

The run this day was a comparatively easy thirty-three miles. Easy, that is, except that we are then to engage in a ferocious battle shortly after that.

Conserving our energy in any way possible seemed an excellent idea. Using support runners to reduce our burdens had worked so well that we decided to use the method again. This time a support team would accompany us more than halfway before transferring their payload to us and turning back.

When we assumed the load for the closing leg of the journey, we were comparatively fresh, and the final run to the portal site allowed an easy lope that got us there with hours to spare. We did not have to carry supplies for more than the run to the gateway. Once we reached our departure point, anything we still held must be eaten, drank, or dropped to be left behind. Carrying anything more than what we needed to reach that point was pointless.

Once in the vicinity of the portal, we had the challenge of locating it. This portal is in an unpopulated area and not known to the natives. Fortunately, unknown to me, those who planned this attack were meticulous and left no detail to chance. The plans for our mission had been developing over several decades. Recognizing and locating a portal, especially one that has not appeared in recent memory, is neither easy nor straightforward for those untrained in the art and science behind the gateways.

You're golden if you have the tools and training of a hyper-dimensional physicist at hand. If not, then it is a little more challenging. Further, after it has opened, even if you know exactly where it is, just recognizing that it is active can be tricky. An open portal has a precise angle from which it may be seen or approached. Unless you hit it square on, you will miss it entirely and walk right past the edge of another world, blissfully unaware.

That explains how portals could exist right in the middle of a city without being noticed. I speculated whether these portals might also explain some otherwise unexplained 'supernatural' phenomena, particularly visions — not to mention many mysterious disappearances. Someone in just the right place, peering in precisely the right direction, might glimpse another world and mistakenly attribute their vision to the supernatural. Someone coincidentally walking in the perfect direction at the right moment could easily step through an active portal.

I had picked up all this detail in bits and pieces in our conversations over recent weeks. Teena's hyper-dimensional physicists had charted this portal carefully. It is a portal never before used for a variety of reasons. One reason is that it infrequently appears with years between active cycles.

The mission to use this portal had been, as I said, planned for decades, and if we had missed this opportunity, it would again be decades before anyone could make another attempt along these lines. It is altogether too remote and inaccessible, too small and delicate to seem of much value in attacking the enemy, any conventional attack that is. Our strategy and approach planned to leverage precisely the factors that disqualified the portal from use in a more direct assault in hopes of catching the enemy by surprise, making possible an attack the enemy had not prepared to counter. We hoped there would be almost no resistance to entering via this obscure and nearly inaccessible back door.

A massive stone marked the exact location, not unlike the stone mile-markers along the highway. You were correctly aligned to pass the portal when you stood just in front of the stone. You merely needed to know when to do so. That too had been provided for, although I am unsure how. There was a 'portal detector' embedded in the stone. A small piece of quartz, merely a simple liquid crystal display, arranged so that if you stood directly in front of the marker at the precise, perfect angle to traverse the portal, the quartz would subtly change color when it opened.

I was puzzled by this. Technology does not work on this planet, so I've been told. So how could the marker for the portal include a hyper-dimensional detector? The answer turned out to be relatively simple. The technology, I learned, would indeed not work in this world. The sensor was aligned so that when the portal opened, it was within the field of the wormhole itself. Hence, effectively shielded from this world's influence, it could work its subtle magic as long as the gateway was held open. The indication, the slight color change, was intentionally designed so that it would not be likely to be noticed by a native. You had to know what you were looking for or be incredibly lucky. We couldn't risk an indication blatant enough to attract a native into the portal. A blinking light would be a dangerous temptation.

I realized that it had long been the practice to subtly mark locations where portals appear on every planet, particularly those frequently used by travelers. I learned that the portal pair in the city where I had watched Teena transit that day were, in fact, quite well marked to the trained eye. Who notices every faint mark or scratch on the street, or a wall, particularly amongst graffiti?

I also learned that someone well-practiced in accessing portals could recognize an active wormhole visually by the slight shimmer in the air and even sense the air movement across the open gateway. Of course, you still need to know precisely when it is supposed to appear and where. Teena and Petch are both well practiced at this. I was not. We should be able to find the aids placed for us by previous adventurers to this realm using their experience and knowledge of the portals. Our very lives depended on doing so.

We arrived at the portal marker a little past noon. We had several hours to wait. We took up our station in front of the portal where we could watch for its appearance. I decided we should take a nap for at least an hour before doing anything else.

Nap! Ha! Who was I kidding? We had just run 35 miles and were keyed up, ready for the opening salvo of a great fight with galaxy-wide consequences. Indeed, a battle in which we were likely to die. Yeah, we could nap! We could drift off while watching the winged pigs soar high above our heads!

Okay, napping wasn't going to work. However, resting was still a good idea. So, we stretched out on the grass for a little over an hour and lay quietly. Sleep, not so much. After a while, conceding that actual sleep was not happening, we again sat up and began to chat as we waited for the zero hour.

While waiting, we went over our battle plans, rehashed the previous afternoon's briefing, consumed what little remained of our supplies, and prepared any way we could.

No doubt my timing was unfortunate, but rightly or wrongly, I decided that an issue was weighing on my mind, and sitting here in enforced idleness, I could not leave it alone. Unquestionably this was the wrong time to raise any issue, much less a highly problematic one, but we might not have another chance. I recognize I should have accepted that and left it alone, but the engineer in me can never merely leave something broken. If something's broken, I honestly must fix it, even if it carries unintended consequences. Some have told me that this is a character flaw. Perhaps it is.

I had noticed a worrying tension between Petchy and Teena the last several days, as if they had been fighting. At first, I considered it none of my business and butted out. But I suppose that having made that decision, I should have stuck with it or else cleared the air days ago to place it far behind us well before battle time.

Each time some minor incivility reared its head, I gritted my teeth and turned away. But unfortunately, it seemed to stay there, bubbling softly under the surface, popping up in rude comments and curt, almost hostile exchanges between Petch and Teena. Then, as we sat and talked about the upcoming battle, it surfaced again, with the two sniping at each other in subtle exchanges.

Finally, after the third curt exchange between them, I decided that it was a threat to our mission, whatever the issue was. Given my self-appointed role as a de facto leader of our team, I stepped boldly up to the problem. Determined to bring it out into the open and air it, resolve it if possible, I confronted them. At first, they denied anything was wrong.

I refused to permit it; some might suggest I acted like a leader. The less charitable might call me a busybody. Teena was annoyed with me. Petch was downright surly. I pressured them anew, rejecting their position that it was not my business. Petch was upset about something, Teena was acting guilty, and I worried it would endanger our mission. I insisted they come clean, and right now. I demanded we clear the air about whatever the problem was before entering the battle.

That might have been a mistake.

Chapter 26

TABOOS

I could see Petchy was upset, clouding up for a severe blow, and I was still wondering why. He paced back and forth, muttering and gesticulating incoherently for several seconds. Then he settled down and confronted the question. Finally, lowering his voice and pointedly excluding me from the conversation, Petchy asked Teena, "Are you going to tell him?" She shakes her head and motions for him to shush.

He wasn't buying it. His voice elevated as his anger gelled. "He deserves to know. I mean it, Athena! Once you bedded him, the equation changed. You placed him in a situation of violating his taboos. But you violated your taboos and his without giving him a chance to decide any of it for himself. By withholding the true nature of what was happening, you raped him as brutally as that act has ever been performed!"

Well! We know now that Petchy had not been so soundly asleep that night in the Dark Castle!

Petch continued, "He is in love with you. He probably has been since he first laid eyes on you. You certainly know your face is the perfect 'golden ratio' and your body sculpted, every inch, every curve carefully fine-tuned, and even your pheromones are enhanced to have that instant arousal. Any human male is SUPPOSED to get an erection on the mere sight of you. But, shucks, it even affects women, even those not so inclined will swing into your orbit given half a chance.

"Look at how the fur-people gravitate to you! Those ladies are almost as eager to bed you as they are Fitz! Men are drawn to you like a moth to a flame. Even I am not immune, and I KNOW what an old witch you are. Even I get aroused when I see you if I don't keep a firm rein on my libido, and I well know why and that it's not real. Hell, I understand it inside and out. But what chance does a child like him have?

"You have been using him shamefully. It's bad enough that you used your enhanced seductive powers to sucker him into this suicide mission. We excused that because of the lives at risk. But it was over the top to use those same powers to sucker him into gratifying your own sexual needs. That was rape, pure and simple, no matter that he enjoyed it too. It was rape because of the deception involved. We all have a great chance of dying in the next few hours. He deserves to know the full truth before he dies."

She burst into tears. Suddenly, my super-woman was uncharacteristically reduced to tears over a sexual liaison with me. I was standing there looking at her, my mouth opening and closing with nothing coming out, unable to make the ostensible connection between my brain and mouth function.

After a moment, she collected herself. "Fitz, Petch is right. I don't like that he says it, and it's painful to admit, but he is right. I am a shameless old harridan who has taken shameful advantage of a child. When you first came to this planet, you balked at what you thought was jailbait, refusing to violate a significant social taboo."

So Petch had told her about that too! Must a man's errors always dog his every step?

She continued, "From where I sit, you are my jailbait, my taboo, and I cannot help myself. I can only plead that many of the same elements of my enhanced attractiveness extend to you too. You must recognize that you have never lacked bedmates when you wanted them. Why do you think the ladies here are so eager for your bed? True enough, here they want your seed for practical, well-understood reasons. Those reasons are enough to ensure you had plenty of eager, furry bedmates regardless if you had been entirely unattractive. That, however, is not the case. The ladies of this world are falling all over themselves for your attention. Quite a few who had no possible hope of being fertile were guilty of deceiving themselves and their sisters to climb into your bed. Yes, my bed too, for that matter, if that matters to you."

I just stared at her, comprehending, yet not comprehending, in mute silence.

She went on, "Quite beyond that basic need for your y-chromosome, they find you utterly irresistible — as do I. Your natural attractiveness to women is scarcely less than my carefully engineered attractiveness to men. Even though, unlike them, I know I understand the basis of that attraction intimately, I still feel it. More than feeling it, I am drawn to you against all my judgment. Maturity, experience, and logic, even higher mission, all too easily become pushed aside in pursuit of lust. Such is human nature, and I am as human as you.

"You have come to sense that we are very old by your standards. It is true. I was an old hag, nearing the end of my childbearing years when your father was born."

I stared for several seconds, digesting all I had heard. My head was reeling from too much information, deciding which of the several broken taboos still mattered to me. Finally, I simultaneously engaged both cerebrum and larynx after a struggle and mounted a semi-coherent response.

"Y-You may have a few years on me. I don't know when my father was born or even who he was. I don't care. We have been through an awful lot together, and I have watched you fight, run, and face death. No other woman could ever live up to the standard you have set. If I am your jailbait, then you are my cougar. All that remains is to decide what we are to do about it."

She took my arm. "Fitz, you do not know the whole story. Petch said my body; my very pheromones were enhanced to give me power over men. That is very true, as my role has often been that of a seductress, getting my way using artificially enhanced feminine wiles. You said no woman could ever live up to the standard I set. That is literally true and by design. I am a product of the same miraculous genetic engineering that now threatens the very universe. I tried very hard not to seduce you, but truly you had no chance, even without my consciously trying. I am as programmed to use the weapons of seduction as men are naturally engineered to fall for them."

She sighed. I had a chance to interrupt, but I was too busy spinning. She collected her thoughts and went on. "You said you do not know who your father was. I do. I know him well. I was there when HE was born!

"Do you know the etymological meaning behind your name, the meaning of Fitz?" I nodded, but she continued anyway, "Fitz is a prefix in patronymic Anglo-Saxon surnames. It means Son of — as in Fitzpatrick means son of Patrick, or Fitzjohn, son of John. Or, as in Henry Fitzroy, the bastard son of King Henry VIII. But more than that, it means 'bastard son of' and is usually applied to royalty. Thus, the illegitimate son of King James was called Fitzjames. This usage dates from the 1600s."

I asked, "So, are you saying I am an illegitimate son of royalty. That sounds suspect. The royalty part, not the bastardy. The irony that

I am leaving bastard babies all over this world, and somehow that's a good thing, desired by these people, is just too delicious!"

I gave way to raucous laughter as I digested the irony. For a few moments, the pain was nearly too much to bear.

"Who is this royal son-of-a-bitch who sired me. You used the present tense, so I assume he is still alive. Tell me who he is. I owe him a swift kick in the ass, at the very least!" I suppose I got a little testy; I seemed to have jumped up and raised my voice ominously.

Petchy and Teena looked at one another, surprised by my fierce reaction. I was too. Then they looked at me. Then at each other again. Realization dawned. "YOU???" I exploded at Petchy. "You are my father?"

He dropped his eyes and shrugged.

"Why? How?" I demanded, "Explain this to me."

She laid a hand on my arm. "Fitz, we have been on a critical mission for many decades. We needed a man of special qualifications who could fulfill a crucial role in that mission. So, we spread our genetically enhanced chromosomes far and wide. We had over ten thousand possible candidates.

"You are not Petchy's only progeny, not by a long shot. On the contrary, you are the most successful result of a long, complicated, and often painful eugenics program. It is not for no reason you were raised as an orphan. You were not born so much as built to specification, engineered to exacting tolerances, and honed for a specific task.

"I have watched over you since your birth.

"Recognize that you have developed from a stereotypical 'computer nerd' over the months here into a super-athlete. Didn't you wonder how that came to be?" She held up a hand to forestall my response. "I know Petchy gave you some nonsensical tripe about nutrition in the root vegetables, and you have been religiously drinking that foul-tasting *Grow-Juice* that the fur-people use.

"But didn't you ever wonder why the natives didn't develop huge muscles if those things were so powerful? Yes, the root vegetables, as Petch called them, are indeed powerful and nutritious, but that's not the whole story. When pushed, you became strong and fast; you responded spectacularly to aggressive training, not because of a magic elixir but because it was always in your genes. Some of it was naturally there from birth; some resulted from a final touch of genetic tweaking in our lab before you came to this planet. True, the nutrition was beneficial. But we cannot exceed that which is in our genes. Sometimes we can manipulate those genes to stimulate the full expression of specific characteristics, which is what we have done. Still, if the genes for intelligence, strength, speed, or endurance aren't in you, no amount of training or nutrition will make you strong, fast, or intelligent.

"You are not even aware of how much you exceed Earthly norms. But, again, that was a part of the plan and a reason for training here, where it would be difficult for you to measure your performance objectively. You can outrun, out climb, outfight, and endure any man ever to have lived on Earth before now. You also have a better memory and quicker mind than anyone, including ourselves. You see now why Petchy referred to himself as coming from 'Krypton.' You are a Superman on Earth, exceeding Earth norms and your progenitor's as well. We built you that way to be our weapon, just as I was engineered the way I am to be a different kind of weapon. We need these weapons far more than you could have grasped.

"There are many others like you, but your results were the best. That silly game we played back on Earth with the goofy advertisement was a calculated trap to bring in our carefully nurtured crop of potentials. Carefully loaded with keywords designed to draw our flock and be ignored by the un-genetically enhanced sons of Earth. Those who responded were overwhelmingly your siblings, drawn by carefully orchestrated psychological cues. Not all, but most. The promise of a job in hard times is a powerful magnet. But you had no choice. We had a larger mission of evaluating their progress and potential to be used in our mission or other future missions. So many of the warriors assaulting the citadel to draw fire to allow us to cross today are your genetic brothers. For this mission, you were and still are our best hope."

I stared blankly at her. Then, I thought about the transexual I had met in the waiting room for a moment. Was he, or should I say she a sibling of mine too? Is he, or she, out there now, cannon fodder to mask our penetration? Was his gender identity issue caused as a side-effect of this mysterious genetics program? Was she a genetic failure? Do I lean toward such gender-identity issues too? Or is that factor completely unrelated, merely another aspect of being human? I need to think about this.

"So where does that leave us. You came into my bed. We were lovers. I have fantasized about you endlessly. I burn for your touch even at this very moment!"

She looked at her feet, "and I, you. Even I am not immune to the very instincts I unconsciously exploit. I truly meant it when I said you were my jailbait. And worse. You see, not only is Petch your father, genetically, he is my grandson." She paused about two heartbeats to let that sink in. "I am your great-grandmother! Your taboos are not my taboos, true, but Petch is right when he says I have abused you shamefully, and you deserve to know!

"My fear now, by being weak and needy and being unable to resist a trap I set and baited, I have torpedoed our mission. I have played with your emotions and messed with your mind and heart by my inability to stay out of your bed. The act itself technically constituted incest is just one more minor plot twist in this matrix of social taboos."

She suddenly looked troubled. Staring at the ground for a moment longer, she wrung her hands in frustration and sniffed back tears before continuing. Then she raised her head and looked me squarely in the eye.

"Can you forgive me? You now know more than I ever intended you should. You were meant to remain ignorant of everything non-essential to our mission, not to be burdened by painful internal conflicts. We knew you would fall in love with me or at least be strongly lustful. That was unavoidable; lust is my stock in trade. I was not, however, supposed to reciprocate, to fall in love with you. That was unplanned, perhaps unfortunate — it may have cost us the mission. It may have cost us our very lives.

"My weakness has placed a burden on you that you should not have carried. Can you now shoulder this awful burden and carry on? Can you complete the mission without letting this burden kill us all?"

I answered by taking her into my arms and kissing her. Petch turned away apparently in disgust. She returned my kiss, then, almost in tears, I pushed her away.

Steeling myself, I stood and faced her squarely. I said, "I think I know what you mean. I cannot afford to think of you as a lover, a bedmate, or even a woman. I must harden my heart, no matter how strong the need; like an addict going cold turkey, the slightest break in my resolve would result in complete relapse. So you are my fellow warrior and nothing more."

I put my hands on her shoulders. I went on, "For the duration of this mission, we are brothers at arms, but that alone. I need to be able to steel myself so that, if need be, I can muster the strength to cut into your flesh with a knife to retrieve the data capsule within. If you fall in battle, I need to be able to do whatever is necessary to carry on, without hesitation, without recriminations."

I kissed her again, "I must put my heart on hold until after the mission. I will not make you any promises for then, and I ask none of you. After the mission, if we both live, we start anew."

She pulled me to her, gave me one last passionate kiss, then drew back. "After the mission!"

I heard Petchy whisper softly to himself, "Oh, Brother!"

CHAPTER 27

LOOKING GLASS

I sat in stunned silence after that. I no longer wanted to know more about the mission. I needed time to think, process, and digest all I had learned. I needed to screw my head on straight to face what was on the other side of the portal. I needed time, but I had almost none. Our date with the AI of Planet K could not be postponed!

I began to understand why Petchy had been so upset. If she is almost supernaturally able to manipulate males using her looks and pheromones, then any thought I had about her was suspect. Any feeling I had was handed to me by my own lizard brain. She had shamelessly manipulated me from the moment I first met her. Since that day in the plaza, really. Had any thought since that moment been my own?

I saw why Petch had called her an old hag. He was not just talking about her age, which I realized I STILL didn't know! He also meant her almost supernatural, witch-like power to manipulate. Could a man around her ever be his own man? Could a mortal man under her influence ever make any decision on his own and honestly trust he was free of manipulation?

I recognized that this was not so strange. The game of sexual roulette demands a suspension of logic and reason when passion reigns. Nature has always provided women with a touch of power over men, even without her artificial enhancements. But oh! Those enhancements. I burned for her still, even in my growing anger! One smile from her, and I would forgive everything.

She was, to put it colloquially, a witch. A cast-iron, cold-blooded triple-plated witch. A scheming bitch of a witch, willing to do anything, stoop to any level, use her supernatural powers without any limit to attain her goals. That her goals included saving all of humanity changed not a thing. Ends never justify means, we are told, right?

I think I understand Petch's original colorfully descriptive rant now.

Despite my anger, despite feeling betrayed, manipulated, and sucker punched, I still felt the passion she incited. A part of me would forgive anything, accept any abuse merely to have her smile at me. That magical, arousing smile. What man would not do anything for her? Her pheromone-enhanced smile alone could move mountains. Could any drug be more addicting? Could any narcotic warp a man's judgment more?

Could I handle it if she fell in battle? Could I lock away my emotions and soldier on, no matter what? I resolved I would. I must. I must harden my heart and forget that we had made love. We are brothers at arms and nothing more. So it must be. But how? What man has that kind of willpower?

I was still ruminating on the subject, in a way working up to a solid hatred for my newly unveiled great-grandmother when the portal opened!

Teena touched my arm and pointed. Startled, I jumped, returning from the deep recesses of my psyche to the harsh world before me with a start. Collecting myself, I looked where she pointed. I saw nothing. She pointed again, and then I realized what I was looking at. On the stone side of the marker, the quartz stone that had been pointed out to me had darkened. I looked critically at the portal itself and realized I could see a faint shimmer in the air, like heat rising off of a sun-drenched highway.

I examined it minutely. I angled my head back and forth, trying to find the optimal angle to view a screen. There, at just the perfect spot, I could see through the haze, and mirage-like, see something dark, with flashes of light behind it. At the ideal location and angle, I could see through to another world. The slightest shift and it was gone!

I asked, "How long will it stay open?" Teena responded, "This opening lasts for just under twenty minutes."

"Should we go right away, or wait a few minutes, that vigilance on the other side might relax. If the other side knew it would open, perhaps they would give it the most scrutiny immediately, then less if nothing comes through right away."

Teena and Petch looked at one another. Petch said, "These are machines; they don't get tired or complacent. I don't think it would matter."

Teena shook her head. "What you say is true enough, but Fitz has a point. All computers, no matter how powerful, have finite resources. Knowing that the portal will appear would focus attention there. But like any process in any computer, if a process is idle for a while and especially if there are other demands on the system — and we sincerely hope our brothers are placing other demands on the system — idle processes get swapped out of memory. That's the principle behind virtual memory, where unused memory is moved to storage and priority in the run queue lowered. So, Fitz is right; waiting a little while might work in our favor. But only a tiny amount. Once it sees us, it can elevate the run queue and swap back into memory very quickly. At best, the advantage will be milliseconds and will depend on precisely how busy the system is. But milliseconds count!"

That made sense to my systems engineering mindset. At times in my career, I had spent hours optimizing systems for precisely those reasons, hoping to shave a few milliseconds off the response time for some critical process. So I said, "Then we wait. But for how long?"

We debated it for a while — I realized Teena knew quite a lot about computers, memory allocation stacks, run queues, etc. She had evidently worked as a systems engineer. Finally, we settled on about five minutes as our best guess of the optimal wait time.

In truth, we had too little data about what was happening in the system to make any intelligent judgment; for that matter, we had no way to know when five minutes had passed anyway. Perhaps we could count our heartbeats.

We had divested ourselves of all our supplies, travel packs, and weaponry. I looked longingly at my exquisitely crafted bow, The Lady Seven, and her equally exquisite ammunition. Too bad I could not take them with me as I suspected we could seriously use them on the other side. I should have left her in the care of our support team and asked them to send her back to Stapleya. I had become used to running with a weapon at the ready. Doing otherwise, those last fifteen or so miles had not even crossed my mind. I packed her carefully and stored her beneath some rocks. I promised her that I would do all within my power to return and claim her again soon.

As we paused, I suddenly noticed Teena had forgotten her hair restraint. She had been forced to restrain her long crimson mop for our runs, and I assume she had become so used to it that she had forgotten. I quickly motioned to her to remove it. She was surprised and hastily yanked it away. Disaster was narrowly averted at the last instant.

Perhaps the minor mass of the bit of string and leather would have passed the portal, but maybe not. Teena had said this particular portal was more finicky than most. Quite likely, had she tried to enter the wormhole with that in her hair, the portal would have popped and disappeared. Of course, that would have invited her and anyone with her to a sumptuous feast; as the main course! Petch and I both checked ourselves for any other forgotten objects. Whew!

Very shortly, Petch called 'TIME.' We chug-a-lugged the last of our water as there wouldn't be any on *Planet K*. Then, taking a deep breath, we jumped for the portal. Perhaps our strategy worked; at least we were not shot down instantly as we popped out into the hostile land.

I burst through the portal and hit the ground in a roll. I leaped to my feet and began running. Much too late, I realized I had not asked what direction I was supposed to run, so I just ran straight away from the portal.

Petch and Teena hit the ground milliseconds behind me and launched themselves in a different direction, yelling, 'This way!' I executed a hard 90-degree turn and headed in their direction just as an explosion erupted right where I would have been had I not turned. We later decided that by coming thru first and inadvertently charging directly toward the citadel, I had drawn the machine's attention and fire, allowing Teena and Petch to come through unscathed. Their yell and my sudden, unplanned course correction had saved my very life. My unintended 'wrong-way Corrigan' and sudden course correction might have saved us all.

Several more explosions ranged around us, making my ears ring, and bullets stitched the soil around us. After our adrenalin augmented calisthenics, we dove over a small outcropping and hugged the ground, off the radar and out of the enemy's line of sight. We hoped.

We heard weapons fire in the distance, but the worst noise near us died away when we jumped over the outcropping.

Ignoring the minor injuries and doing my best to ignore the heat and control my breathing, we lay in the dirt for a few moments waiting to see if the enemy would let us go or continue to attack us. Scant moments later, I heard a mechanical whirring and scanned the sky above us for the source. At first, I saw nothing, but then against the heavy overcast, I saw movement, and my ears tracked the sounds to the object I saw.

A small drone was circling our position at a low altitude. It appeared too small to carry a weapon but certainly had a camera. No doubt we were under surveillance by an eye in the sky. I judged its position and range, deciding to have a try at it. Then, scooping up the nearest fist-sized rock from the rough terrain, I suddenly stood up and hurled the missile at the flying camera with all my strength.

Missed! Dodging slightly in response to my effort signaled it was indeed under intelligent real-time control. Our every action was being watched and evaluated for threat-level. We could not move until this was taken care of, lest the enemy predicts our next moves. We believed the enemy did not know about the small cave and wanted to keep it that way.

I heaved another missile at it, and again it dodged precisely the same. Then, with sudden inspiration, I handed Petchy a rock, instructed him to take his best shot, and grabbed another of my own. Watching him wind up, I targeted the space just below the drone, timing my drawdown to release scant milliseconds after his. Since it could evaluate our trajectory and dodge, hitting it with a single missile was improbable; it was quick enough to move out of the way of anything we could hurl. I was hoping that it would dodge Petchy's effort in precisely the same manner and direction it had in my two previous shots.

The strategy worked! The crafty machine indeed ducked under Petch's hard-thrown projectile just as I had expected. It, however, had not anticipated my incoming bolt and dipped right into my path. The drone rewarded our efforts with a most satisfying crunch as the machine fell to the ground mere feet from our position. I smashed it again with another rock to ensure it was well and truly dead.

Petch turned to look at me with a look of disbelief on his face as he divined what had just happened. His awe only lasted an instant, but I felt satisfaction, having not only defeated an enemy agent but also attained a new level of respect from my former mentor. Furthermore, I began to believe I was earning my leadership position on our team.

Flying spy camera defeated, Teena pushed some debris away and revealed a small cave in the side of the hill. We crawled inside before the A.I. could send another drone. The next one might carry more than a camera!

Now that I was not running and fighting for my life, I was suddenly overwhelmed by the heat. Teena had promised it would be hot here. Like a blast furnace. Like the engine room of a steam-powered freighter in the tropics. The hottest day on 'Planet Oz' was a balmy spring morning compared to this.

It was clear that the heat would rapidly kill us due to dehydration if nothing else. The sweat was pouring off my body, and I had trouble breathing. In addition, we were scraped and bruised from our dive into the dirt. Walking barefoot to the chin on the exquisitely groomed forest trails maintained by the fur-people was one thing; diving unprotected into the harsh rocky soil of this rough terrain was quite another! Bare skin has no place on this battlefield!

Cursing the improbable and circuitous logic that had brought us to this battleground naked and vulnerable, I turned my attention to the promised weapons cache, hoping that we would find weapons and supplies that would better prepare us for the fight ahead.

I'm not sure what I expected. I mean, in all the Sci-Fi action movies, when the hero needs to weaponize, there is a huge closet with a formidable display of weaponry neatly racked, ready for use. Sliding racks and racks of everything from knives to full automatics are all carefully displayed.

Weapons cache my clavicle! We had a hole in the ground and a pair of canvas bags wrapped in a tarp. In the dirt!

Chapter 28

CITADEL

Grabbing the tarp, I unwrapped it and took inventory. Short inventory! We had a small quantity of diddly, a helping of naught, a touch of zilch, a smidgen of swabo, and a whole lot of nada. As a weapons cache, this hole in the ground is a bust. Haven't these folks seen any action movies? Guess not. Well, here we are, and this is what we've got to work with; Not much!

We had a huge tarp, much larger than what was required to wrap a pair of canvas bags. We had some rope tying them together and the two small canvas bags.

Firearms? No AK-47, no grenade launchers for us. We had two ancient revolvers, six shots each, and no additional ammunition. That doesn't seem like much to storm a citadel. There was also a military-grade multi-tool with pliers and knife blades, some string, tape, and two vests with pockets.

The smaller bag contained the most promising, weapon-like items; two more-or-less textbook WWI hand-grenades and a small block of what appeared to be modeling clay. Not being an expert in explosives, I was puzzled at first. I turned it over, looked carefully at it, and smelled it. Then, finally, realization dawned; this was the promised high explosive. Or so I hoped. It must be!

I stared at it for a moment, wondering how I could use it. I am not an expert, but I was pretty sure that C4 would not explode without a severe concussion, typically delivered via a blasting cap, which we didn't have. I searched the bags and the pockets of the vests. Here was our Nada.

I dug into the ground, searching for more materials. I quizzed my companions and got nothing but a shrug.

It is what it is. I shrugged back!

I thought about how to storm the citadel with our meager resources. It seemed impossible. We were several hundred feet from the nearest access point, a drain covered by a fully automatic weapon aimed by a computer that would be unrelenting and merciless. Any approach to that drain would draw weapons fire, certain death. It seemed that our world-saving ambitions and ourselves were to die right here in this hole.

Examining our resources, I asked Petch about the weapon threatening us. Did simple motion-sensing activate it, or was it more sophisticated?

Petch responded, "What are you getting at?" I answered, "I mean, does it simply fire at anything that moves, or does it seek only humans or human artifacts and only fire on things it considers a threat?"

Teena interjected, "Do you think you can simply raise your hands and say, 'Don't Shoot,' and it won't consider you a threat?"

Petch shook his head as he responded, "It is an AI and knows humans and many types of equipment that humans use. It won't waste ammunition on things that aren't threats. You cannot exhaust its ammunition by making it shoot at meaningless targets. It's too smart for that."

"That's not exactly my plan. My idea was more along the lines of disguising myself so the machine would not recognize me, and then just walking right up to it and poking its eyes out."

Teena squinted at me like a mother of a child who had just said something extraordinarily foolish. "How do you propose to do that?"

I elaborated, "I was thinking I could take the tarp, and get under it, and crawl along the ground slowly, slowly, as if the wind were merely blowing the tarp along. Once I was inside the range of fire, I would then stand up and simply throw rocks at it, breaking the camera so it can't see, or even knocking the gun mount askew."

I was about to bet my very life and the mission's success on a harebrained scheme. I insisted we needed to test the idea before trying it for real. We experimented using the rope and various sticks and branches to push and drag the tarp around within sight of the camera watching the area. We could see the gun swivel and track the tarp, but it did not open fire. After several minutes of taunting the machine, we concluded it would not fire on us. This part of my harebrained scheme might actually work.

Teena looked pensive as she thought about the idea. Petch objected. "Those are armored. Do you think you can throw a rock hard enough to inflict serious damage?"

"I'm not sure," I answered, "but we practiced throwing rocks back on Planet Oz a lot, and I got pretty good. I can throw a big rock awfully hard. We have some rope; I can rig a sling too. I also plan to try shooting it with the revolver, although I never got the chance to practice with that sort of weapon."

Teena voiced her thoughts. "Once you are inside the minimum weapons range, you can climb up the wall. Use the rope, climb up and put this explosive under the camera and the gun. Then climb down and shoot it or hit it hard enough to detonate it."

"Maybe. Although I seriously doubt I can shoot accurately enough to hit the target. I can probably hit it with a rock, but I seriously doubt hitting the explosive with a rock or even a bullet will set it off. This stuff is very stable."

"I can shoot it," she responded. "I have good marksmanship and lots and lots of practice." Petch chimed in, "So can I!"

"Okay, which one of you is the best marksman. And think carefully, as our lives depend on this!"

They looked at each other. Then, after a second, Petch dropped his gaze slightly. "She is, much as it pains me to admit. Teena is the best shot I know. If any of us can hit something under those conditions, she can. If she can't, then it can't be done."

I turned to Teena, "Do we need both of us. How's your rope-climbing skill?"

"Not as good as yours, and we still might need to throw rocks at it, and I can't use a sling. We need your biceps!"

"We still need some way to detonate the explosive reliably. We need a detonator. I am certain that shooting it with a gun or hitting it with a rock will not do it!"

Petchy added with deadly seriousness. "I think you're right. I have no experience with the stuff, but I know people that do, and they have talked about that sort of thing. Nothing short of a forceful and hot bang will set it off. The mere impact won't do it. Even fire won't do it. I recall claims that you could ignite the stuff and cook your dinner over it without fear of it exploding."

Inventorying our skimpy supplies, I thought a while, then hatched an idea. First, I took out one of the revolvers, extracted a round, and looked it over. Then, picking up the multi-tool and opening the pliers, I carefully separated the lead bullet from the brass. Next, pinching off a tiny bit of the C4, then molding it like modeling clay, I rolled it up and pushed it into the shell-casing to hold the powder in place; effectively, I now had a C4 "Bullet."

Holding it up, I said, "I think this will work as a detonator. The percussion cap in this casing will go bang when the revolver's firing pin hits it. That, in turn, sets off the gunpowder, and that, I think, will detonate the explosive."

I divided our meager C4 supply into four equal pieces using the multi-tool knife. One would go under the camera, one under the gun itself, and the other two kept in reserve.

Petch and Teena examined my handiwork, then wordlessly, Petch picked up the multi-tool and fashioned a second detonator identical to mine. Then picking up two blocks of our C4, he pushed the ersatz detonators into them, much as a typical blasting cap.

He held them up and smiled. "I bet this will explode, but how are you gonna hit it to set off the percussion cap?"

While he had been doing that, I had been probing around our cave space for rocks. Finally, I found two small stones with sharp edges and just the right shape. I held them up, took some tape, and taped them securely in place, almost but not quite touching the shell's percussion cap. I placed a small strip of folded tape between the cap and the rock as a safety strip, so it could be removed when we were ready to "go live" with the boom-boom-maker.

"If we can hit these rocks squarely and drive the pointy edge sharply into the cap, it should act as a firing pin, explode the cap and set off the chain reaction." I placed our makeshift weapons into one of the canvas bags and handed it to Teena. I also put the grenades in the sack.

"Okay, can we both get under that tarp?"

We tried it. Teena could get on my back and press herself into me with a bit of scrunching around, and Petch could cover us with the tarp, tying it onto us. Teena would hold the smaller canvas bag with the makeshift explosives, a few handy rocks, and the rope sling I had fashioned. The longer rope I then tied around her waist. Then with her as my burden, I would crawl on my belly, very slowly toward the weapon. We hoped the AI would see us as a simple piece of wind-blown debris.

We speculated about the steepest angle the gun could reach to fire downward. We had to be inside that angle before we could reveal ourselves. We finally decided to play it safe and not do so until we were hard against the wall.

The plan was simple. We would knock out the gun emplacement, and then Petch would trot over and join us, bringing the rest of the supplies, such as they were.

We set off. Teena's weight drove my knees and elbows into the rough ground; she is a big girl. Despite the pain and the damage I was doing to my body, I crawled slowly and carefully toward the objective.

After several minutes of blind crawling, I bumped my head on the wall. I raised my head and looked around; we had arrived. Teena climbed off and stood; I expected gunfire to erupt any instant, but it seemed we were unnoticed by the AI. Too close to be seen, I surmised. I motioned for her to sit down by the wall and sit still while placing our explosives.

Slinging the rope, I took the C4 pieces in my mouth; we should have brought one of those vests. No pockets, darn it. I had learned to be supremely comfortable nude, scarcely noticed any lack, but even once you have abandoned the societal taboos, some things about clothing are still handy. I had occasionally wondered about the practicality of genetic manipulation to grow marsupial-like pockets. That seems like an advantageous adaptation.

I climbed the rope. Petch had been right about one thing; adrenalin made it a lot easier! I was able to squish the C4 under the gun mount and camera, align our makeshift detonators, pull the plastic tape safety strip, and retreat. Once I was safely back on the ground, Teena pulled out the revolver. We had left the weapon which had sacrificed two bullets to make detonators with Petch. She carefully aimed and fired at the rock under the camera.

She missed!

We only had six rounds, now five left. I had always heard that hitting anything accurately with a handgun was difficult. She motioned for me to kneel, and she rested her arm against my shoulder and whispered: "Don't move!" I held my breath and froze as motionless as possible, doing my best to imitate a tripod.

Again, she missed!

We shifted positions, and she took careful aim once again. She steadied, and I held my position rock solid. Time stretched out, and it seemed like it took forever. Then BANG!

Third-time charm. We were showered with debris and camera parts. I was relieved to know my makeshift detonator had worked.

We resumed our positions, and she tried again, aiming for the gun mount. She steadied herself against my shoulder and took careful aim.

Again, she missed!

We were down four bullets. Two left, and we still had to take out the gun, although, with the camera gone, the weapon was far less dangerous.

There were, however, other cameras, and we didn't want to take chances on the AI finding targets by other means. It could fly a camera drone to our position at any moment. We resumed our positions and steadied again.

Missed again; Predictable, really!

We took deep breaths, which induced a spasm of coughing, and the overpowering heat was making everything more difficult. Finally, after a few moments, we steadied ourselves into position, and once again, she took aim.

Missed again! We were out of shells, and we still had a rather ominous gun staring down at us, blinded though the camera might be, it nonetheless covered our goal and could not be ignored. I got out my rope sling. I hoped I could hit the detonator hard enough to do the trick.

I picked up a nice-sized rock and placed it in the pocket of my sling; then, I stepped out to where I could draw an accurate bead on the target. The gun swiveled toward me, and I hurriedly ducked back! Even though blinded in this eye, I realized the machine could still see us from other more distant cameras, and it seemed to have a clue of what we were trying to do.

I looked around for another drone, but nothing was in sight. Possibly the one I smashed was the only one in this area. Fortunately, we were still within the space dictated by the gun mount's minimum deflection angle — it could not quite reach me. It rocked back and forth as it tried futilely to draw down on us. Stepping out again, this time more mindful of the gun angle, I wound up my sling and let go.

OH! So Close. But no joy, again I missed!

I repeated the process, wound up, and let fly. This time I over-corrected, my missile sailing to the starboard side of my stony ersatz firing pin. The third time's charmed, you say? Tell that to the rocks! The heat and pressure were affecting my aim. After flinging five more rocks, each one passing further away from the target, I sat down and hung my head in disgust. I had to calm my racing pulse, relax, and mentally walk away from the tension and pressure. Too much adrenalin over too long a period, the heat, and dehydration had taken their toll.

I closed my eyes, concentrating on calm and peacefulness; ignoring the heat, I focused on my breathing, on finding my spiritual center.

After several drawn-out moments, I again stood, wound up the sling, and let fly. This time I was rewarded with a most satisfying BANG!

Debris and gun parts again rained down on us. Painful, but welcome. With all six bullets expended, the revolver was now a paperweight. I debated dropping it but stuffed it into the bag anyway. You never know...

I stood up and waved to Petch, and he came over on the run. Gunfire stitched the ground around him as he ran, barely missing him. Unfortunately, the AI had figured out what was going on and was trying to hit him from another more distant gun emplacement. Fortunately for Petch, we were too far away for accuracy. It did liven up his stride, though; his feet grew wings that last 50 feet!

Automated weapons neutralized; we now must get inside the wall. A giant security grate covered the drain. The pipe was huge, big enough for the three of us to walk side-by-side comfortably, although my head nearly brushed the ceiling. The security grate was monstrous. Even if it weren't securely welded in place, the three of us together could not even begin to lift it.

I pulled out one of the grenades and wedged it between two of the bars. I nodded at Teena and Petch and pointed down the wall. They retreated to safety. I pulled the pin and ran to join them. A few seconds later, a satisfying boom rattled our teeth. The debris that pelted us told us we had stayed a little too close.

Inspecting the results, I was disappointed; one bar was broken, and the other severely bent, but the gap was not nearly big enough for me to squeeze through. We had one more grenade and two small pieces of C4. I considered the bars, trying to visualize the explosive force at various locations. Then I placed our final grenade between an adjacent set of bars and wedged it firmly in place with another of our endless supply of rocks.

I considered my handiwork and examined the damage the first grenade had done. Then, giving the matter some thought, I pulled out the two small pieces of C4 and added them to either side of the grenade, smooshing it right against the steel of the grate and again using rocks to confine the blast. I wished I had more explosives.

Motioning to my companions, they retreated considerably further this time, and I pulled the pin and ran like hell. This time the kaboom was much more satisfactory. Despite being a greater distance away, we were still severely pelted with gravel and debris. I was impressed by the amount of kaboom in that tiny chunk of 'modeling clay.'

The grate was still substantially together, but there was a hole big enough, barely, to crawl through. We had access to the inside now, but we had used the last of our explosives. We had a rope sling, a long piece of rope, a few hand tools and supplies in the vests, and a pair of canvas bags. No more explosives, but we had a revolver with four rounds. We made a decidedly unimpressive attack force.

The metal grate was hot after the explosion, and we had no time to wait for it to cool, not that it would rapidly do so in this environment. I arranged the tarp for protection and motioned Petchy to crawl through the opening. Teena followed, and I went last. I am the largest, of course, and despite the tarp, I managed to burn my leg on the hot metal. I added that pain to the running tab of injuries we were accumulating and did my best to ignore it.

We were finally inside. Foul-smelling water was ankle-deep in the tunnel. The air was hot and smelled like something had burned. We did have a stiff breeze, airflow exhausting from the fortress via this large vent. Although the wind was insanely hot, its flow helped some with the heat.

The heat was taking a toll, but we were dehydrated and desperate for water. So, we sloshed the malodorous wastewater over our bodies and drank a little, hoping the poisonous effluent would not kill us before we completed our mission. We were so dehydrated we would have drunk our urine if we had any.

We sloshed our way along, searching for an opening, any way into the complex.

We came to a grate and tried to open it. But unfortunately, it was solid, unmovable, and we had nothing with which to force it. So, we continued sloshing along, penetrating deeper and deeper into the complex.

We came to a fork, three smaller branches making a trident, a three-pronged 'Y' into the larger drain. I glanced at my companions questioningly, wondering which branch to take.

I said, "Rock, Paper, Scissors," while motioning to Teena to step toward one side as I took the other. "Tie says we take the third branch!" Teena's paper and my rock decided; we took her branch. I had to stoop to walk.

Another grill in the ceiling gave us one more tantalizing view of the floor above, to no avail. This one, too, was impregnable to our meager resources. We continued onward; three more grates, three more failures. Then, we reached the end of the tunnel!

Retreating to the branching point, I glanced at Petch. Another round of Rock wrapped paper to choose one of the two remaining tunnels. Again, grate after grate, none of which we had the power to breach. Once again, we reached the end of the line.

"Third time's charmed," I muttered to the ether as we retreated to the branching point. No further need for games; we were out of options. Only one tunnel remained; we took it.

As before, grate after grate was impregnable to everything we had at our disposal; this was getting repetitive, boring, and disappointing.

Instead of hitting the end of the drain tunnel, this time, we came to another branch, a 'Y' with two still smaller shafts. Another quick game of Rock, Paper, Scissors picked one of the two. We had to crawl on hands and knees. Groveling in the mud now, we came to grate after grate in the floor above, all impossible to open. Finally, we approached the end of the tunnel and a final grill.

As we were struggling in our failure to move it, suddenly Teena exclaimed, "Whoa," and put her hand to her belly. "Nematode has found a signal!" We froze in place for a few moments. Then she said, "It's no good; the signal is too weak. We must get closer!" I attacked the grate with renewed vigor. Laying on my back in the muck, I pushed my feet against the bars. Not enough leverage!

I piled our packs, the tarp, some debris in the tunnel, and everything I had, directly under the grate and under my hips to gain maximum leverage. I pushed for all I was worth, muscles and tendons straining almost to the point of injury!

Nada!!

I pushed again. Teena and Petch positioned themselves on either side, although they could not get the leverage I had. Then, grunting in a chorus, we all three heaved for all we were worth!

Again, Nada! I smacked my forehead and let loose a stream of invective I would never use in polite company.

We were so close! So VERY close.

Chapter 29

NEMATODE

We regrouped. We were so tantalizingly near our objective. On a sudden inspiration, I dropped to a position on my hands and knees. "Lay on my back and press your abdomen against the grate," I instructed.

With sudden comprehension, she grasped what I was suggesting. Place the device as close to the grillwork as possible in hopes it can find a sufficient signal to connect and upload its virulent payload. She climbed aboard and balanced on her back, lying against my back. I arched my back and pressed her into the grate. She shifted a few times, trying to get a better signal. Finally, after a few moments, she whispered, "It's working. Don't move!"

Minutes passed, then Teena unleashed her own invective, impressing me with her vocabulary. The first profanity I had heard from her, but it was unequivocal that she was not ignorant of the art form. After the expletives subsided, she said, "It almost worked but failed before completing the upload."

We repositioned and tried again. "Harder," she said. Then, seconds later, "Push Harder." She exhorted me to press her harder and harder, to push her body against the underside of the grate. I arched my back and thrust her upward with all the strength I could muster. She squirmed around a couple of times, seeking an optimal position.

A few seconds later, she grunted, "Right there! Right there!" and we froze, her perfect golden ratio face pressed harshly into the rough concrete ceiling, her torso pressed against the steel grate until it threatened to cut into her flesh. Time entered slow-motion, with my back, arms, and hips complaining vociferously, screaming at the effort. Finally, she whelped: "OMG! Done!"

We collapsed in a heap, huffing, and puffing, struggling to breathe without coughing in the heat and caustic atmosphere. Face bruised, nose bloodied, shoulders bruised, abdomen crisscrossed with the grating pattern; Teena looked a mess! I wanted to hold her and kiss the hurt I had inflicted. Pressing her against the rough ceiling and pressing her abdomen against the grate hurt me nearly as much as it did her.

I had to remind myself that I had hardened my heart, and she was not my lover. Not now. I wanted to cry. A single touch would violate my sobriety, false sobriety that I really, really wanted to violate! One slip and I would melt, I knew.

We were so spent we rested for a few moments. Then I asked, "So we succeeded. The system is infected?"

She nodded, wiping the blood streaming from a small but nasty gash in her chin with the back of her hand while rubbing the red welts crisscrossing her chest with the other. "Yes, I believe so. If the software team that built it got it right, we should soon see beginning signs of the system shutting down. Of course, it will take hours, days, before it's truly dead, but Nematode should be propagating itself throughout the system even now!"

"Now, how do we get the database?" I asked.

"We need to move deeper into the complex. There is another segmented secure network. We must penetrate the Encrypted Core!"

"But how? We can't get inside at all; even getting this far was dumb luck."

She shrugged. Petch sat beside us, helpless.

The only option was to retreat to the last branch and explore the one remaining path before us.

We crawled along the final path, passing several grates. We tried each one, hoping for one that might be loose enough to pry open. They were all solid, unmoving. We kept going. This tunnel did not end at a wall; instead, it went on and on and on. I wish we had a way to measure how long it went, but we crawled for what seemed like hours, passing grate after impregnable grate, pausing at each one to rattle the bars for any weakness and to give Teena's implant a chance to sniff for a signal. Not a peep!

Finally, we hit a 'T' with another even smaller line, this one too small for us to crawl into easily. We might crawl into it by crawling on our bellies but could not hope to turn around. That is to say, Teena might crawl into it. I didn't think my shoulders or those of Petch would even fit. Even so, her very womanly hips would be tight. Either way, crawling in reverse to get out would be slow and painful, if even possible.

Before the 'T,' the last grate felt like it could almost move. As before, we leaned into it with all we could muster, but it was bolted, latched, or something. It would move a little but not yield.

We were stymied. Staring at the smaller pipe of the 'T,' I wished we could get into it. Too bad we didn't have a hobbit on our team!

Teena refused to concede defeat. Instead, she was determined to crawl into that line in hopes of either finding an opening into the inside or at least a signal she could use to access the Encrypted Core and retrieve the database.

We discussed the idea at some length as we took stock of our situation. Succinctly put, we were a mess. We were bloodied, tired, spent. We didn't know how long we had been here, when our exit portal would open, or even how much longer we could survive. Crawling into a tight space that might be difficult to get out of seemed a prescription for dying a horrible, claustrophobic death on this forsaken planet!

I argued that we had completed the most crucial part of the mission, killing the runaway system. Even without the database, it might be possible that scientists may yet puzzle out the solution, even without the research data used to instigate the process. Knowing the specific research underlying the approach taken to reduce human fertility would make it a lot easier, but we still might succeed without it.

Teena shook her head. "I am not optimistic. Our best scientists, the best geneticists in the known universe, have been working on it for over a century without significant progress. Genetics is complicated, Fitz, far more complex than most people know about, and it's hard. We need that database. If I don't get it here and now, before the machine is dead, it may well be unrecoverable."

"Couldn't computer forensics recover the data from the dead system?" I asked.

"Admittedly, it might be possible," was the response. "But it's a long shot. To ensure the machine stays dead, the Nematode completely wipes all storage. All writable memory down to low-level machine bios code on every node, every server pod, is filled with random garbage, rendering it incapable of booting or even running a power-on-self-test. If we didn't do that, the system would isolate affected nodes and restore them individually. Therefore, we must take them all down, virtually at once, and make sure they stay dead, or else the machine will rebuild itself one node at a time until it is again fully operational. There is no expectation that once Nematode has done its work, there will be any functioning data processing hardware or any structured data of any sort. Anything left to recover would be an accident, pure dumb luck.

"I, for one, have no wish to bet the future of the human race on dumb luck. Not while I have a breath left in my body!"

Petch chimed in, "Killing the machine buys us little. If not for the genetic database, we could block off the portals and abandon it. But, no! We simply MUST have that database. That is far more important than simply killing the machine."

That made sense!

We considered our options. Teena thought she could crawl forward into the pipe. Crawling backward to get out would be much more difficult. We decided to tie our rope to her feet, allowing her to crawl but so we could help pull her back out.

We experimented by having her crawl just a few feet in; then, I pulled her back. Painful and difficult, she acquired additional scrapes and bruises in the process, but it's doable.

She took the left side of the 'T' and began crawling. I played out the rope to her and watched her progress. I had played out about three-quarters of the line when she stopped. She was still for a very long time. I began to worry. Finally, she signaled for assistance in retreating.

She was scraped and bloodied from head to toe, and by her expression, I could see there had been no success. She shook her head. "There was a grate but I couldn't budge it. I tried and tried. There was no signal either. Just a dead end."

She started for the right side of the 'T.' I stopped her. "Are you sure?" I asked with my eyes. She avoided my gaze, pulled away, and moved toward the pipe. Once again, she crawled into the tight space, inching forward. Again about three-quarters of the length of my rope disappeared, and then she stopped. Once again, there was silence for a very long time.

The bad air and the heat were taking their toll. I was having a harder and harder time staying focused; I must have faded out for a second or two because when I looked again, the rope was gone!

Nightmare scenario after nightmare scenario played through my brain as I lunged for the pipe access. I reached inside as far as I could, feeling for the rope's end. What had happened? Had something grabbed her. Had she fallen into an intersecting down-pipe?

I stared dumbfounded. Then I shouted into the pipe. No good; we had tried that before; the overall ambient noise and the echoey nature of the environment made understanding our distorted voices impossible.

Ever the optimist, Petchy suggested she might have found a grate she could open and now be inside the complex. I had seen so many that were so impossible to move, I doubted it, but I knew there was nothing I could do. I could not go after her.

We waited a while. Then we waited some more. Then, finally, Petch said something; I didn't understand him at first. The heat and bad air were taking their toll on us both, and I was pretty well wiped out.

"Maybe we should head for a portal," he finally got my attention. I shook my head. "When you're going through hell, keep going," I quoted, "Let's at least give her a few more minutes."

He shrugged.

We probably sat there in the muck and mire, covered in mud and crud, for an hour; actually, I don't know how long. Hard to judge, no way to mark time. I wished for a simple wristwatch. I wished for lots of things.

I stuck my head into the pipe, listening for any sound, any indication of what had happened to her. Petch was again making the case that we should go, and I still refused. I was having more and more difficulty staying cogent, and so was Petchy. If we did not go soon, we would probably die here, rather soon, I suspect. We were overheated, dehydrated, and had ever-increasing difficulty breathing. I realized we were very likely to die right where we sat. Soon.

Just as I was coming to terms with failure and the prospect of my imminent death, I heard banging! It was hollow and echoey, but definitely, someone was banging something on the other end of the pipe. Or was it gunfire? Hard to tell, but there was life of some sort in that pipe.

Moments later, I heard a voice. I could not understand the words, but it was unquestionably Teena. I couldn't make out what she was saying. Neither could Petch. We heard more banging, then silence for a time. Several minutes elapsed, then we heard a grinding sound much closer at hand, apparently not weapons, more like metal-on-metal scrunching and squeaking.

Suddenly we heard her voice clearly, but not from within the pipe. Instead, she was above the grate behind us, which had seemed almost loose. We scooted over to her and gaped in astonishment.

"I think I managed to undo the clamps. It's too heavy for me, though. Can you lift it?" Petch and I lifted the grate, pushed it aside, then climbed through to the upper level. We were in!

It was much cooler inside, owing to the machines' need for a controlled environment. Earthly data centers are virtual refrigerators; this one not so much, but much improved over the outside air.

Teena was a bloody mess. She explained that she had found a grate that was loose and managed to open it and crawl into the complex. Thanks to her implant's security override software, Teena had succeeded in making her way from one secure area to another. She was searching for a connection to the internal network when a security bot found her. Though wounded, Teena had managed to disable it and take its weapon. She brandished a formidable piece of artillery!

She was excited and hopped up on adrenaline, but success had not come without a price. She had taken two bullets and had a nasty burn on her leg as though raked by a powerful laser beam. Her wounds appeared non-life-threatening but bloody, messy, and very serious. She was bleeding and virtually unable to walk, a makeshift rope tourniquet somewhat stemming the worst bleeding from her leg wound.

Weapon or no, a hasty retreat and urgent medical care seemed in order, but we still had to find and connect to the secure internal network, the Encrypted Core she had called it, and download that database!

The temperature dropped as we ventured further into the facility; I carried Teena not to aggravate her bleeding. Nevertheless, we left a trail of her blood. At each nodal cluster we passed, I cocked an eyebrow questioningly at her. Any signal? She shook her head.

With no way to track time, it seemed as if we spent hours exploring deeper and deeper, searching for a connection.

Twice we were accosted by a bot. They were indeed like something out of a bad Science Fiction TV show, and I would have laughed at them if they weren't firing real, deadly weapons at us. As it was, I almost imagined I could hear a high-pitched '*Exterminate*' echoing the corridors. Fortunately, we were armed and able to defend ourselves. Each time we were able to take their weapon, re-arming ourselves and dropping our spent ones. They turned out to be relatively easy to 'kill' with their own weapon if you hit them just right. Surprisingly fragile, really, though if they came at us in significant numbers, they could be very bad news. Their primary strategy seemed to swarm any threat as a coordinated phalanx of attackers. Individuals alone were more dangerous than comical. Barely.

So far, the ones we had seen were few and solitary. However, our luck was overdue to run out. The AI was aware of our existence and must have a fair idea of where we were. Frankly, we were amazed at encountering so few internal forces. Even though the frontal attack occupied most of its forces, it was only a matter of time before it mobilized sufficient bots to overcome us with sheer numbers.

Despite our fatigue and Teena's worrying bleeding, our only hope was to move quickly. Petch and I took turns carrying our wounded warrior, but we were both tiring fast, and Teena herself was fading due to blood loss. If we did not find a signal soon, we faced dying here in abject failure or abandoning our mission and retreating. Neither option was palatable.

As we moved, I examined the various pipes in the hopes of finding one carrying desperately needed water. However, I feared breaking one, lest it might discharge something poisonous, coolant, or a fire suppressant.

We came to a monstrous security gate, unable to proceed further; we could see past it into the corridor beyond, which housed cluster after cluster of server pods.

Suddenly, the gate opened. Teena's override had worked once more; luck was still with us. We hobbled down the corridor, following the curving pathway, deeper into the machine's bowels, deeper into the massed hardware clusters.

As we rounded one bend, Teena hoarsely whispered: "Stop!" We froze. She pointed ahead. There, ahead of us, lay what I could only describe as a communications hub. Massive numbers of fiber optic cables converged into a multi-tiered conglomeration of hardware. It seemed a candidate to have the communications access we sought, but a camera and gun emplacement covered it!

Petch raised the weapon commandeered from our last encounter. I shook my head, vetoing it. "Too noisy!" I whispered hoarsely—no reason to advertise our presence more than necessary. Besides, we had limited ammunition. Rocks were reusable!

The camera was scanning a cyclical surveillance pattern, covering the entire corridor, each direction, one at a time, and oscillating back and forth. I unlimbered my sling and waited just out of sight behind a rack until it scanned our direction and then turned away. Then, holding my breath until it was pointed directly away from us, I stepped out, wound up, and let fly. My hard-flung missile caught the camera squarely, knocking it from its mount and smashing it to pieces.

Blind it may now be, but the machine deduced the direction of the threat. The weapon whirled around and opened fire, blindly sweeping our area. We dove back around the bend and watched as the gun scanned the area, spraying bullets until we heard its magazine spin emptily. It was out of ammunition and blind. No doubt it knew we were here now, guaranteeing reinforcement bots were on their way.

The flying bullets had damaged some plumbing, and various fluids hissed and spewed at us. Unfortunately, none of them was water. After a time, the AI must have detected the leaks because the flows stopped, leaving a nasty, stinking, slippery mess in the hallway.

I carried the injured Teena to the hub, and she smiled weakly. A few seconds and she began nodding. Petch and I abandoned her briefly as the download commenced and placed ourselves down the hallway in either direction from her location to guard against incoming bots.

We waited for what seemed like ages — periodically, we raised a questioning thumb at Teena, and she would give us a weak thumbs up — still going. It was too noisy to communicate otherwise. I never imagined computers could be so loud.

Again and again, we repeated the cycle. Once Petch engaged fire with a solitary bot that had come from his direction. He knocked it out, ran over, and yanked its weapon. He tossed it to me, and I stuffed the revolver and its four lonely pips into my vest. It felt good to have a real firearm. Of course, it was meant to be used by a robot and not a human, but although it was awkward, we could manage. But, of course, humans are much more flexible than any robot.

The download continued. We knew the data was massive; we didn't know how long to expect it to take. We only knew we would hold this position as long as it took or until we died. As long as we secured the data, we were expendable. Of course, subsequent forces could extract the data from Teena's corpse, if necessary, but needless to say, that would not be our preferred outcome.

We expected more bots to appear, but our luck was still holding. Our brethren making the frontal assault must be taking most of the machine's attention and resources. We could occasionally hear distant thunder that must be weapons fire. Despite our fears, bots had been few and far between. I was astonished that we had not seen more flying drones.

Between vigilant scans for bots and drones, I studied the plumbing. I noticed one smaller line color-coded differently than those leaking a suspect mixture into the adjacent hallway. On a whim, I raised my weapon and smashed it, breaking the pipe. I was rewarded with a gush of water, pure water! Petch and I refreshed ourselves, filled the canvas bags, and carried water to Teena. With the more tolerable temperature and water, we could hold our position for a very long time. Unfortunately, within about ten minutes, the flow stopped. That damned AI again, I suppose.

Teena's download went on for what seemed like hours. Then, finally, after an eternity, Teena circled her thumb and forefinger in the universal sign of success. We ran to her; I scooped her up, and we headed home! We had succeeded; now, we just needed to get out alive.

We retraced our steps at a dead run, following the trail of Teena's blood. We were virtually running now, heedless of the danger. But unfortunately, our attempts at battlefield medicine were inadequate; Teena was unconscious, and we were leaving a fresh trail of her blood. Eventually, we reached the massive grate I had blown up — how many hours ago?

Bad news.

Three security bots had stationed themselves outside the opening. How to cope with them, I wondered. I set the now unconscious Teena down inside the grate. I carefully checked her breathing and pulse. She was fading fast. Petch took our one useful revolver with its four shots, removed two shells, and loaded them into the empty one, handing it to me. I appreciated the resource sharing, though I was unsure how effective a revolver with two cartridges would be against the bots. We each took a purloined automatic rifle, mine nearly half-full, Petchy's almost empty.

We could not hope to crawl out through the grate. We would be attacked immediately, with fatal results. We could sit inside and shoot at them from there until they returned fire. Once they knew we were there, it would be hard to do anything but duck and run. Worse, their bullets would ricochet off the concrete walls, making almost anywhere unsafe, even if they couldn't get a direct shot.

Teena's burn confirmed they had beam weapons too. Even mere light can be deadly with enough energy behind it.

We couldn't sit there forever. The unconscious Teena was still bleeding! We all needed medical attention, but Teena's need was more urgent. We couldn't go out there because they would shoot us. If we shot at them, they would shoot back; we were at an impasse for the moment, only because the bots had not yet detected our presence.

Petch and I talked it over and decided to go for whatever we could do. The worst-case scenario was now that a rescue party would eventually find our bodies, with the precious database information intact in Teena's implant. So, we had succeeded, kinda. Some might argue that success called for returning alive, and I agreed, but a pyrrhic victory was marginally better than abject failure and defeat.

We planned to position Teena far back in the tunnel and then carefully position ourselves at the grate. Then, we would fire on the two bots nearest us simultaneously and try to disable them, and then run for it before the third one could hit us.

It almost worked to perfection. Almost. We waited until one bot had moved further away from the grate and then opened fire on the two closest to us. The third one came rapidly toward us, firing on the move. Petchy had emptied his revolver into his target, and surprisingly, it went down, though not before firing several shots in our direction. I got off my two shots before the incoming fire from the third bot forced us to retreat. We dropped the revolvers, ducked, and ran, but a ricochet creased my shoulder. It wasn't bad, missed the bones, didn't damage the joint, but I lost some tissue. I would heal, but it hurt like hell and was bleeding. Even so, compared to Teena, I was barely scratched!

The third bot fired several rounds into the grate, but not seeing us and with no target in sight, it soon retreated and again took up position outside the grate. We surmised it had called for reinforcements and would not attack until it had support. We had moments to escape before those reinforcements arrived.

After the fire had settled down, we again sneaked up to the grate and peered out. The bot had stationed itself a few feet from the entry and was keeping watch. Either it hadn't noticed us behind the massive grate, or it interpreted our movements as non-threatening. On the other hand, perhaps it was merely watching, waiting for reinforcements to arrive. Petchy and I took positions on either side of the opening, each of us with one of the same weapons the robot possessed. Petch had one round left in his weapon. I had not counted mine, but I had more than he. We were sure it had a laser weapon too, but so far had not used it.

With an injured shoulder, I was not as able to shoot as I wished, and Petch was covered in blood; whether it was all Teena's or some of it his I did not then know, but he was moving painfully. I later learned he had taken two ricochets, much more severe than my shoulder scratch, yet somehow, he remained upright and mobile despite pain and blood loss. We drew down together, aimed, and opened fire simultaneously. The bot went down, but not before getting off multiple shots. One creased my side, digging an open furrow in the flesh, more than a scratch, exquisitely painful but a long way from life-threatening. The bot was vanquished far easier than we had dared hope.

We scrambled back to where we had left Teena. She was unconscious and breathing shallowly. Her pulse seemed weak. We had to go for it; it was now or never. Reinforcements, theirs, were on the way.

We got ourselves out through the grate, some difficulty with an unconscious woman. Teena's a big gal and limply unconscious; she's a burden. With my injured shoulder and knife-edged pain in my side, I was somewhat hampered and the stream of blood leaking down my arm from the shoulder wound made things slippery and painful, but we managed. Petchy slung her over his shoulders in a 'fireman's carry,' and we took off on a fast hobble. Distant weapons began firing in our direction, though thankfully ineffectively. I felt dirt and gravel hit my legs several times as bullets stitched the ground around our path.

I had started for the portal location where we had arrived, expecting the portal back to Planet Oz. Instead, Petchy shouted, "No. This way!" I turned to follow him. We went over the outcropping, past the cave, and straight away from the citadel. We ran a while and then had to stop, out of breath. We had been running, fueled by adrenalin, for a time now, and even that was running out. We were close to the absolute end of our endurance. The heat, bad air, lack of water, and blood loss took their toll.

Petchy collapsed, dropping his burden. He was exhausted, nearly unconscious, unable to continue. I reached deep inside, found one last reserve, and picked up the comatose Teena, my injured shoulder screaming in pain, the furrow in my side chiming in with its exquisite chorus. Then, steadying my burden and prodding

Petchy, we started again. Petch struggled to his feet, leaning on my arm even as I held Teena. We were both barely able to hobble, propping each other up as we staggered forward. Petch said there was a friendly portal ahead, just a little way. We started for it, stumbling along like zombies, supporting each other and carrying the unconscious Teena.

Brain fog was descending. If we didn't get water and some decent air soon, we would just lay down and die right here. And I mean within seconds! But somehow, we staggered forward. Petch stopped, looking around as if studying the terrain. "It should be here," he muttered. Moments passed, and brain fog descended. I put Teena down and felt for her pulse; I couldn't find it.

Finally, Petch found the friendly portal he sought, and it was open. I shucked myself of everything I was carrying. Mostly that meant dropping the vest with the tools in it. Petch dropped his vest and checked that there were no other foreign objects on our bodies. Then with my last ounce of strength, steadying Petch and shouldering Teena again, we stumbled through the portal!

CHAPTER 30

PLAZA

We staggered through the portal into bright sunlight and a crowd of people. We collapsed in a heap, bloody, bruised, with several gunshot wounds; Petchy had picked up two bullet wounds, neither too severe ordinarily, but he had lost a lot of blood. One grazed his side, and one nipped him in his buttocks. I hadn't even been aware of his wounds at the time. I had no idea what condition Teena was in, but she was not yet dead, or else we would not have made it through the portal.

We had emerged right into the middle of the plaza where this whole adventure had started, a naked and bloody mess. I must have passed out, and someone must have called 911 because I was in a hospital bed the next thing I knew, and some very serious cops were standing over me demanding explanations.

What could I tell them? Let's see how that plays out!

"Officer, you see, I was recruited, really kidnapped, by aliens from another planet, taken to a stone-age world infested with dinosaurs, where I was meticulously trained to be a hero. Then we went to a dead planet controlled by an evil Artificial Intelligence that was destroying all human life in the galaxy. We destroyed the AI and saved the galaxy, and oh, by the way, the beautiful young woman

with me is my great-grandmother, and the older man with us is her grandson and my father."

Yeah, that's not gonna go far.

I played dumb, pleaded ignorance, and refused to talk. Along the way, someone told me Teena had died of her injuries, and they were going to book me either for murder or manslaughter, depending on what story I could make them believe.

I broke down in tears and asked to see her body. They refused, nor would they let me see Petch. We played that game for two days, and finally, someone claiming to be my lawyer came to see me.

The cops initially refused to leave us alone. It took some arguing, but pleading attorney-client privilege, my visitor finally got me alone. He pulled out his phone, launched a music app, and turned the volume up to the maximum.

Then he leaned in close, put his lips next to my ear, and in a whisper, he asked me, "Did you succeed. Did you infect the AI?" I stared dumbly. Then comprehending he was in on the joke, I nodded imperceptibly. "Whew, what a relief. We have been working on that my entire life, since long before I was born, in fact. Great job! Did you get the database?"

"Teena said she had it, but they said she died. So, I don't know what became of it, her body, or anything."

At that, his face fell. Then he said, "I am not the only asset from the off-world team here, others are to address those two, but I don't have any information about that. I do not know what happened. I have a limited mission. I am here to get you out, and beyond that, you know far more about it than I do. We had a devil of a time finding you. You were not supposed to come here, but it's ok; it all worked out. I would have been here a lot sooner otherwise."

I nodded. Apparently, he was a limited clandestine 'asset' unaware of much of the larger organization. "They're trying to charge me with all sorts of murder and mayhem. What about the charges? Will they stick? What is gonna happen next?"

He replied, "Again, I don't have all of the data, but in a few hours, I will be back. This time I won't be a lawyer; I will be an NSA agent. Have to wait until after shift change, so the cops won't remember I was your 'lawyer.' You are going to be 'renditioned' to a so-called 'black site,' or so they will come to believe, because of 'terrorist connections.' We will simply walk out the front door, and all police and hospital records will be purged. This never happened."

"Where am I going?" I wanted to know.

"I don't know. My task is to get you away from the cops, erase any record of your presence here, and take you to a safehouse. Beyond that, you will be guided by someone else. You will probably need to be off-Earth for a little while until we clean up all of the mess, but then you can come back and resume your old life if you want. None of that is my call, though. I'm just to get you to the safe-house and purge the records."

That made sense, I guess. I needed to be scarce until the data of my appearance here was erased, and local cops had forgotten me. Then it should be safe. "If anyone asks, I would like to spend the off-Earth time on our 'Planet Oz.' I have friends there." He nodded and then shut off his phone, stepped to the door, had a few words with the cops, and then left.

I relaxed after that, trusting that I would shortly be rescued and hopefully be back with my dear Lolita soon. I was not surprised then when a 'man from the Government' visited me. Fortunately, my silent act was well ingrained. I was naturally tight-lipped after the last few days with the cops hovering over me.

He came in and showed his government badge. I should have twigged when I saw my 'NSA guy' was not the same man as my 'lawyer,' and the shift had not yet changed. I guess I was slow today. But, silly me, I just assumed that they were anxious to get me out and had pulled in another agent.

Oops!

When he pulled out a thick file and started asking me question after question about things I had no clue about, I soon realized that this was not my extradition team. He was, in fact, from the Government! He interrogated me for two solid hours!

His first question immediately put me on guard. "What were you and your sister doing in Australia last year?" I said, "I don't have a sister and have never been to Australia!" He didn't like that. "We ran your DNA. You and that woman you came in with are closely related. I think she's your younger sister. Is that right?"

Hmm, I wonder what he would say if I told him she was my great-grandmother. I said, "Who?"

He became exasperated. "Your DNA or that of a close relative was connected to a terrorist act last year. We're running a full panel on you all now, and I am betting it will confirm that she is your sister, and he is your father and one or all of you are our terrorists!"

"I don't have a sister, and I am an orphan, never knew my father." Well, it was mostly true.

"If you don't have a sister, who was the naked broad who came in with you?"

I reverted to my initial cover story. "I don't know who you're talking about. I was mugged and shot. I was going about my private business, alone, when a big gorilla of a guy stuck a gun in my face and demanded everything I had, shot me, and I woke up here!"

This was not going to go well!

On and on it went. We did that dance until he got tired of my 'attitude.' I even gave him my real name and told him I was an unemployed engineer in pressing need of a job. I had just come from a job interview when I was mugged.

I even asked him for a job!

He didn't buy it. Along the way, through our little dance, he insultingly commented that no one with my physique could be a computer engineer. What can I say?

I told him that just because I keep fit does not diminish my computer skills. Being unemployed left me with time on my hands.

If he didn't think I was an engineer, I told him to have one of his techie types question me.

That might have been a mistake; It gave him ideas!

He decided that he would take me to their facility rather than bring someone else here. So, he called the doctor in and consulted with him, and then moments later, I was in a wheelchair, handcuffed to the chair, hands, and feet, and being wheeled out of the hospital!

What happened after that is a blur. I was put in a room and questioned. Mostly I just sat and practiced my stupid face. Occasionally I would rotate my dumb face into view to break the monotony. Once or twice, I trotted out incredulous and stupefied to see if my questioners were paying attention. Finally, several hours into our session, three guys in white shirts with pocket protectors came in, looking so much like they stepped out of a 1950s sci-fi movie that I laughed at them. Government geeks! Were they kidding me? Hilarious! Was I supposed to take this seriously?

They started peppering me with questions. At first, I resisted, thinking this was all some kind of joke, but I quickly realized they were just what they appeared to be; computer nerds pulled straight from the IT department, sent in to find out if I had mad skills or was a poser. Their starched, unlikely appearance aside, they were my kind of people after all. I started talking to them as long as they stayed on matters of technology. They quizzed me on everything from WiFi to ISDN, from firewalls to honeypots. Finally, the lead guy called a halt when I started explaining IPchains, how to configure it, and the differences between IPchains and IPtables. He said I was the real deal and that I should be working there with them. I said, "Make me an offer!"

I guess I passed muster as a techie. That's something no one is going to be able to fake.

They left me alone after that for several hours. I took a nap.

Hours later, it might have been the next day, I'm unsure, my Agent came back. His name was Alex, he said, and he was suddenly much more friendly. His demeanor changed from antagonistic to friendly, almost familial.

He brought me street clothes. I eyed them curiously. How long since I wore something like that. A year? More? I didn't know, but a long time. The time on Planet Oz had been many months. I thought again of Lolita and my son. Indeed, he had been born months ago. Was he walking yet? Probably not, but soon, I guessed. Then I thought of Teena. What had become of her?

As I was dressing, an apologetic Alex fawned all over me. He said the initial DNA analysis had been flawed. They had done their own analysis with entirely different results. They no longer thought I was in any way connected to the events in Australia, whatever they were, and no relation to the mysterious woman or the man. He had confirmed my identity, tech cred, and probably my bank account. At least they recognized I was a solid citizen and not connected to whatever terrorists they might be hunting.

Casually, feigning a lack of interest, I asked what happened to the other two. Suddenly tight-lipped, Alex claimed he didn't know, but his downcast eyes betrayed him. He was lying. That puzzled me; I wondered why he would lie and what happened to Teena's corpse. But I dared not ask. Had Teena indeed died? Or was that misdirection. I had no clue and dared not betray the depth of my interest.

When he gave me the clothes, he apologized again for the inconvenience, saying he now knew I was a solid citizen, but without my wallet and ID, it would be inconvenient at first. He even gave me a little 'walking around money,' as he called it, to help until I got squared away. He apologized again for the harsh questioning and shook my hand. A few minutes later, I was on the street, wondering what to do now!

Someone was still pulling strings for me. Something odd happened to that DNA data. I was free, out of jail, and mostly recovered from our ordeal on 'Planet K.' Well, I was ambulatory, rehydrated, and functional. I still had a wracking cough, numerous scrapes, some terrible-looking bruises, an extremely sore shoulder, painful stitches in my shoulder and side, and I felt weak and fragile. I'll take it.

I walked almost twenty blocks to the old, dilapidated storefront where this had all started. It was boarded up, now, apparently vacant. I thought I had understood this was an essential facility for them, a stable, reliable portal that they kept watch on and guarded. I camped out in front of the building for a while and people-watched. No one came or went, no sign of life. Just ordinary pedestrians and the occasional colorful counter-culture type passed the storefront without a glance.

Finally, I abandoned my vigil and walked up the hill toward my old bedroom. I wondered if my landlady remembered me, wondered if my things were still there. I wondered if my bank account was still active, and my meager funds were intact. I was going to need to eat soon, and the few bucks Alex gave me were not going to buy much more than perhaps a fast-food meal or two. I was feeling pretty scared. If I had no home and no money, I was in a bad way. Sleeping under the overpass was not attractive.

I was in luck. My worries were groundless. My landlady was glad to see me, and my room was just as I had left it. Except cleaner? Yeah, someone had definitely cleaned. My landlady had not re-rented it, which was a surprise, but it turned out my rent was paid up; the room was still mine. The plastic bag of clothes, wallet, Droid, keys and assorted miscellany I had thought abandoned so many months ago was in the top drawer of my dresser. The Droid was even charged!

I pulled out my tired old laptop, and it booted right up despite months of sitting idle. I logged into my bank account and let out a low whistle. I had scarily few bucks the last time I logged in. Now the number was so large I considered it must be an error. But no, there had been a considerable deposit the 16th of every month since I left, and my rent had been paid in full and on time.

It's now been six weeks. I have heard 'nothing from no one.' I have money in the bank and time on my hands. I bought a lovely, costly, state-of-the-art laptop and have spent the last few weeks writing this memoir of my adventures, most of that time spent sitting right here in the plaza, sipping my Arabian Mocha-Java.

People-watching, reading the flashy ads in the urban rag and writing. No one would believe me if I tried to sell it as factual, but it might find an audience in the science fiction marketplace. I can always self-publish it as an eBook.

Still, though my memory is clear, I find myself occasionally wondering if it all really happened. I am confident, make no mistake, but I have absolutely nothing to prove it. I often find myself wishing I was back with my Lolita. I think I miss her the most. She's a sweet, fun, and enticing bedmate, a wonderful gal. I wondered about her baby, my son, and what sort of father I would make. I knew enough about their society to know he would be well cared for and loved. I refused to burden myself with the guilt of being a drive-by baby-daddy. That society looks at these things differently.

Still...

I always carry a raincoat these days. You never know when someone might find themselves naked in the plaza, in urgent need of civilized camouflage.

Once satisfied that my bank account was flush and it wasn't a clerical error, I approached my landlady, and we reached a deal to sell me the house. The cash infusion ensured her financial health, and we made arrangements that she would continue to run the place as she saw fit, collect the rents from the other tenants and keep anything left over after expenses.

I only wanted a dependable place to live that I didn't have to work to keep. So, I moved from the tiny, tiny sleeping room to one of the larger apartments, a space large enough for two, should I have a guest, and large enough to allow for a decent desk.

I required one additional duty of my former landlady. Care for my pets. I now have two cats and a dog. I named the tiny, saucy gray feline Lolita and the big orange one I named Athena. The stocky, good-natured bulldog is Petchy. I wanted to ensure someone took care of them when I traveled.

I joined a gym and have been regularly working out. After spending so much energy and effort on my physical training on Planet Oz, I felt I had an obligation to maintain myself. I had no wish to turn soft and flabby again. I found myself 'going easy' when others were around, not wishing to risk unmasking as a superman. I suppose whatever genetic endowment I had, either from birth or as a result of manipulation for the mission, has put me beyond the capabilities of anyone I am likely to meet here. I wasn't doing the hard training Petch and I had subjected ourselves to; I had no wish to spend six or seven hours a day at it. A good hour or so, three or four times a week, seemed enough for maintenance.

It also seems good for my social life and allows me to meet people. I am trying to be more outgoing and more social these days. Gone is the whiny nerd I now understood myself to have been. Mostly.

I had learned a lot about opening up and enjoying life at those big group dinners on 'Planet Oz' and have no wish to retreat from that. I am still an introvert at heart, but that does not mean I must indulge those feelings. I now understand the rewards of a robust social life. At times, it is challenging, but I am a different man and up to the challenge.

I took up running and ran a couple of marathons. But again, I found I must hold back. Compared to our brutal runs, a 12K city marathon was hardly even a run, almost laughable. It would not do to outrun the entire field, breaking course records and attracting attention. I debated running nude in the upcoming 'Bare to Breakers,' naked runners are well received in the city.

Maybe. We'll see.

I also bought some classy clothing, a couple of Brooks Brothers suits, and several of their beautiful, if expensive, shirts. Custom-tailored, of course, to compliment my newly developed physique. **I've never been big on fancy clothes, but I have had enough running around naked for a while. So, I'm going to try it the other way, just for now.**

Please visit the Chromosome Quest Reviews Page and leave a nice review.

https://www.amazon.com/review/create-review?&asin=B00R8NXS56

If you've enjoyed the story, please help an author out by leaving a nice review on Amazon. We authors need your reviews.

Please visit the **Chromosome Conspiracy: The Aliens, The Agency, and the Dark Lensmen** Amazon page. Now available in eBook, paperback, and audiobook.

https://amazon.com/dp/B00ZM3RTP4

Continue the Adventure: Chromosome Conspiracy: The Aliens, The Agency, and the Dark Lensmen (Chromosome Adventures Book 2)

continues the saga when the Fur-Girls come to Earth in search of Fitz, and Alex Marco, head "Man in Black" wants to capture the aliens.

 Please visit the **Undercover Alien: The Hat, The Agency, and the Quantum War** Amazon page. Now available in eBook, and soon in paperback, and audiobook.

https://www.amazon.com/dp/B09YNG2JD3

If you want to learn the incredible backstory of Fitz, claim your copy of Undercover Alien: The Hat, The Alien, and the Quantum War.

THE STORY CONTINUES...

Continue the adventure: *Chromosome Conspiracy: The Aliens, The Agency, and the Dark Lensmen (Chromosome Adventures Book 2)* continues the saga when the Fur-Girls come to Earth in search of Fitz, and Alex Marco, head "Man in Black" wants to capture the aliens.

In between, I wrote a short story titled *The Threshold* to serve as a bridge between the two books, telling how one of the fur girls made her way to Earth, setting the scene for the 'Planet Oz' women to come to earth in *Chromosome Conspiracy*.

The third installment, *Chromosome Warrior*, completes the saga with the story of G.I. Jill, the lady "MiB" and her quest to defeat humanity's greatest enemies.

COMING IN SEPTEMBER 2022: A new series set in the Chromosome Adventures Universe: *Undercover Alien: The Hat, The Alien, and the Quantum War*

If you want to learn the incredible backstory of Fitz, claim your copy of *Undercover Alien: The Hat, The Alien, and the Quantum War*.

Did you ever wish to be a superhero?
Rithwick Jahi Pringle, a.k.a. Ritz, has a keen
imagination, vivid dreams, and unparalleled cyber
skills, but his neurodivergent brain is out to
get him! Paralyzing anxieties, symmetry-demanding
OCD, and unbridled geekiness hobble his superhero
missions.
He dons the superhero cape on The Dark Web. He
wears a White Hat for the Agency by day but patrols
the shadowy dark-web realm by night, dispensing
Vigilante Justice to those beyond the Law's reach.
When a new, otherworldly Director takes charge
of The Agency's cyberwarriors, he is captivated,
seduced, and drawn into a shadowy world beyond
cybercrime, a deep underworld of dark alien villainy.
They come not in spacecraft, and they fight not
with particle beams and lasers. They seek not to kill,
enslave, or even dominate humanity but to dismantle
civilization and return humankind to the stone age.
Allied with a friendly Alien faction and a budding
young sidekick, his near-supernatural gift for cyber
warfare is a powerful asset, but is it enough? Can
the Hat turn the trick against humanity's would-be
oppressors?
Join in this action-packed tale of Hackers and Spies;
Aliens and Earthlings; Superheroes and Hats.
*Read **Undercover Alien** today!*
There has never been a superhero like The Hat!

ABOUT THE AUTHOR

Nathan Gregory writes books, which shouldn't surprise you since you are reading one. Nathan believes there is nothing inherently wrong with writing, as long as you do it in private and wash your hands after.

Before he succumbed to the nasty habit, he was a respected engineer, contributing significantly to the practice of networking and the commercial Internet we know today. Moreover, previously he was a highly sought-after electronics technician in the days when electrons were aggressive, vicious little beasts that required wielding a hot soldering iron and holding raw, leaded solder in one's teeth to subdue them.

When not chasing rogue electrons, he often played a mean game of billiards, made awesome **Pool Hall Chili**, and cooked incredible, mouth-watering hamburgers.

Nathan's journey with Science Fiction began even before electrons, chili, or hamburgers; you see, he came of age during the Space Race!

When, on September 12, 1962, JFK said, "We choose to go to the moon," Nathan had already launched a rocket to the moon with **Rick Brant** in John Blaine's "*The Rocket's Shadow.*" He went to Mars with Heinlein's "*Red Planet*" and "*Podkayne of Mars,*" became a "*Space Cadet,*" trekked across the moon with Kip and the Mother Thing in "*Have Space Suit, Will Travel,*" and trod the "*Glory Road.*"

Edgar Rice Burroughs' Barzoom Epics with **John Carter** and the "*Princess of Mars*" were inspirational classics. A Keto devotee, he fully intends to live long enough to, like "*The Man Who Sold the Moon,*" **Delos D. Harriman**, die on the moon.

Note to Elon: You two really should talk!

By the time "Star Wars" captured the public imagination in 1977, Nathan had already dreamed it a million times. So naturally, it should be no surprise that he should eventually degenerate into a Science Fiction writer.

Check out my author's website for FREE material and subscribe to my BLOG

https://www.nathangregoryauthor.com/

Please visit my Facebook page for various posts, old family photos and more.

https://www.facebook.com/nathan.gregory.923

Please visit my Bookbub Author's Page.

https://www.bookbub.com/profile/nathan-gregory

Please check out my Amazon Author Central page.

https://www.amazon.com/Nathan-Gregory/e/B00QZHIIBK

Please check out my YouTube channel. I have many good videos you might enjoy.

https://www.youtube.com/channel/UCD4vPm_YoJvInuWhF2IICJQ

Please follow me on Twitter.

https://twitter.com/nathan_gregory

Please check out my Pinterest pages. Tons of interesting stuff there, including my recipe for Pool Hall Chili.

https://www.pinterest.com/wa4otj/

Please visit my LinkedIn page for a peak into my professional life.

https://www.linkedin.com/in/nathantgregory/

Please visit my Instagram page. You never know what you will find there.

https://www.instagram.com/nathan.gregory.923/

Please check out my Goodreads public page.

https://www.goodreads.com/author/show/8578172.Nathan_Gregory

THE WRITINGS OF NATHAN GREGORY

Science Fiction

Chromosome Quest is the opening story in the *Chromosome Adventures Series*, introducing the protagonist 'Fitz,' the Mentor 'Petchy,' the crimson-haired Goddess 'Teena,' and the stone-age world he dubbed 'Planet Oz.' Their epic fight was to shut down the runaway AI on Teena and Petchy's home planet and retrieve the genetic database at the heart of the fertility plague.

Chromosome Conspiracy brings the stone-age 'Fur girls' to Earth looking for Fitz's help with a new problem. The adventure begins as he seeks to protect the fur-bearing alien women from the machinations of Alex Marco and the 'Men in Black,' that is until Fitz's girlfriend and several others are killed, and MiB Agent Jill Smith is badly wounded at the hands of a new super-villain. Facing a common foe, Fitz joins the Men in Black to fight the evil Gharlane.

Chromosome Warrior sees the fate of all human civilization hanging in the balance as Fitz, Jill, Petchy, Teena, Alex, and the Fur girls ally with a strange other-worldly energy-being against the evil Gharlane.

Non-Fiction

Nathan Gregory's non-fiction features a pair of documentaries that tell the untold origin backstory of today's commercial Internet. The creation and funding of the ARPANET and the technologies we use today are well told, but there is another side to the story that academia has overlooked.

From its cold-war beginnings until its commercialization beginning in 1992, the Internet forbade any form of commerce. Yet, globe-spanning commercial networks existed for more than two decades before the Internet legitimized online eCommerce.

The story of the creation of the concept of remote computing we call 'Cloud Computing' today began in the 1960s, with the first globe-spanning commercial cloud coming online in 1972. From February 1972 until well beyond the end of 1992, these commercial networks carried the world's e-Commerce traffic while ARPANET and its cousins remained the private playground of academics and politicians.

The Tym Before... tells the story of creating these first commercial networks and the remote cloud services they powered.

Securing the Network tells the story of the subsequent commercialization of the Internet, beginning with the first commercial peering point, MAE-East, for which the initial order was placed on September 29, 1992. By mid-1993, the MAE was in place, and by 1994 it was carrying 90% of the world's commercial Internet traffic.

Kindle Vella Episodic Fiction

With the advent of Kindle Vella, I have begun some serials for publication in the episodic format.

A Walk in the Woods, a one-of-a-kind first-contact story is my first story in this format.

Tommie Powers and the Time Machine stands at four completed episodes. This story is a juvenile that is perhaps closer to a Tom Swift or Rick Brant story. Its fate depends on feedback from you, dear reader.

Made in the USA
Las Vegas, NV
29 October 2023

79901089R00157